LISTEN FOR THE ANGELS

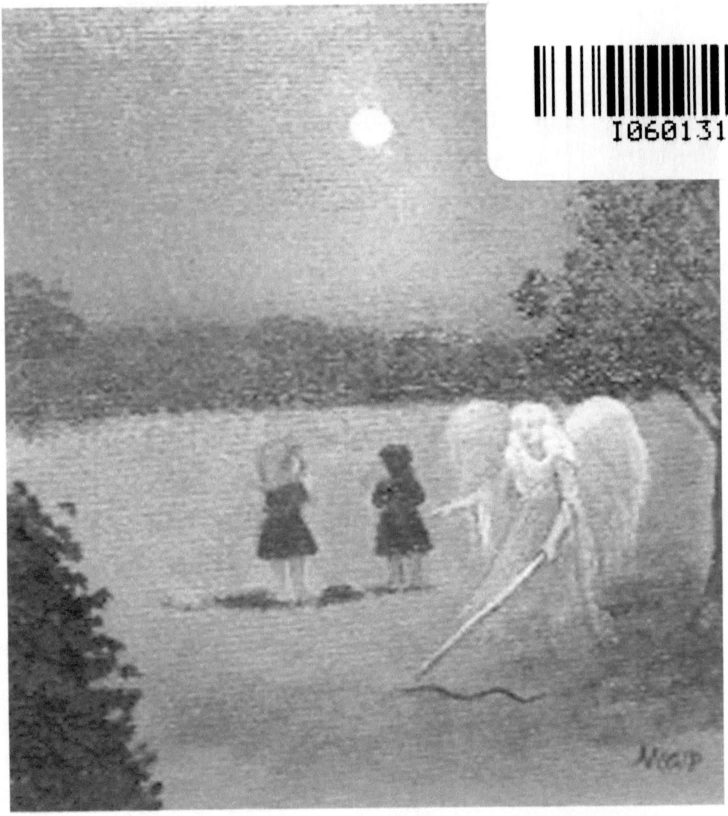

Nancy Powell

Book Three of the Ollie's Angels™ Series

RTP

ISBN: 978-1-59095-592-5
UPC: 6-43977-45927-5
Copyright © 2014 by: Nancy Powell
Edited by: Jessica D. Caruso and Elizabeth Easter

Library of Congress Control Number: 2013952270

TotalRecall Publications, Inc.
1103 Middlecreek, Friendswood, Texas 77546
281-992-3131 281 - 482-5390 Fax
6 Precedent Drive Rooksley, Milton Keynes, MK13 8PR, UK
1385 Woodroffe Av, Ottawa, ON K2G 1V8

Printed in the United States of America with simultaneous printings in Australia, Canada, and United Kingdom.

FIRST EDITION

1 2 3 4 5 6 7 8 9 10

TO MY FAMILY

The Roy and Ollie Glenn family

Acknowledgement

I want to thank my family for their love and support, and my writing friends for their help and encouragement.

Table of Contents

About the Book

Listen for the Angels, the third book in the Ollie's Angels Series, begins on the road to California where Ollie and Roy move with three young daughters in search of a prosperous life following struggles on an Arkansas farm during the Great Depression. Roy works at farm labor. Ollie joins him in the fields during cotton-picking season, and becomes infected with a disease that the newspapers call Sleeping Sickness. Several people have died from the illness, but doctors do not know the cause. Ollie's intuition tells her that mosquitoes cause it—she takes a quinine tonic and recovers. They move back to Arkansas, after hearing that Roy's ma has cancer.

They buy a small farm and continue the struggle of rural life. Almost every fall, Roy goes away to work in other states to earn money for the mortgage, to buy seed and fertilizer for the next year's crop, and to pay doctor bills.

In 1946, Roy and Ollie buy the farm of their dreams, but drought destroys the harvest. In 1950, while expecting her seventh child, Ollie, gets strep throat and loses her hearing. Uterine tumors dictate induced labor. She has twins. Four years pass before she can afford a hearing aid to enable her to hear her babies laugh or cry.

Roy tries to borrow money to start a Grade 'A' dairy farm, but cannot get a loan. Fire destroys the pasture, corn and cotton crops, and a tornado hits the farm.

List of Main Characters

Ollie McNew, born in 1908, (POV Character), light brown hair, blue eyes, olive complexion, slim, smart, helpful, competitive, strong willed, loves children and animals, skilled with a pistol, competent horseback rider, and has premonitions that alert her of dangers.

Roy Glenn, Ollie's husband, tall, dark hair, blue eyes, olive skin, excellent horseman, a farmer.

Morene Glenn, daughter born 1928, brown hair, blue eyes, olive skin.

Syble Glenn, daughter born 1930, brown hair, blue eyes, olive skin.

Mary Ann Glenn, daughter, called Ann, brown hair, blue eyes, fair skin.

John Glenn, Ollie and Roy's only son, brown hair, blue eyes.

Nancy Glenn, Ollie and Roy's fifth child, blond hair, blue eyes.

Patty Glenn, Ollie and Roy's sixth child, brown hair, blue eyes.

Robbie Glenn, Ollie and Roy's seventh child, blond hair, blue eyes.

Bobbie Glenn, Ollie and Roy's eighth child, blond hair, blue eyes.

Artie McNew, Ollie's mama, small and thin, dark hair, blue eyes, olive skin.

Robert McNew, Ollie's Papa, dark curly hair, dark eyes, olive skin.

Bertha McNew, Ollie's older sister, light brown hair, blue eyes, olive skin, plays the organ.

Earl McNew, Ollie's oldest brother, brown hair, blue eyes, olive skin.

Herbert McNew, younger brother, died as a baby.

Eldridge McNew, brother four years younger than Ollie, brown hair, blue eyes, olive skin.

Bronnie McNew, Ollie's youngest sister, black hair, dark eyes, darker olive skin.

Sherrill McNew, brother nine years younger than Ollie, black hair, dark eyes, olive skin.

Eugene McNew, asthmatic brother, eleven years younger than Ollie, brown hair, blue eyes, olive skin.

John McNew, Ollie's youngest brother, black hair, blue eyes, olive skin, winning smile.

Ma Glenn, Roy's mother.

Pa Glenn, Roy's father.

Doctor Hart, the community doctor and good friend of the family.

Doctor Williams, the family doctor at Greenbrier.

Chapter 1
New Dreams

He turns the truck onto a narrow dirt road that does not look familiar to Ollie. "Roy, are you sure this is the right way? This is an awfully rough road."

"I've rode horses through here. It's a shortcut to the highway that'll take us to the state line. Don't start worrying until we leave Arkansas."

She sighs and lifts the baby onto her lap.

Everything looks new after they leave Faulkner County. The tree-lined pavement stretches out like a gaping throat ready to swallow them. *Will I ever again see Mama, Papa, my brothers and my older sister, Bertha?* Panic rising, she wants to yell, *"Stop. Let's go back."* Instead, she hugs little Ann, takes a few deep breaths, and glances at Roy. Seeing his wrinkled forehead and shiny eyes, she looks away to pray in silence.

Miles of farms, houses, trees, and brushy road ditches roll by before Roy speaks. "Ollie, this is an adventure. Let's at least give it a year. If we hate it, we can go home. In the meantime, we'll save all we can toward another place of our own."

"One minute I'm eager to see what's over the next hill, but before we get there I'm afraid. We have so many things to worry about. My biggest concern is that if both of us were to get sick at the same time, who would take care of our girls?"

"You can't worry about what *might* happen."

"But I do. My grandpa took his buggy and went two counties over to pick up three orphans with the same last name as his. The children's parents died with a fever, leaving a boy and two girls on a farm near White River. When Grandpa found them, they were chasing their last chicken to kill. The kids didn't know what they would eat after that was gone."

"Were they relatives?"

"Grandpa never found definite evidence that they were, but he raised them like family."

"That was in the 1800's. Things are different now, and your sister, Bronnie is with us, for a while anyway, until she finds a job. Morene is nine years old, and acts more sensible than some grown women. We'll be fine." He grins and pats her leg. "Remember, we're going to the land of sunshine—it could be our place of milk and honey."

Laughing, she pushes his hand away. "Keep both hands on the steering wheel. I don't wanna get killed before we get out of Arkansas."

She twists to look through the back window at the girls in the truck bed. "I can hardly believe it's 1937. We've been married a decade. In another ten years, Morene will be grown, maybe married, and Syble right behind. Where did the time go?" She shakes her head, still staring through the glass.

"It passed while we were working, and trying to build a future."

"For sure, but things would have been different if the South hadn't been hit by drought and the Depression. Thank God, we survived, and didn't have to move in with family or give our babies away because we couldn't feed them."

"The hardest thing for me was working away in other states where I couldn't be with you and my girls, but I didn't know of any other way."

Ollie pats his leg before shifting Ann on her lap. "Those were the hardest times for me, too. Way down on that farm with only the babies for company, problems with animals, snakes, and those thieving neighbors. They worried me a lot more than animals and snakes." She sighs and pushes a lock of hair away from the baby's forehead.

"Every night, I was exhausted from work, but I couldn't sleep soundly for worrying that someone might break in. Especially in summer, when the heat forced me to leave windows open. I felt as if every outlaw and piece of scum in the country knew I was alone with two little girls."

Roy smiles and glances at her. "I laughed when I heard about you shooting a prowler in the rump. Word of it traveled fast. Pa said people down his way were entertained with that story for a long time."

She frowns. "That guy was lucky it wasn't buckshot."

"He had a grudge against you after you made him the laughingstock of the county. It's a good thing we left. Eventually, I would have tangled with him."

She leans her head against the seat, looking straight ahead. "Will we get to Fort Smith before dark?"

"We should. I'd like to park close to the river, near where the old fort stood, but as warm as it's been lately, the mosquitoes might carry us away. If we get there early enough, we'll drive by for a look and find another place to spend the night."

"I was surprised when you said your friend Snake wanted to

ride with us. I didn't like the idea at first, but he seems like a nice man stuck with an awful nickname."

"He's a good guy. He'll help pay for gas, and he knows a little about mechanic work. That could come in handy if we break down somewhere."

She slaps a hand to her face. "Don't give me something else to worry about."

At four o'clock, they stop for gasoline on the edge of Fort Smith. Everyone climbs out to stretch and move around. Roy walks to the back of the truck. "Snake and Bronnie, what do you think about stopping near the old fort for a picnic supper, then driving until almost dark before pulling off for the night?"

They nod in agreement, but before they can speak Morene and Syble start asking questions about the fort: "Does it have real soldiers? And Indians with arrows?"

Roy walks toward the gas pumps. "It's not used as a fort now, but it was originally built to control rowdy Indians."

When they stop near the old fort site, the girls continue with questions.

"Girls, I don't know much more than you. Only that this is the fort location."

An elderly man walking by smiles and speaks to the girls. "I can answer some of your questions. I've lived in Fort Smith all my life." He points toward where the Arkansas and Poteau rivers join, and tells of Indian tribes in the area, the original fort, Cherokees from the Trail of Tears, the gallows and Judge Parker, the hanging judge.

Ollie spreads food, from the baskets prepared by her mama and Roy's ma, onto the truck's tailgate. The others listen to the old man's stories.

Roy invites him to eat with them, but he declines. "My wife will have supper ready by now. May God bless and keep you safe on your journey." He waves and starts to go, then turns back. "You're not planning on staying here for the night are you?"

"We wanted to travel another hour before stopping, but it's getting late. I guess here is as good as any place we might find."

The man shakes his head. "The last ten years have been mighty hard for some, and a lot of vagrants loiter along the river. There's a church next to my home; you can park in the churchyard tonight. It has a toilet outside that will be convenient for your family. The location is much safer than here." He takes a tiny pencil and pad from his jacket pocket, writes the address, hands it to Roy and gives directions. "I'll walk on while you eat your supper. It's a green house next to the church. You'll find it easy enough."

The next morning, Ollie wakes in the tarp covered truck bed to the smell of bacon and fresh coffee. She pulls back the tarp. "Roy, it's time to roll out of your cot."

The moment Roy stands, the old man calls to him from his porch. "Mr. Glenn, come over and have coffee with me while your family's waking. My wife's cooking breakfast for all of you—side meat, fried eggs and the best cinnamon bread you ever tasted."

"Coffee sounds good, but first let me run over to that toilet in the church yard. I'll be right back."

"Roy," Ollie calls, "wait till I get my shoes on. I want to walk with you."

After breakfast, Mrs. Smith gives Ollie a self-addressed

postcard and requests a note when they are settled in California. She packs the extra cinnamon bread, enough fried eggs and bacon to feed them through the day, and fills two glass jugs with ice and fresh water. "Ollie, don't forget the rest of your mama's fried chicken that you put in my ice-box, and the ham from Roy's ma. Smoked ham will keep without ice, but you should eat the chicken at your first stop."

"Yes, I was going to put it in the trash last night, but Roy suggested that you might have room in your ice-box. I appreciate you letting me use it." She pauses and looks into the woman's smoky blue eyes. "Mrs. Smith, it was so nice of you to cook breakfast for us. It will be a long time before we eat like that again."

"The Bible tells us to help others, and I thoroughly enjoyed sharing with you."

That day, they travel across Oklahoma to the outskirts of Elk City before stopping for the night. They eat the chicken, fried eggs and cinnamon bread for lunch; supper is cold bacon on Ma Glenn's home-baked yeast bread with boiled eggs. When everyone is finished, Ollie says, "Tomorrow morning, we'll eat the last of our yeast bread and ham. From there on to California, we'll eat cheese and crackers, or bologna sandwiches. Maybe cornflakes for breakfast, if we stop near a store where we can buy milk."

Morene and Syble squeal, "Cornflakes! We love cornflakes."

"You may change your minds before we get settled in a new home."

They shake their heads. Syble answers, "I could eat them every day for a year."

Not wanting to miss any sights along the road, Morene and

Syble talk Roy into tying up the wagon sheet so they can look out from between the sideboards. After two days on the road, they are quite brown from the wind and heat. Sometimes the sun shines directly on them, but they do not burn; their olive skin simply tans a little darker.

On the third day, they stop at a store in Texas where a beautiful Indian girl is tending the counter. Syble keeps watching her, and follows when she goes to slice bologna and cheese for Ollie. The girl smiles.

Ollie comes up behind Syble with money to pay for the meat and cheese. "Go get in the truck. We have to leave."

"Wait." the girl calls to Syble, and turns to take three pieces of candy from a jar on the counter. "These are for you and your sisters."

"Thank you. I hope you live happy ever after."

The girl's eyes sparkle. "Thank you. I wish the same for you, little friend."

Morene reaches to help Syble climb into the truck. "Hurry, get in so we can go. Maybe we'll see a buffalo today."

"I want to see a *big* buffalo—and a grizzly bear, but not up close." Syble huddles near the back so she can catch sight of everything interesting.

Ollie, putting her change pocket into her purse, walks behind the truck. "Syble, get up to the front, and don't let me catch you near the tailgate again. If it came loose, you'd fall out on the highway and be killed."

Syble does not argue, but after Ollie is inside the truck, she hears the girls grumbling with low voices.

One place where Roy stops for gas has an animal exhibit. The sign advertizes snakes, giant lizards, wolves, and a dancing bear. Morene and Syble walk to the side of the building to listen for sounds from the creatures. A brown bear, chained to a tree behind the gas station, catches Syble's attention.

"Look, Morene. There's the bear."

"He looks sad, and tired. They probably made him dance too much."

"I bet he's hot. His bucket is turned on its side, and the water spilled."

"Let's go tell the people inside."

Morene walks to the counter where a large man sits on a stool fanning himself. "Mister, your bear needs his water bucket refilled. He's really hot under all that fur."

Syble leans on the counter. "He's breathing hard. Did you make him dance a lot?"

"That lazy bear. I told his owner to get a bigger bucket. Every time he sticks his fat head in to get a drink, it gets stuck and he spills the water." The man runs a yellowed handkerchief over his face and neck to dry away the sweat. "I can't run outside every hour to water that stupid thing. I have to take care of the store."

Morene frowns at him. "Where is his owner?"

"I don't know, I don't care, and I'd like it fine if the bear was gone."

Ollie has been watching and listening from a distance. "Mister, the girls are worried for the safety of the bear. If you don't give it some water, it'll die before dark in this heat."

"That would suit me fine."

"Surely, you're not so cruel as to keep an animal chained without water until it dies."

"Look at this scratch." He turns slightly and points to the

back of his arm. A red mark runs from his shoulder to his elbow. "This is what that thing did to me the last time I tried to help him." He opens the cash register and puts the money inside that Roy has counted. "Hey, lady, I bet if you lived on a farm, you've seen many an animal killed."

Instantly, Ollie's temper rises. "Yes, I've killed animals for food, and others in self-defense, but there is a big difference between that and letting something suffer."

Snake, listening from the doorway, walks to the gas pumps and takes a tub of water left for washing windshields, dumps it, and drapes the dripping rag over a hose from one of the pumps. After filling the tub at a faucet on the side of the station, he takes it to the bear. As he approaches, the big furry critter ambles to the end of the chain and immediately begins drinking when Snake lowers the container.

While the bear's muzzle is immersed, Roy grabs the dry bucket. He fills and sets it between the gas pumps. "Girls, get in the truck. Now the bear can drink without getting his head stuck and spilling his water."

That night they stop in New Mexico, the next in Arizona. At last, they see the Colorado River and a big *California* sign. Roy stops the truck close to where some children are playing in the river. Everyone wades into the cool water. Ollie puts a bonnet, long pants and a long-sleeve shirt on Ann so she will not blister. Morene and Syble play and try to swim in their dresses. The adults take turns walking in the water and huddling in the shade of a small tree.

The sky is turning pink when Roy tells them to get in the truck. "I'll drive across this desert tonight and stop when we reach a cooler place." Sometime in the early morning, he pulls into the parking lot of a gas station.

A sign states, "Open 6 a.m. to 10 p.m." The restrooms are unlocked, but giant roaches are crawling everywhere. Ollie laughs as her sister Bronnie goes inside, stomping and squealing at the bugs. Ollie leads the little girls behind the station and tells them to squat in the shadows.

Returning to the truck, she finds Roy asleep across the front seat with his feet hanging out the driver's side. She slides a pillow under his head and eases the passenger door closed.

Snake unties his army cot from the frame covering the sideboards. "Ollie, if Bronnie can crowd onto the mattress in the truck bed, beside you and the children, I'll put my cot here by the tailgate. We only have a couple of hours before daylight. I have a gun, in case anyone comes around."

Ollie tucks Roy's wallet under the mattress, and puts Ann in a corner at the front of the bed with the other girls beside her. After Syble, Morene and Bronnie settle down, Ollie slides her feet close to Ann, places a pillow on the tailgate, and straightens out. Before closing her eyes, she runs her hand across the pistol.

Ollie has held Ann and watched every mile of highway, especially after dark, and is exhausted, but afraid to sleep—Roy and Snake are both snoring. She is aware of each dog that barks and every passing car. As the eastern sky pales with misty shades of gold, she hears someone walking along the sidewalk in front of the station. Lifting herself onto her elbows, she watches while holding the pistol under her pillow. He passes, but before she can snuggle under a thin blanket, the owner comes to open the station. "Good morning, sir."

"Hey, lady, you people will have to move on. Cars will be driving through here."

"Yes, sir, as soon as I wake my husband."

Roy sits up in the front seat.

Snake crawls from his cot.

Ollie slides off the tailgate, and goes to Roy with his wallet. While he fills the truck's gas tank, she takes the girls to the bathroom; no roaches are in sight.

Ollie lifts Ann into the truck bed. "Snake, you ride up front with Roy. I'll stay here with the girls until we stop for breakfast." She is asleep when Roy stops at a roadside diner and comes back to the truck with seven paper-wrapped biscuits filled with sausage and fried eggs, and four bottles of chocolate milk for Bronnie and the little girls.

Snake is behind Roy with three cups of black coffee. "The woman inside said we should sit at the picnic table by the building, and she'll return the price of these cups and bottles when we bring them back."

"Girls, go sit at the table, and don't drop those bottles." Ollie blinks. "I really need coffee. I feel like I haven't slept in days."

Roy looks around at the surroundings. "I feel rested. That seat made a pretty good bed. Snake, did you get any sleep last night?"

"I planned to keep an eye out for robbers, but I don't remember a thing after my head hit the cot."

Ollie sighs. "Well, in case anyone is interested, I didn't sleep. I heard every dog, car, and person moving within a quarter-of-a-mile, and my gun was ready."

Chuckling, Roy winks at Snake. "We brought along a good bodyguard."

The quiet man grins, and pushes a brown felt hat to the back of his head. "Roy, I appreciate you letting me travel with your family. I've really enjoyed the trip. Someday, I hope to find a good wife and have some little girls as sweet as yours. I hate to leave all of you, but relatives in Bakersfield are expecting me. I'll stop-off there."

Roy's cousin Charlie and his wife Vera live in Shafter. Roy pulls the truck into the driveway as Charlie gets home from work. He takes Roy to talk to his boss, a landowner with large fruit orchards.

While Roy is gone, Ollie goes to look at a nearby house with a For Rent sign in the yard. The house is reasonably clean with no signs of bugs or mice. She pays the owner for the first month's rent, borrows a broom from Vera, and has it swept and most of their belongings moved inside by the time Roy returns.

"Ollie, I got a job picking fruit. I start tomorrow." He walks through the little house. "I'm glad you rented this place. It's close enough that Charlie and I can ride to work together."

"I thought you'd like it. The girls can walk to school. Did you notice the little ice-box in the kitchen, and the gas stove?"

"I saw them. Let's go find a store and buy some food so you can try out the stove. Have you ever cooked on one where you just turn a knob?"

She shakes her head. "Only wood stoves—I may burn everything. Have the girls come in and wash their hands." She points to the sink. "Look, we have running water. No more going to the well."

"That would be handy in canning season, if we had a garden."

"I'll comb my hair and get my purse. Oh, tell me about your job. Do you think you'll like working there?"

"I think so. Charlie said the boss is honest and reasonable. I'll get paid according to how much I pick, and if I'm lucky, he'll keep me for maintenance work during the off-season." Roy puts an arm around her shoulders. "Maybe this will truly be our place of milk and honey."

Chapter 2
Getting Acquainted

Morene and Syble run into the house after the first day of school. "Mama," Morene calls. "A girl tried to take Syble's new pencil. She told Syble she'd better trade with her or else. Then she made a sign like a knife cutting her throat."

"Syble, did you do something to make that little girl mad at you?"

"No, except for not trading my new pencil for her old chewed-up one."

Morene interrupts. "Mama, we met her and Bella, her sister, on our way to school this morning. Mable is in Syble's class. Mable told Syble that their teacher is mean and really hates girls with blue eyes. She said, 'Girl, you might as well turn around and go home, right now, 'cause you'll be gettin' a whippin' before this day is gone.'"

Morene stops and motions for Syble to come over, but Syble shakes her head and turns her face toward the floor.

"Mama, Bella yelled at her to stop it. She said, 'Mable, 'cause you get a whippin' almost every day, don't mean she'll get one. I never got whipped when I had that teacher.'"

Ollie walks over, takes hold of Syble's chin, and tilts her face up. "Was your teacher nice to you?"

Syble nods. "I tried real hard not to do anything bad, and to stay away from Mable, but she kept following me. Because her last name starts with "*F*" and mine with "*G*," I have to sit right behind her. I saw her poking the girl in front of her and pulling her hair. She even tried to trip me when I went to take my paper to the teacher."

"I hate that you had problems the first day. I'll go to school and talk to the teacher tomorrow. Maybe we can figure out a solution to this problem."

When Roy comes home, Morene tells him what happened. "Syble, the only way to stop her is to get in her face and tell her to leave you alone or you'll clean her plow."

"What does that mean?"

He laughs. "It's a country expression. It means you'll scrape your knuckles on her nose."

Syble's lips curl into a grin. "Then I would get a whipping at school."

The next morning Ann is sick. Ollie, places a cold cloth on the baby's forehead before turning to Syble. "I can't take Ann out with a fever. Maybe tomorrow I can go talk to your teacher. Try harder to stay away from Mable."

That afternoon Morene rushes in the door and yells, "Mama, that girl kept picking on Syble all day, and Syble beat her up after school. I don't think she'll mess with us again."

"Do you mean Syble started a fight with her?"

"Mable pestered her all day—she ripped Syble's homework paper, pushed her, dumped her lunch on the floor, and in the bathroom she threw water on the back of Syble's dress to make it look like she wet her pants. After school, we walked fast away from the building and stopped behind a tree. As Mable began to pass, Syble jumped on her. She screamed and tried to get away, but Syble pounded her face. Bella helped me pull Syble off of her." Morene stops to catch her breath before continuing.

"Mable yelled, 'I'm gonna tell, and you'll get a whippin' tomorrow.'" Morene glances toward the door, but Syble is not coming in.

"Syble yelled at her, 'Go ahead. If you tattle, I'll beat you up again'"

Ollie walks out on the porch where Syble is sitting. "Young lady, I've told you not to start a fight. We'll have a talk when your Daddy gets home."

"Daddy told me to clean her plow, and that's what I tried to do."

"Tomorrow, I think you need to tell her you're sorry."

"But I'm not sorry. Do you want me to lie?"

Ollie sighs. She would like to give that little girl a good spanking, but knows better than to tell that to her girls. "We'll see what your daddy says about this."

Syble walks out to meet Roy as he comes across the yard. He stops to sit on the porch until she finishes telling the story. Ollie listens from inside. Syble's account is exactly like Morene's.

Roy spits tobacco juice into the yard and rubs his mouth with a blue handkerchief. "It sounds like you cleaned her plow."

Syble looks at the ground. "I had to. I meant to stay away from her, but she followed me. I tried to be her friend, but she kept doing bad things when the teacher wasn't looking. After school, I jumped on her and was trying to make sure she didn't bother me again, but Morene and Bella pulled me off." She stops talking and begins to pull at a dried scab on the side of her hand. "Daddy—"

"Is there something else you want to say?"

"I'm not sorry I hit her, but Mama says I should tell her that I am. Won't that be telling a lie?"

"You don't have to tell her you're sorry. Tomorrow, act as if nothing happened. I bet she'll be trying to be your friend." He stands, but sits again and puts his arm around her. "If that girl tattles, but I don't think she will, you tell the teacher your side of the story and I'll go talk to her, if need be."

"Roy!"

He looks at Ollie as she speaks from inside the door.

"I don't want you teaching these girls to fight. I want them to act like young ladies."

"Ollie, I'm not gonna teach them to be cowards. I bet, when you were her age, you would have jumped on a bully long before Syble did." He turns to Syble. "I wouldn't like it at all if you were picking on kids. Like your mama, I want you to be ladylike, but I don't expect you to let someone run over you."

Ollie watches out the window as the girls leave for school the next morning. Bella waits to walk with them. Mable, walking fast, is a long way in front.

If Mable told the teacher about the fight, Ollie does not hear of it. Syble comes home happy and tells Ollie of a new friend— a little girl from Oklahoma.

Within a few days, Bronnie finds work in a large dairy at the edge of town and rents a one-bedroom apartment. Ollie wants to work, but does not ask for a job in the orchards. She cannot find anyone nearby who is willing to watch Ann.

Roy's boss allows him to bring home culled fruit from the

orchards—peaches, oranges and lemons. Everything else they eat comes from the store. By the time they pay the rent and buy food, most of Roy's paycheck is spent.

Not realizing California nights are usually cool in comparison to the hot days, Ollie left the girls' flannel nightgowns and most of their quilts in Arkansas with her mama. The three girls snuggle together to sleep, but Ann kicks off the blanket. *They need long gowns to keep their arms and legs warm, but the ones in the store cost more than I can pay.*

Finding some pretty material on sale, Ollie buys enough for three gowns. She cuts them out at home before going to Charlie and Vera's house. It never occurred to Ollie that Vera would mind letting her make the gowns on her machine.

"Are you sure you know how to use a sewing machine like mine?" the woman asks.

"It's a Singer, just like Mama's. I've been sewing on a machine since I was thirteen. I brought my own thread and scissors. If a needle breaks, I'll replace it, but it shouldn't—this is soft material."

"All right, but be careful. Sewing machines are expensive." She stands watching every move until the gowns are finished.

Playing with her doll and a scrap of cloth, Ann sits beside Ollie's chair. She will not raise her head to look at Vera.

Ollie used a simple pattern. In little more than an hour, she closes the lid, picks up a few pieces of loose thread, and thanks Vera. Ollie is glad to go home to hem the nightgowns by hand, although she could have completed them within a few minutes on the machine.

When Roy comes in, she shows him the gowns and tells of her experience. "I won't ask to borrow anything else from her.

When we're settled in a more permanent place, we'll have to buy a machine. Store bought clothes for three girls are too expensive."

Their savings dwindle, and Roy may not have a job after the fruit harvest is over. Thrifty in every way she knows, Ollie walks across town, carrying Ann on her hip, to an outdoor market where she can buy produce cheaper than at the grocery store.

When Ollie finds bargains that weigh more than she can tote along with the baby, she asks the merchant to hold them until after Roy gets off from work and can come get them in the truck. More often than not, she walks home carrying loads heavier than she should.

She plants onions, cabbage, and tomatoes on the east side of the house and keeps them watered, but they do not grow. The soil is poor and neighborhood cats select the tilled soil as their litter box. She sprinkles red pepper and garlic powder around the plants—the cats are not discouraged.

"Ollie, I can borrow a steel trap from the orchard, but it will probably kill whatever it catches."

"I don't want to destroy the neighbor's pets. They catch rodents coming out of the orchards. We might have something worse if we eliminate cats."

Ollie has been corresponding with her cousin's wife, Floy McDougal, who lives farther north. In a letter, Floy invites Roy and Ollie to come to Tulare for a visit and to look around for work. "Ollie, these farms have some of the finest cotton fields you've ever seen. The stalks are taller than a man's head, and loaded with large bolls. You and Roy can do well up here. The cotton is not ready to pick, but this is farming country. There's lots of work."

That evening Roy is very quiet, does not eat much supper, and immediately goes to sit on the porch instead of waiting at the table to talk while Ollie washes the dishes. Morene and Syble try to tell him about their day, but he seems disinterested. They leave to pet one of the neighborhood cats.

Ollie takes the letter and sits beside him. "This came today from Floy."

He turns the paper to let light from inside shine on it and reads as the twilight darkens, hands the letter back to her, and removes the pipe from his mouth. "When do you want to move?"

"You mean you want to go? Without thinking it over?" The paper is shaking in her hand.

"I'll be out of a job on Friday, until another orchard ripens. The boss told me today. He doesn't need any more handymen to work full time. Her letter seems like a blessing."

"Maybe we should leave Saturday morning. Our rent will be due again on Monday. If you can ride to work with Charlie on Friday, I'll get most everything packed. In the morning, I'll write to Floy that we're coming."

"I hate to take the girls out of school?"

"Tomorrow is their last day. That's what they were trying to tell you."

He turns to stare at the girls sitting on some rocks, picking burs from a yellow cat's fur. "I guess I was too worried about a job to hear what they were saying."

That night, Ollie can hardly sleep for thinking of moving. She likes the little house, but the neighbors all seem to be too busy for anything more than a quick hello. *Maybe in Tulare we'll find some friendly families.*

In the morning, she pulls out her rub-board and washes sheets, blankets, and dirty clothes. While the laundry dries, she walks to the post office and mails a letter to Floy; we *may beat that letter to her door.* On the way home, Ollie stops at the grocery store for packing boxes. That afternoon, she bakes enough yeast bread and sugar cookies to last a week and then packs everything from the kitchen cabinets.

Supper is batter-fried onions, and a sausage-and-potato pie, to use up the sausage from the icebox. Roy whistles when he comes in the door. "Man, it smells good in here." He reaches for a handful of the crispy onions.

Ollie slaps him lightly on the arm in protest.

He grins and grabs a hot ring, blowing on it as he goes to the door. "Girls, come wash your hands. Hurry before the onions get cold."

Using folded dishtowels to protect her hands, Ollie takes a pie from the oven. "I made this from the last of those peaches you brought home."

Morene looks at the pie and licks her lips. "We have yeast bread and cookies, too. What are we celebrating?"

"Stay out of the cookies. Those are for the trip. It may be a while before we find a house and I get to bake again. Tonight, we'll have pie."

The morning sky is a soft gauzy pink when Ollie plops bacon into a long-handled skillet and cracks the last six eggs into another frying pan. While they sizzle and the coffee perks, Ollie washes the icebox with baking soda. She butters slices of yeast bread and sets them in the oven to toast. They will not have gravy this morning; the flour is already packed, and there is only enough milk for the girls to drink.

"Morene, wash your hands and face, and do the same for Ann. Syble, after you've washed, set the table. Get a move on, girls. We have to clean this house before we leave."

Carefully, Syble sets the dishes on the table. "Daddy, how many days will it take to get to our new town?"

"Oh, we'll be in *Tulare* within a few hours unless we have troubles, but we want to get there early so we can look for a good place to live."

The girls are waiting on the porch, Roy is tying rope over the mattresses where Morene and Syble will sit, and Ollie is mopping the kitchen when the property owner comes by to collect the key. He sticks his head in the door. "Hello. I want to tell you, before you leave, to open every cabinet, every drawer, and the oven to make sure you haven't left anything. Most people forget something."

"I've already looked, but I'll check one more time." The second drawer she opens contains silverware, and the bread pan is in the oven. "Thanks for reminding me. I've been rushing all morning, and I would have left them for sure. I couldn't replace that silverware. My grandma gave it to me."

He nods, smiles and waits to lock the door behind them. "I hope you have good luck in finding work and a new home."

Roy stands talking to him while Ollie pushes the mop handle between boxes tied-down in the truck bed. Gray cotton strings drip water over the tailgate.

"Morene, Syble, it makes me nervous for you girls to ride back here alone, but I'm counting on you being grown-up enough to stay seated until we stop. You'll get a better view of the country than you would up front between your daddy and me."

Soon they are rolling past vegetable farms, pastures, hay meadows, creeks, and hills. They stop in a park at the edge of a small town to eat the bologna sandwiches and sugar cookies Ollie packed for lunch.

It is early afternoon when they arrive in Tulare. Floy and Morris greet them with hugs and handshakes. Floy is still holding Ollie's arm when she exclaims, "There's a vacant house next door to Morris's mama. It has a double kitchen sink and an icebox, but no stove. It's close enough to walk from here, so I can visit often."

Morris interrupts with his smooth deep voice, "Roy, you can buy a portable kerosene-burning stove pretty cheap. It will fit on a cabinet top. Then, if you move someplace with a regular stove, you can easily sell the portable, or keep it for picnics and camping trips."

Ann is alternately tugging on Ollie's dress and reaching for Ollie to pick her up.

Ollie lifts the baby and turns to Roy. "Let's go look at the house. I'm anxious to get settled."

The house is not as nice as the one in Shafter, but Ollie likes the area. The surrounding land is level farmland with tall mountains in the distance. From the porch, they can see for miles. There are not many trees except in orchards or someone's yard.

Floy raises her hand and points. "Ollie, in the winter those mountains are topped with snow. They're gorgeous, like a storybook picture."

Roy pays the rent to the property owner, then he and Morris

walk with the older girls to look at the school. Floy helps Ollie unpack dishes and housewares while Grandma McDougal plays with Ann.

Grandma McDougal says she will be glad to watch the baby if Ollie finds a job. "She's walking, so I won't have to lift her. We'll get along fine."

Roy stays busy with odd jobs for a few weeks until the cotton is ready to pick, then he and Ollie start with a large crew—most of them from Arkansas, Oklahoma, Texas, and Mexico.

Ollie works side by side with Roy, as they did in the Arkansas fields. When her sack gets full, he takes it to the scales. She continues picking on his rows while he is gone. Ollie cannot lift the heavy sack when it is full of cotton, but her hands are quick. Very few workers accumulate more weight on the chart than she does.

Chapter 3
Temptation

After they have been in the fields for a week, Grandma McDougal tells Ollie that Morris is afraid she will lose her pension if someone discovers she is working. "There is a daycare center in town where you can leave Ann during the day. If you work on a Saturday when they're closed, I'll keep her without charging you. She's no trouble at all. I enjoy her company, but I need my pension money to live on."

The next morning, Ollie, in her best dress, waits for the daycare center to opens. She fills out the paperwork, pays the fee, and starts to leave. Ann reaches, screaming, "Mama, Mama."

With tears streaming down her face, Ollie can hardly see to walk home. The girls have left for school, and Roy has gone to work. Sobbing, she changes into work clothes and washes her face in cold water before going to the field.

All day, she can think of little else except Ann. *What if she gets hurt or sick? I wouldn't know about it until I get off work.* For two weeks, Ann continues to cry when Ollie leaves her. The third week, she runs off to play with other children, hardly looking back.

A teacher brings Ann home each afternoon.

Grandma McDougal watches the child from her window, until Morene and Syble get home from school. She refuses pay, insisting it never takes more than five minutes for the older girls to arrive.

One day Grandma McDougal rushes out to meet Ollie and Roy as they walk home from the field. "Ann's playing with toys in my living room, but the older girls have not come home."

Roy runs toward the school, asking children along the way if they have seen the girls. Soon, he is back. "Ollie, they're not at school or in the park. I'm going to the police station."

He is about to get into the truck when Ollie sees three small figures coming across an open field. "Roy! Over there!" Shielding her eyes, she cranes her neck and watches from the porch as he hurries to meet them.

Morene and Syble wave timidly. The other child turns toward school.

Hands on his hips, Roy pauses to catch his breath.

Careful not to get within his reach, the girls run ahead to Ollie.

Roy trudges up, and drops down on the porch. "All right, start explaining."

Both girls stare at the ground. Morene's voice is soft and low. "We went with, uh—"

"Speak so we can hear you."

Morene clears her throat. "Lilly wanted to show us a place where she goes to play and jump on some old bedsprings stuck in the top of a hole."

Syble looks up at her daddy. "We told her we were supposed to go right home, but she said it wasn't far. If we ran, we could be home at the regular time."

"Girls, remember the Bible story about Adam and Eve—she listened to the serpent's lies because she wanted to taste a pretty apple that she thought would make her wise like God. Now everyone suffers because she was bad and brought sin into the world. You listened to your friend instead of doing what you knew was right. Now, you have to suffer the consequence."

Morene interrupts, "But, we ran as fast as we could to get

there, and only jumped a little."

"You were gone over an hour while the baby and Grandma McDougal waited."

Roy goes inside, gets his leather belt, gives both girls a hard spanking, and tells them to sit on the porch until bedtime. "I better not ever hear of you going near that place again."

The next day after work, Roy walks over to see where the girls were jumping. It is an abandoned oil well. Morris told him those old wells are usually several hundred feet deep. If the bedsprings had come free, the girls would have fallen into the well and been killed.

That night, while supper is cooking, Ollie sits in a chair near the front window to read a newspaper. Morene and Syble are talking on the front porch. "Syble, I don't want to walk home with those kids tomorrow. That woman might think *we* were throwing apples."

"Well, we can't stand around waiting. We'll get in trouble for not watching Ann. Why don't we walk over one block and come back to our street after we're past the apple tree?"

Ollie walks onto the porch. "Who's been throwing apples? Was Lilly doing it?"

"No, not Lilly." Syble shakes her head. "She walks with us. It was some other kids."

"Morene, start at the beginning and tell me the whole story."

"Syble knows as much as I do."

"You're the oldest. Hurry up—I don't want to burn supper."

Morene looks at Syble and frowns. "An old woman, who lives near the school, has an apple tree in her yard. Some of the kids went inside the fence, stole some apples, and threw them in the street. They made a terrible mess."

"How awful."

"The woman was really mad. She came out with her broom, chased and yelled at them. One kid threw an apple at Syble. She caught it, but dropped it real quick. Now we're afraid to walk by that house. Is it all right if we walk around the block?"

"No, I don't want you walking off by yourselves. Hurry along in front, or linger behind if they get ahead of you."

The girls look at each other with somber faces. Ollie hears them whispering as she walks into the kitchen.

The next day when Roy and Ollie get home, a dishpan of apples sets on the table. Ollie's voice reveals alarm. "Girls, where did you get these?"

Syble is quick to answer. "We didn't steal them. That woman gave them to us."

Ollie frowns. "She gave them to you." She looks at Morene. "Explain why."

Morene takes a deep breath. "We left school as soon as we could after the bell rang. When we got close to that woman's house, no one else was around. Lilly said she bet we could grab some apples off the ground, run away to eat them, and no one would know."

Ollie slaps a hand to her chest. "Oh, my goodness."

"We didn't, Mama. We wouldn't steal. Syble told Lilly we couldn't, but Syble had two pennies in her shoe. She walked up to the porch with Lilly pulling on her arm and telling her that woman was gonna kill her with a broom." Morene pauses to look at Syble.

"She went inside the gate? Did she knock on the door?"

"Yes," Morene nods. "When that woman opened the screen,

Syble held out the pennies and asked if it was enough to buy three apples."

Ollie grins. "Two pennies?"

Morene nods. "The woman said, 'Honey, I don't want your pennies. You can have all the apples you can carry away. Only don't throw them and make a mess.'"

"She gave them to you—but how did you carry them home?"

"We put them in our dress tails. Mama, our panties didn't show. We had slips on."

"Lilly filled her dress tail too. That woman's not mean, not like those kids said. She's nice. Her name is Rose. She told Lilly that roses and lilies make pretty bouquets."

Ollie stoops to hug them. "Would you like for me to make a couple of pies with some of your apples?"

They smile, and nod vigorously.

"All right, they can bake while we eat, and later we'll sit on the porch and enjoy pie in the cool evening air."

The girls are washing dishes when Floy sticks her head in the front door. "Ollie, I sure picked a good time to drop by." She giggles. "It smells like apple pie in here."

Ollie laughs. "Help me dish this up, and we'll see if it's fit to eat."

"I know it is. Anything smelling this good has to be delicious."

During dessert, the conversation turns to the giant redwood forest. Roy sets his empty plate on the porch. "I want to go see those big trees. My pa said his grandpa used to tell him about giant oaks and other hardwoods on the mountains of Georgia. After the government moved the Cherokees to Oklahoma, loggers cut the timber and literally rolled it off the mountaintops because the mountains were so steep and the trees so big. All those logs rolling downhill to the rivers knocked over and killed the small timber. Afterwards, when the rains came, tons of mud, rocks, and brush rolled toward the rivers. Erosion was terrible."

Morris nods. "If it hadn't been for John Muir fighting for these redwoods, the loggers would have done the same here. They destroyed a lot of them before he got the government to set aside areas for national parks. You know, they claim some of those trees were here before the time of Christ."

Roy rubs his hands together. "Let's go see them. Ollie, how about frying a chicken early Saturday morning so we can picnic on the mountain? I've been looking at the map—it won't take long to get there. Morris, will you and Floy go with us?"

"Sure! You'd like that, wouldn't you, Floy?"

"You know I would. I'll fry a chicken, too, and do some baking. I can hardly wait."

Early Saturday morning, they leave on the trip to the Redwood Forest. The sky is bright blue and seems to increase in brightness as they go up the steep mountains.

They stop at a little store and buy bottles of grape soda. Ollie thinks she will share with Ann, but that is a mistake. Ann clings to the bottle. After the baby drools into the drink, Ollie does not want to share. All three girls have purple mouths.

Roy walks around with Morris, reading every sign, feeling the bark, and examining the small cones. "You'd think trees this big would have giant cones instead of such small compact things, but I guess these survive a forest fire better than big brittle ones."

The girls, Ann included, want to run around the trees, collect and toss cones, and climb on the big rocks. Ollie is afraid they will run in front of a car, fall off the rocks, or step on a rattlesnake. "I'm sure I would have enjoyed this much more before I had little girls to worry about."

"It's beautiful up here"—Floy draws a deep breath and looks around—"but I'm watching where I put my feet. I've heard some of those awful stories about rattlers in the mountains."

The day passes quickly. They are in the truck ready to start home when Roy asks, "Who would like to stop at one of those mountain streams and look for gold nuggets?"

"We do! We do!" the girls shout.

Morris, Floy, and Ollie smile and nod.

They stop at a stream flowing over and around a bed of rocks and gravel. Morene picks up a round stone about the size of an egg. "Daddy, why are all these rocks so smooth? None of them have rough edges."

"That's because they've rolled for miles through the water. All the rough edges have worn away."

"But all of them are that way, even the ones not in the water."

"All of these rocks have tumbled for miles. In the spring, when melting snow runs off the mountains, and heavy rains pour down this little stream will look like a raging river. Rushing water will be so swift that a man couldn't stand. When it's like that, gravel and rocks rub together as they roll along until they become round or egg-shaped."

Upstream, where a few trees cluster, an old man pans for gold. "Are you having any luck?" Roy asks.

"I found a small nugget last Saturday. Only a few flakes today."

"Do you pan gold for a living?"

The man shakes his head. "No. I like to eat, and this is not profitable enough to buy my groceries. I work in a bank during the week, but on Saturdays, I like solitude. I come up here to enjoy nature."

"Don't you have a wife?" Syble asks.

"Not anymore."

Roy takes Morene's arm. "Come on, girls."

"But I want to watch him find gold." Syble stares at the sand and water swirling in the flat pan.

Roy's voice is stern. "I said, come on. He came here for solitude."

Floy and Morris walk toward the truck. Ollie lingers, waiting for Syble to get closer to Roy.

The old man continues shaking and draining the pan without saying another word.

Syble runs to keep up with Roy's long steps. "Daddy, what does sol-i-tude mean?"

"It means he wants to be left alone, probably because he lost his wife."

"Lost? Why's he not looking for her instead of gold?"

"Not that kind of *lost*. She probably divorced him, or she may be dead."

"Oh. He wants to be left alone because he's sad."

Roy is carrying Ann in his right arm, but he pats Syble's shoulder with his left hand. "I believe that's right."

After setting Ann in the back of the truck, Roy rubs his stomach. "Do we have any scraps left from the picnic lunch? I'm hungry again."

Ollie picks up her basket. "The chicken and potato salad are gone, but I still have boiled eggs and fried apple pies."

"I have enough corn fritters for everyone"—Floy rummages through her basket—"some pickles and a sack of raisin cookies."

Holding pie tins as plates, the men and children sit on rocks. Ollie divides the pies and cookies. Floy dishes out fritters, pickles, and boiled eggs. "Morris, you have to wait until last for sweets." She winks at the girls and goes to sit near Ollie on the truck's tailgate.

On the way home, distant hills and mountains are a dark navy contrast against the tangerine-streaked sky. Ollie blinks and strains to stay focused so she can talk to Roy and keep him awake, but cannot help yawning as he speaks with Morris and Floy at their driveway.

Roy leaves the headlights on until Ollie carries Ann inside the house. Morene and Syble, still half-asleep, stagger inside and curl-up on top of their beds, offering no resistance as Ollie washes their faces, hands, and feet.

Roy sits on the porch, smoking his pipe while Ollie cleans the picnic dishes, then he comes inside, stretches, yawns, and heads for the bedroom.

Ollie intends to sit and read the Bible while the house is quiet. Since she has been working in the fields, there has been little time to read, but like so many times lately, she is startled awake when the book plops onto the floor. She fumbles with her apron strings, turns out the light, and moves toward the sound of Roy's snoring.

A few days later, Morene runs to meet Ollie and Roy as they walk to the house after work. "Mama, Daddy, my teacher signed me up for art class. It doesn't cost anything. I go to the art room with a special teacher while the other kids in my class color."

Morene draws on every scrap of paper she finds that is not covered in print—in the newspaper margins, on the back of old homework papers, and in the sand beside the house. One evening she brings out a picture of a rooster. "Daddy, look at the picture I drew in class."

"You mean traced, don't you?"

"No, I didn't trace it."

"Morene, it's very good tracing, but you need to admit you didn't draw it. I won't put up with you telling lies."

"I'm not telling a lie. I drew it in art class."

Roy reaches for his belt, but stops. "All right, prove it. Get your notebook and draw another one."

Wiping away tears, she brings her art book and sits at the table.

Roy watches as a rooster, even more lifelike than the first one, materializes before his eyes. "I'm sorry for accusing you. I had no idea you could draw like that. Your teacher was right. You have an unusual talent for your age."

Morene looks at him, her face beaming.

Chapter 4
Sleeping Sickness

Roy and Ollie are pleased at the money they make picking cotton. Irrigation during the hot growing season made the stalks grow tall and loaded them with large bolls bursting with long, snow-white strands. Watering has stopped for picking season, yet many wet places remain in the fields. Shaded by large green leaves, every damp area harbors swarms of mosquitoes.

Roy and Ollie walk to their rows wearing long-sleeved shirts to protect their arms. Still, large red bumps frequently appear on hands, faces, necks and ears even though they apply kerosene each morning to help repel the insects.

"Roy, I've never seen such aggressive mosquitoes." She slaps at one flying toward her face. "You'd think they couldn't settle on our hands because we're continually moving, but these big critters fly in and stick. I worry about the chance of us getting mosquito fever like you had when Morene was a baby."

"I don't want that again. I've never been so sick. Do you think your mama could get some quinine medicine from Dr. Hart and mail it to us?"

"I'll ask when I write to her." She slaps at another insect. "I wish I had a sewing machine so I could make us some hoods out of mosquito netting."

A man calls to Roy. "Did you read last night's newspaper?"

"No, I didn't get out and buy a paper."

"Folks around this area are getting a sleeping sickness" — the man steps closer — "no one knows the cause. A few people have died from it."

Everyone talks at once, panic in their voices. The workers discuss the news as they pick and while getting their cotton weighed. One man demands his pay at the end of the day. He says he is moving his family before one of them falls asleep and dies.

A few days later, in the afternoon, Ollie is so tired that she fears she will not be able to work until quitting time, but she is afraid to start home alone. *What if I pass out on the side of the road? People will think I'm drunk.*

Roy leaves early to get her cotton weighed. When he comes back, she is leaning on his sack trying to stay awake. He goes for the truck while a friend weighs-in his cotton.

Ollie is vaguely aware of workers on adjacent rows picking extra fast with faces turned away. One woman pulls her shirt collar around her face and drags her sack about twenty feet past Ollie before starting to pick again. She declares, "I have a baby to take care of. I can't afford to get sick."

The next day, Ollie wants to go to the field with Roy, but before they are finished with breakfast, she feels faint. He helps her to bed.

She insists that Roy go to the field. "The cotton is at peak condition for picking. I'll be fine. Ann will stay beside me and play with her doll."

Ollie hears Roy call to Grandma McDougal, asking if she will watch the house to make sure Ann does not go outside to play.

"Do you want me to come over and stay with Ollie?"

"No, but I'll feel better if you'll look this way once in a while."

When a few days pass and Ollie is not better, she worries that she has the sleeping sickness. Roy wants to take her to the doctor, but she refuses. "Why go to the doctor when the paper says they don't know what's causing this?"

The spells become more frequent. Sometimes she will be in the kitchen and start feeling as if she is going to fall asleep. If she is washing dishes, she does not take time to grab a towel to dry her hands before rushing to the bedroom. As she goes, she tells Ann to come sit beside her. Ollie never remembers getting past the doorway, but when she wakes, the baby is always playing on the floor near the bed.

One day, after an attack, she remembers dreaming: an angel held out a bottle filled with yellow liquid.

When Roy comes home, Ollie asks him to go to the store and buy two bottles of a yellow-colored chill tonic. She has felt all along that mosquitoes cause the illness. "That tonic has quinine in it. After my dream, I'm sure it's what I need."

She is soon feeling better. Within two weeks, Ollie is back at work. She and Roy buy several bottles of the tonic and continue taking it until all the cotton is gone from the fields.

Bronnie writes to say she is coming to visit on the weekend, her days off from the dairy. Ollie goes to the station to meet her and smiles as she watches her young sister gracefully exiting the big Greyhound bus.

They embrace and stand at arm's-length, looking at each other.

Who would ever think they are sisters? Ollie has Irish blue

eyes and hair the color of dark honey. Bronnie has black hair, brown eyes, and coppery skin inherited from their Cherokee ancestors. "Bronnie, you look more beautiful today than I've ever seen you."

"Maybe it's because I'm in love."

Ollie squeezes her arm. "You don't mean it?"

Bronnie nods. "His name is Herbert and he's from Arkansas."

Laughing and talking, they walk slowly back to the house. The girls race to meet them. Bronnie hugs Morene and Syble, lifts Ann high and then squeezes her tight. "Oh, I've missed all of you so much."

"Why don't you look for a job up here? You can stay with us until you find work."

"I was considering that very thing, until I met Herbert. This is too far away for courting."

Ollie smiles. "Romance complicates things."

The weekend passes too quickly. On Sunday afternoon, Bronnie hugs them all before climbing onto the bus for her return trip to Shafter.

Ollie's eyes fill with tears as she watches the bus pull away.

Roy puts his arm around her shoulders. "We'll see her again before too long."

"Seeing her makes me miss my family even more. Most of the time I'm too busy to be lonesome for very long." She looks away toward the mountains, and wipes her eyes. "I hope Herbert's a good man. If he's not, Bronnie will never suspect until after he's done her wrong. She sees the good side of everyone."

"Your sister's a pretty woman, has a sweet personality, and

she's not lazy. I can't think of a reason he wouldn't love her."

"Some people think so highly of themselves that love of anyone else is only temporary. I do hope Bronnie will be happy."

"Well, you couldn't change her mind now, even if you knew he was a rascal."

"He's handsome, and she's crazy about him. Did she show you his picture?"

Roy nods. "They'll make a good-looking pair."

Monday afternoon, as they walk home from the field, Roy and Ollie talk about their future and the money they are saving. Roy squeezes her hand. "I talked to the boss about doing maintenance work through the winter. He hinted that he might keep me on, but didn't say for sure. If he does, we'll buy you a sewing machine. You might even take in some sewing and mending jobs."

"I would like that. I could keep Ann at home with me while I sew, but we need to make sure you have a job until picking season. I don't want to dig into our farm savings unless we have no other choice." Ollie takes off her bonnet and combs fingers through her hair.

"I've been thinking a lot about that. Farming here is different from the kind we grew up with in Arkansas. We would need a tractor and irrigation equipment." He pauses to spit tobacco juice beside the sandy path. "It'll take a lifetime to save that much. If we stay here, we'll need to buy a small house and plan on working for the big farmers, or I could look for a factory job."

She turns to look at him, squinting against the sunlight. "Would you like working in a factory?"

He draws in a deep breath and spits again. "I'd hate it, but that's not the point. I've gotta make a living for my family."

She stares at the ground and her dusty brown oxfords. "Can we save our money for a few years and go back to Arkansas? I hate for our girls to grow up so far away from family."

He puts an arm around her shoulders. "That's what I'd like to do, but if I don't get a maintenance job, we may have to dig into our savings. Morris told me there are very few farming jobs in the first three months of the year."

"We'll do something. Both of us can look for factory jobs to hold us through until picking season."

Roy's boss keeps him until after Christmas doing carpentry repairs on the barns. In January, the job ends. After looking all day for work, Roy checks the mailbox and takes out a letter from one of his sisters. He rips open the envelope and sits on the porch to read while Ollie cooks supper.

Morene steps softly into the kitchen and whispers to Ollie, "Mama, is Daddy crying?"

"I don't know. You and Syble take Ann and go play in the backyard. Don't come into the house or the front yard until I call you. Your daddy must have read some bad news. I'll let you know later."

Ollie rushes to the porch and sits beside him. "Roy—?"

He clears his throat, wipes his eyes, and turns his face away from her. "They think Ma has cancer."

Ollie lays her head against his shoulder and rubs his arm. She cannot think of any words to ease his pain.

He places the letter on the porch, reaches into his pocket for a handkerchief, and blows his nose. "We've got to go back. I'm not gonna wait until she's gone. As soon as we're packed, we'll take the girls out of school and leave." He picks up the letter, folds and unfolds it. "We need to ask our family to inquire about farms to rent or sharecrop. It'll mean starting over again, but I have to go."

"I know." Ollie smoothes her apron with both hands. "I didn't want to move here, but now I hate to leave. The girls are doing well in school, especially Morene. She loves her teacher and her art class." She reaches for his hand before standing. "I smell cornbread. I'd better take it from the oven before it burns."

Roy remains seated on the step.

She tugs at his hand. "Supper's ready. I'll dish it up."

He shakes his head. "Go ahead. I don't want any."

Chapter 5
Going Home

"Ollie, we'll need to take the southern route on our way to Arkansas. That way is a little longer and the highway may not be as good, but I don't want to get stuck in a snowstorm." He pauses to look up at snow-covered mountains. "The deserts should be pretty this time of year. Wildflowers bloom there in winter and early spring. It's also the best time to see animals. They'll be out searching the lowlands for green grass."

She walks around mumbling and counting off things on her fingers. "We have potatoes and canned meat to fry on the kerosene stove. I made enough cookies and yeast bread to last three days, and bought cornflakes and milk for breakfast. What time do you want to get up?"

"Set the alarm for four. I'll finish loading while you wash the breakfast dishes and get the girls ready. I want to be driving by five."

Ollie shakes her head. "The girls won't be able to eat that early. I'll make us some coffee and buttered bread, then I'll help you load while the girls get dressed. They can eat somewhere along the road when they get hungry."

"Whatever. Tonight, I'm too tired to talk or even listen." Roy moans and stretches out on a mattress. "We've got three or more long days ahead of us."

He has paid the final bill, and the electric company turned off the power, so they drink coffee by lantern light. Before daylight, they are rolling toward San Bernardino, where they will turn east.

Morene and Syble are excited about the trip, although Morene cries over having to leave her friends and art teacher. Roy barely stops long enough to buy gas and allow the girls to visit the restroom. They eat sandwiches while riding. Stopping to see sights along the way is out of the question—he is going home.

The countryside is more beautiful than Ollie imagined. Wildflowers of every color, unlike any she has seen before, blanket deserts and hillsides. In some areas, snow-capped mountains tower in the distance. Antelope and deer seem unafraid of passing vehicles.

Sitting on mattresses lodged between the wheel wells, Morene and Syble bob around, twisting and turning to look over and around boxes of clothing, household furnishings, and Roy's tools. They want to see everything, but viewing space is limited. The truck is packed tight.

Each night Roy removes and stacks the boxes under the truck. He sleeps outside on a cot. Ollie and the girls get the mattress bed, but Ollie stays awake most of the night remembering all the awful stories she has heard about road bandits. Hand on the pistol, she is ready to defend her family.

In Arkansas, they move into a rented house near Centerville. Later, they find a farm in the Happy Valley community. The farm has some good flat ground, fertile for crops. It is a short distance from the high bluffs of Wolf Hollow.

Roy is familiar with the area and tells Ollie and the girls how spring rains turn the hollow into a wonderland with roaring waterfalls rushing off the bluffs to the valley below, and about fishing in the East Cadron creek, and riding horses through the valley when he was a boy.

Morene glances at Syble then at Roy. "Daddy, how old were you then, and who went riding with you?"

"I was about your age when I started riding with boys from the neighborhood. Before, I went with my brothers or Pa."

The girls look at each other, and then Morene asks, "Can Syble go riding with me?"

Before Roy can speak, Ollie answers. "Only when your daddy goes along and that won't be often. He has too much work planned for this spring."

Morene and Syble are back in school with old friends. Roy spends as much time as possible with his ma, but has to break ground and plant crops when the weather allows.

One afternoon, Morene and Syble come home very excited. "Mama! Mama!" they both yell. "Lou's having a birthday party after school tomorrow. She asked us to spend the night."

Ollie frowns. "Well, you'll have to miss it. We're planting corn. You need to hurry home to watch Ann and get the chores done, so I can help Roy." No amount of pleading can convince her to let them go.

The next day, Morene goes to the field where Ollie is hooking up the planter. Ann waits in a shade at the edge of the plowed ground. Morene takes her little sister's hand, waves to Ollie, and turns to go.

Ollie yells to her, "It'll be late when we get in. We want to plant as much as we can."

"All right." The girls giggle as they start toward the house.

When Ollie and Roy come in from the field, Morene has supper warmed and waiting on the table.

Ollie walks through the house. "Where's Syble?"

Morene looks at her shoes. "Her jobs are all done."

"That's not what I asked. Where is she?"

Morene swallows and clears her throat. "She went to the birthday party, but I did her chores."

Ollie slams her hand down on the table. "After I told her not to go? Did you plan this together?"

"No. It wasn't my idea. I told her she'd get a whippin', but she said, 'It'll only hurt for a little while.'"

Roy frowns when Ollie repeats the story to him, but he does not comment. He is in a hurry to go see his ma.

The next afternoon Morene goes to the field to get Ann, while Syble does the chores. When Roy and Ollie come to the house, he breaks a long limb from a bush, stops at the porch, and calls to Syble.

Wearing blue jeans and the thickest long-sleeve shirt she owns, she steps outside.

"Why did you go to the party when your mama told you not to?"

Syble draws in a deep breath. "She's my friend."

"Do you think that's a good enough excuse to not mind your mama?"

"No."

He spits tobacco juice onto a flower bush, grabs Syble's arm, and jerks her off the porch. He whips her until his arm gives out, then he goes to the barn to feed the horses. Morene and

Ann, tears streaming down their faces, try to hug Syble. She grits her teeth and turns away.

Coming from the barn, Roy stops at the porch and asks, "Has it stopped hurting yet?" Before bedtime, she gets two more whippings.

Ollie was angry when she told him to give Syble a whipping she would remember. She forgot to consider Roy's temper, his worry about getting crops planted before heavy spring rains turn the fields into a sea of mud, and the stress of his ma's illness that keeps him awake at night. Lately, Ma is suffering a great deal with the cancer. Ollie's heart aches for Syble, for Roy, and for his ma.

Syble knew she would get a whipping, but not three. Ollie overhears Syble talking to Morene: "No one cares how I feel, except Ann. And I don't like any of you either."

"Why me?" Morene asks.

"Because you told Mama what I said."

"She asked me. I had to tell her."

"You didn't have to tell her I said a whipping will only hurt until it stops hurting. You caused me to get three instead of one. Tattle-tale—you were too scared to go to the party, and you wanted me to get in trouble."

Morene stares at Syble. "I didn't know he would whip you three times."

"You knew that would make them furious. I'll never tell you anything else, 'cause you always tattle to Mama." Syble picks up a stick and throws it at the woodpile. "I hate living in Arkansas. We can't visit friends or have them visit us, because we have to *work*. All the time, nothing but work."

For a week, Syble wears blue jeans to school to hide the red stripes on her legs. It is several weeks before she will voluntarily look at Roy's face, and months before she initiates a conversation with him or Ollie. At home, she has returned to old habits of letting Morene do the talking.

Mary Lou, Ollie's old friend, lives near Ma. Despite a big difference in ages, she and Ma have become good friends. Since the discovery of Ma's illness, Mary gets up early every day to do her own chores, then goes to help Ma.

Mary whispers to Ollie. "She doesn't want some undertaker changing her clothes. Weeks ago, she made me promise I would get her ready for the funeral."

"She told me you promised to do that for her."

"Ollie, you know how Miss Nancy hates flies. At funerals of friends and relatives, she was always near the casket ready to wave her lacy handkerchief if one buzzed into the house, and at every church potluck she stood over the food fanning a wide white dishtowel instead of eating."

Ollie nods. "She was the same at family dinners. Mary, I'll help you when her time comes, but I'll have to bring Ann along if the older girls are in school."

"Ann won't be a problem. She's a quiet little thing. I'll need someone to give me a few breaks to run to the toilet. I swore that no green fly would get near Miss Nancy, and I'll keep my promise if I have to stay beside her 'til the water runs down my leg."

Roy is with Ma when she draws her last breath. He comes home exhausted and stretches out across the bed. Like Roy, most of the family goes home to rest. Mary is left in charge.

Ollie takes Ann and goes to help. Morene and Syble have the measles and must stay home from school until the spots fade, but Ollie does not want to leave Ann with them. The older girls will be quiet, and Roy can rest.

With swollen eyes and clenched teeth, Mary is placing silver combs in Ma's hair when Ollie arrives. She speaks in a low monotone without looking up. "The doctor's already signed the death certificate and left. Like she asked, I washed her face and tied new cheesecloth around her chin and head so that when her jaw locks in place her lips won't separate." Gently, she touches Ma's cheek.

"She told me that, once when she was a little girl, she went to a funeral where a woman's mouth gaped open, showing her tongue. Miss Nancy didn't want to look like that. She was a hard worker, and as neat as anyone I've ever known. I promised she'd look pretty for her funeral."

Neighbors place the varnished casket on a stand in the living room, then lift her from the bed and ease her onto the smooth white pillowcase that will be the final resting place for her tired head. Mary places new copper pennies on Ma's eyelids, and folds the thin muscular hands over her stomach.

Ann tugs at Ollie's dress tail. "Mama, pick me up so I can see Ma."

"Not now, Ann. Mary's not finished making her pretty."

Ollie does not want Ann to see her grandma until Mary removes the pennies and cheesecloth. While Ollie talks to a neighbor bringing a food dish, someone lifts Ann up to see.

"Put me down! Put me down! I don't like Ma in that box." She reaches for her mama.

Ollie places the food item on a table, takes Ann, and stands her on the floor.

Ann wraps herself in the folds of Ollie's dress. "Mama, why does Ma have a bandage tied around her head and money on her eyes? It makes her look scary. And why does it smell like medicine in here?"

Ollie whispers, "The pennies hold her eyes closed. We'll take them off in a little while, but don't ask anyone else to lift you. The medicine smell is camphor. Mary gave Ma a bath with it."

"I don't like it. She should use soap."

Ollie leans close to Ann's ear. "The camphor kills germs and keeps away bugs. Whisper when you need to talk to me. If you don't be quiet, I'm gonna get one of these men to take you home, and you'll have to take a nap with your daddy."

Ann frowns and turns her head to look around the room.

Ollie leads Ann to a corner. "Play with your doll and don't let anyone pick you up."

Nancy Jane (Battles) Glenn died May 29, 1938. The following day, she is buried in the Thorn Cemetery near a young son and her infant twins. Fanny, Roy's oldest sister, moves into the home-place to take care of Pa.

Chapter 6
A Son

After renting for several months, Roy and Ollie buy a farm in Happy Valley. It seems to have good ground for growing cotton and corn. The house has three rooms: a kitchen, one bedroom where the girls will sleep, and a large living room where Roy and Ollie set their bed in a corner across from the rock fireplace—in winter, they will keep a warm fire burning night and day.

In the spring of 1939, Roy works in the fields from daylight until dark, breaking ground, planting, and plowing. Ollie knows he is trying to work too many acres. She prepares a hearty midday meal and then yells, "Din-ner!" as she beats on an old plow point hanging from a post.

Roy comes through the door, lets the screen slam, and drops into a chair. "Ollie, you know the preacher's boy, the red-headed one? He came by today asking for a job. I was tempted to hire him, but I told him I'd think about it and talk it over with you. I really need help to get all this plowing done before the grass and weeds choke out the crops."

A shiver runs up the back of her neck. "Oh Roy, I know you need help, but we can't afford it. Don't go in debt for that. I'd rather you let some of the corn grow up with weeds. Tomorrow, if you'll borrow Papa's team and cultivator, I'll help."

His brow furrows. "You know better than that—with a baby coming in four months." He releases a long sigh and stares at his plate. "I'll do what I can." He eats the meal in silence, takes a long drink of water, and stands.

"Wait. I made a cobbler. It's still hot, but it'll cool pretty quick in a dish."

"I don't have time. Send some in a pie tin with Morene when she brings water. It'll taste better then." He grabs a sweat-stained straw hat and goes out the door.

Ollie saw both disappointment and anger flash across his face when she said they couldn't afford to hire someone. He will have more to say when the girls are not listening. *That boy's from a good family and probably a hard worker. Still, we'll be in trouble if it's another drought year.*

That night, after the girls are in bed, Ollie mentions the subject while he sits on the porch smoking his pipe. "Roy, I know you need help with the work, but I feel like it's the wrong thing to hire that boy."

"Every year can't be a drought, and we'll never get ahead like we're going."

"I'd help if I wasn't expecting."

"But you are, and the baby's due at picking time."

"The girls will have to help."

"It'll take both of them to pick as much as one adult."

"You may have to pay someone then, but not now—not 'til you know the crops are going to produce."

She turns her face toward the sky, hardly noticing lightning bugs twinkling in the darkness, and the painful screeching sounds of tree frogs in nearby maples. "There's something else, something that's hard to explain."

Roy stares at her without speaking.

"A cold chill runs up the back of my neck every time I think about you hiring that boy."

Roy knocks his pipe against the side of the step, runs his work shoe over the ashes, and stands. "I'm going to bed. Wake me as soon as you hear the alarm."

Throughout the summer, rains come when needed, and crops grow well. Every day, Ollie expects Roy to tell her they should have hired help and planted more fields. He never does.

At picking time, the girls stay home from school to help. Ann plays in the shade of the wagon while Ollie picks the rows close by. The first picking is complete, and the second is well underway when labor pains start. Roy saddles Nell and goes to tell Ollie's mama and the doctor.

Within an hour, Mama pulls her buggy into the yard. She has never missed coming to help deliver one of Ollie's babies. Doctor Hart lifts the baby. "Roy, it's a boy this time." John Vernon is born in October of 1939.

Roy never acted disappointed when the girls were born, but he is thrilled with John. So is Syble—she coddles and watches over him as if he were her own. Roy's family celebrates the birth of a son. His Uncle Jim, visiting from Texas, comes to the house to see the baby.

The weather is turning cold before Roy and the girls finish gathering the crops. The stove wood stacked outside the kitchen is almost down to the ground, and there is no pile of wood ready for burning in the fireplace.

The day after the last load of corn is stored in the corncrib, clouds hang low in the sky, thick and heavy. A cold wind blows from the northwest, pulling orange and red leaves from trees on the mountainside. "Roy, those clouds look like they could start dumping snow at any minute. Do you think I should keep the girls home from school?"

"No, I'll go get them in the truck if it gets too bad."

"But I thought you and Eldridge were going to cut wood today."

Roy pushes back his breakfast plate. "We are. He has enough to last him a while, so we'll get ours first. We'll be cutting on the mountain where that storm blew over those big oaks, but I'll go get the girls if it gets too bad for them to walk home."

"All right. Girls, get your lunch pails, and put on your scarves and gloves."

Knowing that her brother will be eating with them, Ollie wants to serve a good meal. All morning the baby whines and fusses. After nursing at ten, he finally falls asleep. She rushes to fry potatoes to go with the ham, beans, cornbread, buttered turnips, and plum cobbler. She sets a fresh pot of coffee on to percolate before spooning food into a plate for Ann. "Hon, come on to the table. I know you're hungry. Daddy and Uncle Eldridge may be a while. They're probably trying to get a good load before starting home."

Ollie puts Ann in her bed for a nap after she finishes eating. "You need to rest a while, but I'll wake you when your daddy and Eldridge get here."

Nibbling a leftover piece of Ann's cornbread, Ollie walks out into the yard to throw scraps to the chickens. Black smoke billows from the mountainside. Sudden fear runs through her.

That smoke is too black for a brushfire, and there are no houses in that area. What could be burning? She stands watching. Chickens peck around her feet. A red rooster grabs for the bread in Ollie's hand. She jumps and kicks at the thief. Frightened birds squawk and fly in various directions and then race for the soiled bread tossed toward the barn.

Snowflakes fall softly, and the sky grows darker. The diminishing smoke blends with gray-black clouds. Ollie shivers and turns to gather the few remaining sticks from the woodpile. *I hope they get here soon.*

After adding wood to the fireplace, Ollie sits at the table to eat alone. "Ollie," Eldridge calls as he steps onto the porch. The door bursts open and closes quickly against the freezing wind. "The truck got away from us."

Ollie jumps up. "What do you mean, it got away from you?"

He sighs, shakes his head, and starts dipping food into a plate. "I thought I'd starve to death before I got here. I rushed off without eating breakfast this morning." He takes a big bite of fried potatoes and chews quickly.

Horrible images race through Ollie's mind. She reaches for the coffee pot and pours him a cupful. "Tell me, what happened to the truck?"

Eldridge is about to bite into a piece of cornbread when Ollie grabs his hand. "Not another taste 'til you tell me about the truck and Roy." Panic rises in her voice. "Where's Roy?"

"He's all right. He went to the store to see if he could get someone to help us cut another load of firewood before this storm hits any harder. The truck was full of wood. We were ready to come unload, but couldn't get the truck started. I hopped out to push from the back. Roy was pushing on the driver's side, ready to jump in and start it when we got rolling, but he tripped or something." Eldridge shoves the bread into his mouth, gulps coffee, and almost chokes.

"Once it began to move down that steep incline with a load of wood pushing, it seemed to fly—there was no catching it. I tried, and for a long way Roy was hanging onto the side, trying to get in, but the truck rolled off the road, tumbled sideways, dribbling our morning's work along the mountainside. I guess it was spilling gas, 'cause it burst into flames the instant it hit that big rock."

Ollie wrings her hands and walks back and forth beside the table. "Oh, Lord, what will happen next? Over half of our savings went into that truck. That was our transportation out of this valley. We can't afford another one—we'll have to use the wagon and team."

He takes another gulp of coffee. "Sis, be thankful Roy lost his grip and fell away from the truck. He would have been killed for sure if he'd held on until it went over the edge."

"Goodness, I didn't think about that." She pats him on the arm. "I'm thankful neither one of you were hurt."

"I've got to catch the team and take the wagon back. Can you fix something for Roy to eat, and put butter and jelly on a piece of that bread for me to eat on the way?"

"Those mares are not accustomed to seeing you. They might take off for the creek. I'll hitch them to the wagon while you fix a pie tin full of food."

That afternoon, Ollie is too nervous to concentrate on sewing, and keeps looking out the window to check on the weather. Sporadic snowflakes continue to fall, although not enough to cover the ground. She lets the fire in the fireplace die down, but keeps the house warm with the cook stove while baking sweet potatoes and a molasses cake.

Ollie has already milked the cows when Roy and the girls come home with a wagon full of wood—some of it already split. She rushes into the wind. Brushing wood chips from the girls' good coats, she tells them to go change into work clothes.

"Morene, stay inside with the babies. Syble, you come back and help unload wood. Gobble a piece of molasses cake before you put on your scarf and gloves, but don't linger. It'll be dark soon."

Roy takes the team to the barn for feed, leaving the wagon beside the house, between the two porches. Ollie steps onto the spokes of a wagon wheel. "Syble, pitch the small sticks near the front porch. I'll toss this split wood toward the back of the house. Later, you can help stack it on the porch for my cook stove, but you'll need to be careful of splinters." She pulls at a sliver jammed into her finger.

The wagon is unloaded when Roy finishes his work at the barn, except for large, heavy pieces that need splitting. He rolls them off before beginning a neat stack across one end of the front porch. He and Ollie work as fast as possible in silence until the chore is complete.

"Ollie, you and Syble get inside. I didn't unharness the horses. I want to put the wagon under the shed to keep it dry."

Morene has built a warm fire in the fireplace, put supper on the table, and filled plates for her sisters.

"When Syble gets her hands washed, you girls can eat and get ready for bed." Ollie removes her gloves and coat. "Your daddy has been out in the cold all day. He needs to eat and get some rest as soon as possible."

"But I have homework, and Syble does, too."

"Then do your homework as soon as you finish eating."

Roy comes in, scrubs his hands, and plops into a chair, his elbow resting on the table, one hand holding up his head. Face still red from the cold, eyelids drooping, he frowns from exhaustion and despair. "I couldn't stop it. All I could do was stand and watch it tumble off the mountain."

"Eldridge told me about it. I'm glad you weren't in the truck when it went off the road."

"It went so fast."

"Roy, eat your supper. You need to get in a warm bed. You've been out in this weather all day, and with the stress of that accident, it'll be a wonder if you don't get sick."

"A couple of neighbors were at the store when I got there. They came down and helped cut that wagon load of wood."

"Did you pay them for helping?"

"I tried, but they refused."

"We live in a good community. The people here are always ready to help someone in need." Ollie lifts a steaming kettle from the stove. "I've got a tub of water in front of the fireplace. With this, it should be just right for your bath. I'll send the girls into the bedroom to finish their homework."

Most of the snowstorm missed the valley. Only a light dusting covers the fields. Before morning, the wind stops blowing, but water in the kitchen bucket is frozen. Ollie sets it on the edge of the stove to thaw.

"I'll have to walk down to the creek and break ice at the edge for the cattle to drink." Roy stomps his feet, settling them in his work boots. "The ice is thin over the deep parts. A cow or calf would fall through when they stray that far. One might drown before it could get out. We've had enough bad luck. We don't want any dead animals."

"I hate for you to go out in this cold. Your face will freeze if you don't cover it. Have you still got that old pair of goggles to wear over your eyes?"

"They're in the barn, but the straps are rotten."

"I'll find a shoestring or a piece of elastic to tie them on. You need to protect your eyes."

Roy puts on gloves, a scarf, goggles and a hat. Ollie stops him before he opens the door. "Take your gun. You might run across something."

"I'll have the axe. It's too cold for hunting."

"I don't mean for hunting—for protection."

He shakes his head. "Ollie, I've been all over this place dozens of times with nothing more than my pocket knife. Now, I have on so many clothes I can hardly walk, and I'll be exhausted from carrying that axe."

"Remember those screams we heard a few nights ago? I have a feeling you need to take the gun. I'm sure there's a panther living along the bluffs. It could come into our pasture."

"Do you want to go along and carry the gun?"

"You know I have to stay here with the babies. I'm only thinking of your safety."

He sighs. "Hand it to me. My arms will be so tired, I'll have to sit and rest before breaking ice."

Ollie grins as she watches Roy waddle away in the heavy clothing, but she is getting worried before she sees him coming back across the field. He drops the axe at the corner of the house and steps onto the porch. She opens the door, takes the gun, and extends her hand for the shells.

"I used the shells." He slumps into a chair and leans his head back. "I shot at something big. It was probably out hunting for meat, but it wasn't black. It was tan, the color of a coyote. It sure looked like a cat." He sighs and grins. "Your intuition was right again. Without the gun to scare it off, I might've had quite a fight with that axe."

"Yeah, and you might have been kitten food about now."

He yanks off his hat and gloves, and fumbles with the buttons of his coat. "Do you remember Mort?"

Ollie nods. "Is he still trapping and selling hides?"

"Yep, and he's got a pack of hounds that I'll bet would search until they found that critter. We sure don't want any panthers hanging around our children and cattle."

"It's awful cold to be out in this weather."

"I know, but we need to get that animal. Some of the kids in this area walk a long way to meet the school bus."

Ollie lifts a potholder and removes a pan of muffins from the oven.

"Let me have a couple of those before I go. I walked off my biscuit and eggs. I'd hate to get hungry enough to eat at Mort's."

"That coffee should still be hot." She fills his cup, checks on the baby asleep in his bed near the fireplace, and peeks into the bedroom. "Girls, the house is warm and we've got hot muffins in here. Are you gonna snuggle under those quilts all day?"

Inside the small house, the morning passes slowly. Ollie worries that something bad might have happened to Roy. *He could freeze to death in weather like this.* It is mid-afternoon before Roy returns. "Ollie, dish me out a plate of food while I wash my hands. I'm starved."

She smiles and turns toward the stove. "I figured you stuffed yourself at Mort's."

"You know better than that. I wouldn't take a bite from that kitchen. Soon as I eat, I have a couple of stories to tell you."

After setting a plate of warm food in front of Roy, Ollie pours his coffee and sits across the table from him. "Is Mort gonna take dogs to look for that cat?"

Roy nods. "In the morning. He wants to get a bunch of his hunting buddies to help."

"I don't have a dessert ready, but I mixed another batch of muffins for snacking this afternoon. The girls and I finished the others. I thought they were pretty good made with chopped dried peaches and hickory nuts."

"They *were* good." He chuckles. "Much better than mouse poop."

"What?" Ollie frowns at him.

"Mort asked me to come in by the fire. His wife offered me a cup of coffee, but I turned it down. I figure they have to be conservative with groceries. Then she told me she fished a mouse out of her churn yesterday morning. The churn lid was cedar with a little chip out of one side, barely big enough for a mouse. She said, 'Mort wouldn't even drink that buttermilk.'"

Ollie grabs her throat. "Oh my goodness."

"I asked her if she drank any of it. She said, 'Sure I did, weren't nuttin wrong with it. It wus good buttermilk. I skimmed all the hairs outta that churn.'"

Shivering, Ollie gets up to open the oven door and check on the muffins. "It'll be a long time before I can drink buttermilk without having bad thoughts."

"She said they're having a terrible time with mice. Last week one chewed a hole in the cornmeal sack and pooped all in it. She scraped off the top but hated to waste the meal so she baked a pan of cornbread to feed the chickens. She went outside to help Mort with something while it cooled. Meantime, the boys came home from school. When she went inside, they had eaten almost all of that mouse-poop bread."

"Did it make them sick?"

"I asked her if they coughed up their boots when she told them. She said, 'I ain't never told 'em, and they's as healthy as ever.'"

Chapter 7
Help Needed

When winter weather allows, Roy turns under the old corn and cotton stalks, tilling them into the soil, then cuts and burns brush, and starts breaking ground for more crops in the spring.

Pushing back his morning coffee, he stands to stretch. "It looks like a nice day for work. I better get to it."

Ollie slides their empty cups into a dishpan of water. "What do you have planned for today?"

"I think the ground's dry enough to turn over the sod in that new ground." He reaches for his hat, hanging on a nail behind the kitchen door. "This coming year, I'm gonna plant as much corn and cotton as I can, and sorghum. Lots of people will buy sorghum molasses. I'll be plowing from sunup to sundown, but we'll never get ahead if we don't work."

"Ann can't go to school this term, but she's old enough to watch Johnny while we work. A fact that really worries me is that by planting time he'll be crawling. Would it cost too much to build a playpen strong enough for them both?"

"I don't think so. I'll get the lumber for it. Building it will be a good rainy-day project."

"If I have a pen to keep the baby out of the dirt and grass, I can run the planter while you put out fertilizer."

"But you can't stay in the fields all day and keep on nursing

Johnny. I think we should hire that redheaded boy. He asked me again about a job."

"Roy, I don't know what it is, but there's something dangerous about hiring that boy. My intuition tells me we should stay away from that."

"We're both so thin we hardly cast a shadow. Does your intuition tell you anything about working ourselves to death?" He opens the door and lets it slam behind him.

Ollie walks to the mirror hanging over the washstand. She stares at her face. Her eyes seem to recede into the sockets. Her breasts, full of milk, fill out the front of her dress, but the sleeves hang off her shoulders. Pinching up a handful of material at her waist, she turns sideways scrutinizing her reflection. *It'll be a while before I have to worry about getting too fat.*

She opens the flour bin. *I'll make a chocolate cake.* Johnny starts to whine before she can set out all the ingredients. "Ann talk to your brother while I butter us some of these biscuits left from breakfast. We'll fill them with plum jam and eat them while the baby gets his milk."

All spring and summer, Ollie sets the alarm clock so she and Roy wake in time to have breakfast, finish the morning chores and be in the field at sunup. Mama tells Ollie that she heard some of the neighbors joking about Roy and Ollie Glenn plowing by lantern light.

"Oh, Mama, we've walked to the field a few times with a lantern, but only when we were worried about getting crops planted before a rain. Most of the time, though, we're ready to go by first light."

"There's nothing wrong with working toward a goal. You'll reap the rewards of honest work."

Crops and gardens are planted and growing well by the time school lets out for the summer. Ollie sends Morene and Syble into the pasture with grubbing hoes to cut persimmon bushes while she sits on the porch shelling early peas.

The Jersey milk cow is grazing closer and closer to the girls. Ollie does not fret; still she keeps an eye on them. The cow has never acted aggressive toward the girls before, but she has a new calf.

Syble yells something Ollie cannot understand, crosses a ditch, and starts for the house. Morene walks toward another clump of bushes. The cow lowers her head, swings her sharp horns from side to side, paws the dirt, bellows, and charges toward Morene.

Syble yells louder, "Mama, the cow's after Morene!"

In the yard, Ann echoes Syble's cries.

Broom in her hand, Ollie runs toward the cow.

Morene jumps the deep ditch, screaming, "Mama, Mama!"

Circling the deepest part of the trench, the heavy cow turns when Ollie confronts her with the broom. She runs to the bushes, and rouses a baby calf.

Ollie walks back to the house, props the broom against the wall where she leaves it after sweeping the porch. "Girls, you can have a glass of milk and a cookie. Then I want you to take the grubbing hoes and cut bushes and weeds from around the garden. I think you need to keep a fence between you and that cow while she has a baby calf."

The summer stretches from one long workday to another. Roy cannot get all the fields plowed before weeds grow up in the first one. Ollie, Morene and Syble hoe after the first and second plowings. When not chopping grass and weeds from crops and gardens, Ollie has the girls cutting bushes with the heavy grubbing hoes.

Sorghum and garden crops grow well. Most are ready for harvest before the cotton and corn. Between working crops, the family picks blackberries and wild plums. The girls have already found vines near the creek that are loaded with green muscadines. They will keep a careful watch until the fruit turns purple. Crows and flocks of migrating birds will strip the vines clean if they are not gathered at the right time. After crop harvest, Roy and the girls will gather black walnuts, hickory nuts, and pecans. Morene and Syble never complain about traipsing through the woods to gather wild fruit and nuts—they love those adventures.

Ollie cans beans, peas, corn, sauerkraut, pickles, black-berries, wild plums, peaches, apples, and she makes jams and jellies from any fruit the girls find. Onions and dried peppers hang by strings along the barn rafters. Dried peaches and apples, wrapped in meal sacks are stored in a large crock. Peanuts in tall shocks, covered with thick sacks to keep out crows, stand in the field to dry. The late crop of potatoes will be dug before frost, and stored in the storm cellar; sweet potatoes, wrapped in newspapers and packed in boxes, will keep in the corncrib.

Ollie and Roy are pleased with crop yields. Morene and Syble grumble about having to work all the time. They can hardly wait until school starts. Ann, anxious to begin first grade, complains that she wants to work with the older girls instead of sitting in the playpen with the baby.

School opens in September. From the cotton field, the girls hear the groaning gears of the school bus as it climbs the mountain. Syble grumbles, "Whoever named this place 'Happy

Valley' didn't live on this farm and have to work like we do."

Ollie straightens and gives her a stern look. "Syble, if you don't stop so much complaining and pick a little faster, I'm gonna put one of you girls to the right of Roy and one on my left. The sooner we get this done, the sooner you can go back to school."

When the first picking is complete, the girls start to school knowing they will have to miss more when the rest of the cotton-boles dry and pop open. Ollie's mama comes every morning for a week to watch Johnny and Ann while Ollie helps Roy gather corn. After school, Morene and Syble help Roy. Ollie leaves the field to nurse the baby, and to allow Mama to get home before dark.

Friday afternoon Mama lingers until the girls go to the field. "Ollie, it's time you stop nursing that baby. He's fat and healthy, but you're not. You have four children to think about. He'll do fine on cow's milk and table food."

"I know, but—"

"Don't use excuses. I know them all. I had nine babies. If you get pregnant, while you are so run down, you could lose it, or you and the baby are likely to be unhealthy." She turns to go, but stops. "I understand that you and Roy want a nice home without a mortgage hanging over your heads. You'll have all of that someday, but take care of your health and be patient."

"Thanks for watching the kids, and Mama, will you check your almanac to find out the best days to wean a baby?"

Mama smiles and pats Ollie's arm. "I'll do that."

Johnny quickly learns to drink from a cup without spilling his milk. He thinks he is a big boy now, and is excited about going with Ann to spend the night at Grandma's house. His doll, Betsy, is under his arm, cloth arms and legs dangling with every toddler step.

Syble grabs Betsy and stuffs her in the bag with Johnny's clothes. "Betsy has to stay in the bag. Some mean kid on the school bus might grab her."

Johnny screams and yanks the doll out, holding her tight, an angry look on his face.

"Syble, leave him alone. He can carry her if he wants. This is all a new experience. Betsy gives him comfort." Ollie smiles, smoothing her little boy's hair. Although her milk has dried up, she longs to sit in the rocker, cuddling and nursing the baby.

"Mama, boys are not supposed to play with dolls, and that thing is dirty."

"It's not dirty. I washed it yesterday. It's a little stained because he loves it so much."

"I don't understand why Grandma didn't come here and get them instead of meeting the bus at school?"

Ollie frowns. "It's a long way down that mountain. The bus driver said it'll be fine for them to ride, and I need to get to the field."

Syble tugs at the doll. "Johnny, let me put Betsy in your sack so kids won't laugh at her."

"Syble!" Ollie's voice is loud and angry. "Take your hands off that doll."

Morene smiles, and holds out her hand to Johnny. "Nobody will laugh at him. He's a baby. They'll think he's cute carrying Betsy."

Ann yells from the porch, "Come on. Come on. I hear the bus."

"Ann, pick up your sack. You'll drag the bottom out of it before you get to the road." Standing on the porch, watching the four children walk away, Ollie feels tears sting her eyes. She takes a deep breath and turns to go inside. *I better get to the field and take advantage of Mama watching Ann and Johnny. Maybe Roy and I can get all the cotton picked without having the girls miss any more school.*

She lifts a newspaper-wrapped jug of water and the sack lunch of bacon and egg biscuits, and molasses cake wrapped in wax paper. The door slams behind her. Ollie strides quickly across trampled corn stalks where they gathered last week. Crows, scavenging for ears missed in the gathering, caw and fly to trees at the edge of the field.

Roy is weighing a sack of cotton when she gets to the wagon. "Let me have a drink of that water. I'm about to starve." He gulps from the jug, some of it drizzling down his chin to the front of his shirt. "Whew. My throat was dry, and I'm hungry already."

Ollie opens the lunch sack. "Eat a piece of cake. I brought all that was left."

He takes a big bite of the spicy treat. "That hits the spot. With this behind my belt, maybe I can survive the rest of the morning."

They drag their long sacks into the large field dotted with white. The sun will be dropping behind the mountain before they leave.

Ollie wonders about Johnny, but knows he is safe with Mama. Now that he is walking, he hates the playpen. Outside of it, Ann cannot keep up with his curious mind and constant energy. Last week he tried to pick up a tarantula—that is when

Ollie decided to accept Mama's offer to keep him until the cotton is picked.

The next week, Roy takes the second bale of cotton to the gin in Conway. It is late in the night when he gets home. At breakfast the next morning, he tells Ollie about his evening.

"Our cotton weighed out good. This morning, while you do your washing, I'm gonna ride Nell over to Enola to make a payment on our farm and deposit the rest. The money's in my shoe—one of those things that hurts and feels good at the same time." He laughs and lifts his foot.

"Yesterday, after they paid me, I went into a bathroom stall where no one could see, folded the large bills, and put them in my shoe. Believe me, I tied my old brogan good and tight before going to Massey's Hardware. After paying for my nails and bolts, I heard someone call my name. Red, that boy I wanted to hire to work on the farm, was motioning to me."

Roy pauses while Ollie gets up to refill the coffee cups.

"I walked over, that heavy sack of nails resting on my hip, and asked him if he ever found work."

"He shook his head. 'An odd job, every now and then. Step out in the alley. We'll talk and finish off a few swigs from this bottle.' He handed me the bottle."

"Oh, Roy, you didn't."

He holds up his hand until she sits back in her chair, folds her arms, and purses her lips in disgust.

"I took a little sip from his almost empty bottle and handed it back. Red took a drink and said, 'Ah, this thing's empty. My car's around the corner. Let's go to Palarm and get another. You ought to be loaded after selling that cotton.'"

Ollie gasps. "He said that to you?"

Roy nods and scoots his chair away from the table. "I said, 'They'll pay me next week when I bring the last load. I spent the last dollar that was in my wallet on these nails and bolts. Thanks for the drink, but I gotta get home. Ollie'll be waitin' up.' I didn't lie—only skirted the truth."

"What did Red say to that?"

"He rubbed his hands together, real nervous-like, and said, 'Roy, you ain't helping much.' I walked back into Massey's and out onto the lighted street and started home."

Lifting his cup, he drinks the last of his coffee. "Pa once told me that no one with common sense will ask a man personal questions about his wife or his money, and a smart man won't answer those questions. I felt uneasy with that boy last night. I'm glad we didn't hire him."

Chapter 8
Helping Hands

In the spring, Morene stays home from school for a week with fever and a sore throat. Syble and Ann have runny noses and croup at night. The girls are almost well when Johnny wakes with a fever. Ollie thinks he has caught a cold from the girls, until he starts gasping for breath.

"Roy, look in this baby's throat. He's having a hard time breathing."

"Hold the lamp close while I pry his mouth open."

She moves the lamp nearer.

"Oh, God! He has white in the back of his throat." Roy runs to the barn to hitch the mares to the wagon. Ollie wraps the baby and gives instructions to the girls.

Roy gallops the horses as much as he can until they reach Centerville. At the doctor's, Roy is running when his feet hit the ground. Rushing into the office, he gasps to the nurse, "My boy can't breathe."

The doctor opens a door.

"Doc, Johnny's having a hard time breathing, and he's got white in his throat just like Morene did when she had diphtheria!"

Dr. Hart takes a quick look in the baby's throat. "You're right, but I'm out of serum. I gave the last dose to a little girl. You'll have to go to Greenbrier for the medicine. Borrow the preacher's car. Ollie, you stay here with the boy, so I can help if he gets worse."

"Wes Cullum steps forward from the waiting room. "Roy, I'll drive if you want me too."

Roy grabs his arm. "Come on."

Ollie sits in a small waiting room, wiping at tears while Roy tells her what happened on his trip to get the medicine:

We ran to the preacher's house, but no one answered the door. I went around back and saw the old man down the hill, in his garden. I yelled, "Mr. Qualls, I gotta borrow your car. My boy has diphtheria and the doc's out of serum. I have to go to the drug store in Greenbrier to get a new bottle."

"Well." The old man scratched his head and drawled, "I guess it'll be all right, but I don't know if it's got enough gas in it to get to Greenbrier and back."

"I'll put some in it."

"Do you boys know how to drive?"

"Yes, yes, both of us. Where are the keys?"

He fumbled in his pockets. "I guess I left them at the house. I'll go get them."

"Tell me where they are. I'll get them. My boy's running out of air."

"Well, they should be hanging on a nail inside the back door."

I left the old man standing with his cabbage plants and ran for the keys. I pitched them to Wes. We jumped in the car, and took off for Greenbrier. I told Wes, "Wind this thing up. Don't let any grass grow under it."

We were nearing town when I remembered what the old man said about the gas. I didn't even grab my wallet when we rushed out this morning, but in my pocket, I had that silver dollar that Uncle Jim gave me after Johnny was born. I gave it to Wes and told him to get a dollar's worth of gas, then meet me back in front of the drug store, with the motor running.

On the way back here, I kept thinking about Uncle Jim and what he told me when he gave me that dollar. He said, "Roy, Pa gave this to me, so I've had it a long time, but I feel a strong impulse to give it to you in honor of that baby boy. Keep it in your pocket. Don't spend it unless it's real important."

I protested, saying, "I might lose it working on the farm. If Grandpa gave it to you, it's too precious for me to carry around in my pocket."

"He grinned and said, 'You won't lose it if you keep it next to that snuff can you always carry. Glue it to the can if you think there's a need, but keep it with you. It'll come in handy someday.'"

"I forgot about that." Ollie stands, and flexes her neck and shoulders. "You never glued it to the can, did you?"

Roy shakes his head. "I was afraid to carry it, until I got new overalls with deep, sturdy pockets. I've been carrying it with my snuff can for the last two days."

"If you didn't have your wallet, how did you pay the druggist for the medicine?"

"When he set it on the counter, I grabbed it and ran out of the store yelling 'Charge it to Roy Glenn! I'll be back next week to pay.'" He takes a deep breath and stares at the closed door in front of them.

"Doc's been in there with him a long time." Roy's hands

start to shake. He stands and walks around the room. "He'd be crying by—" Roy's voice cracks, and he turns toward the window.

Ollie touches his arm. "Johnny was still breathing when the doctor took him. He may have to put a tube in his throat until the medicine gets through his body, but I know Dr. Hart will save him."

"He let me hold Morene when he gave her the diphtheria shot."

"Morene wasn't as far along. Don't worry. Dr Hart knows what to do."

The nurse opens the door and places Johnny in Roy's outstretched arms. Holding an orange sucker in one hand, Johnny smiles at his daddy.

Doctor Hart walks into the room. "We were almost out of time. I thought sure I'd have to do a tracheotomy before that serum got in his system. He's still breathing shallow, so I'd like you to stay here a little longer, until more of that mucus breaks up, but I don't think he'll have any more trouble."

Roy hands the baby to Ollie and walks into the waiting room. Wes stands, and Roy throws his arms around his friend. "He's breathing. He's gonna be fine."

Roy is so busy plowing the fields that grass and weeds around the yard are growing tall. The girls are out of school for the summer, and Ollie worries that a snake hidden in the tall grass might bite one of them. Sunday, Roy tells her he is going to hitch the mares to the mowing machine and cut around the house and barn.

Ollie's mouth gapes open. "Surely you don't mean that. What will the neighbors think about us working on the Lord's Day? It's not right to work on Sunday."

"You cooked this big dinner. That was work."

Ollie squints and looks sideways at him. "You know that's not the same thing. We have to eat."

He grins. "And we have to get the ox out of the ditch. Isn't protecting my kids from snakes as important as an ox?"

"Roy, don't twist things around. You can mow the yard in the morning. I'll keep the kids inside this afternoon."

Ollie has not finished washing breakfast dishes when she hears the mowing machine clicking. "Morene, Syble, Ann, stay in this house and help to make sure Johnny doesn't get out. Your daddy's cutting the yard and barn lot. If you get in front of it, that sickle could cut your foot off as easy as it cuts those weeds."

Morene looks at Syble and grins. "Are you teasing us, Mama? We've got big bones in our feet and legs."

Raising her voice, Ollie twists to face Morene. "I would not tease about your safety. That sickle has knives in it, and they move very fast. Many times, I've heard of dogs getting their feet cut off when they ran in front of a mower."

As soon as Roy leaves for the field, Morene and Syble rake the thick grass and weeds into piles. Ollie looks out the window in time to see Ann dragging a pitchfork across the yard. Ann tries to jab the fork into the ground so it will stand against a tree, but the tines turn out. One of them sticks into her bare foot. She screams and tries to lift her foot, but she is pushing down on the handle.

Morene gets to her first. "Oh my goodness. Syble, pull it

out while I hold her foot."

Carrying the baby, Ollie rushes outside. Syble and Morene help Ann hobble to the porch.

Ollie leans over, squinting to see the wound. "Did it go deep?"

"All the way through to the ground," Morene answers, "but it's not bleeding much."

"Pull it apart and make it bleed. Puncture wounds are dangerous. Bleeding will help to clean it out."

Ann jerks her foot away and screams, "No! Don't pull my foot apart! It's all right."

"Ann, calm down. I only meant for her to hold the cut open so the dirt will come out."

Morene pushes Ann's foot into a pan of kerosene. "This will wash away germs."

Trying to jerk her foot away from Morene's grasp, Ann screams, "No! No! It burns!"

Ollie hands the baby to Syble. "Take him inside." She pulls a ladder-back chair up close, and kneels. "Ann, sit in this chair and let your foot hang down." The tine went between the bones, near her toes—gravity is not going to make it drain much. Massaging, from the ankle to the wound, brings out a few drops of blood.

"Where did you get that pitchfork?"

Rubbing her eyes on her sleeve, Ann mumbles, "In the manure pile, at the barn."

"You're not supposed to be in the barnyard unless someone is with you, and you should never have touched the pitchfork." Ollie frowns. "Morene, why did you let her have that fork?"

"I was raking weeds like you told me to do. I didn't know

she had it until she screamed."

"Dump this kerosene away from the house and get me a pan of warm water with a bar of soap."

Ollie scrubs and squeezes the punctured foot in the soapy water until Ann tries to pull away. "I don't know anything else to do right now. We don't have any Epsom salt. If it starts looking infected, you'll have to go get a tetanus shot."

A week later, Johnny and Ann are still in bed when Roy leaves for the field, a new-ground about a half-mile away from the house.

Ann wakes up crying. "Mama, my foot hurts. It feels like pins are poking it, and it won't stop jumping. My head hurts, too."

Ollie rushes to her. Her swollen foot twitches uncontrollably. "Morene, run get your daddy. Tell him to hurry. He has to take Ann to get a tetanus shot."

"But I still have my gown on."

Ollie's mouth quivers. "Never mind your clothes. Run!"

"I'll go." Syble runs out the door, letting it slam. She races across the field, nightgown flapping behind her.

Ollie dresses Ann, changes her own dress, and looks out the window. Roy is running behind the trotting horses, cutting across corn rows, trace chains dragging against the tender plants. He goes straight to the barn to hook up the wagon. Syble follows, slowing every few minutes to catch her breath.

"Morene, you and Syble take care of Johnny. We'll be back when we can." Carrying Ann wrapped in a blanket, she meets Roy by the road. He takes Ann while she climbs up.

Whipping the lines, Roy yells, "Get-up!" The horses take off running, the wagon rattling and bouncing.

Leaning back against the seat, Ollie braces herself with one foot until it begins to cramp, and then the other. "Roy, hold her and let me drive—my leg's in a cramp." Taking the lines in her right hand allows him to pull the bundled child from her left arm and onto his lap.

Ollie wants to whip the lines and make the horses run faster, but the mountain is steep. At last, she stops in front of the doctor's office. Holding Ann securely, Roy climbs down and rushes into the office. Ollie is close behind.

The doctor comes out of an examination room.

"Doc, my girl has tetanus!"

Seeing Ann's foot, he says, "Follow me."

Roy and Ollie walk into a little room with a sink and cabinets all around the walls. The doctor sets a bottle of medicine on the counter. Reaching for a needle, his sleeve knocks the bottle over. Glass and liquid splatter across the floor.

"Oh, Lord help us. That was my last bottle."

Ollie swallows and looks at Roy. A look of horror covers his face. Blood pounds in her temples, and bitter liquid rises in her throat.

The doctor shakes his head. "Roy, you'll have to take her to Greenbrier and get the doctor there to give her a shot. Leave your wagon here, and borrow the preacher's car again. She needs that shot pretty quick."

Ollie carries Ann outside and sits her in the wagon while Roy runs to the preacher's house to get his car. Within minutes, they are speeding toward Greenbrier. Dr. Williams has the tetanus serum and administers the shot.

"Pretty girl, I want you to stay away from pitchforks." The doctor picks up a box of suckers. "What color do you like best?"

"Yellow."

"Then you can have two yellow. How many brothers and sisters do you have at home?"

She lifts three fingers.

"Take these red ones to them, and you keep off that foot until the swelling goes away."

Ann is depressed about having to stay off her sore foot. Rough wood floors inside the house make crawling difficult, still she crawls until her knees are sore. Sometimes she drags a chair along and hops on one foot.

On Sunday afternoon, Roy and Ollie sit on the front porch enjoying an afternoon of rest.

Ollie fans herself with a folded newspaper. "Roy, have you checked those watermelon plants? We may need to sprinkle a little bug poison on them."

"Not for several days. Let's walk down and look. I'll call Morene and Syble to stay with Ann and Johnny."

Ann throws a ball to her brother. "I don't need someone to stay with me. I'm not a baby. If I had a walking stick, I'd hop down there with you."

"Ollie, if you'll pull John in his wagon, I'll carry Ann on my back."

"Roy, she's too heavy for you to carry that far, and it's an awful rough path for that little wagon."

He shakes his head. "Ah, you worry too much about little things. Come here, Ann. Put your arms around my neck and hold on tight."

They start along the path, the wagon rattling, Ann giggling. They have not reached the watermelon patch when Roy says, "Not so tight, Ann. You're choking me."

"My arms are tired, Daddy."

"Well, put your feet in my back pockets and hold onto the straps of my overalls."

"Roy, if she lets go of those straps, she could fall and hit her head on the ground or a rock before you could catch her, and I'm afraid she'll tear the pockets off those old overalls."

"She's smart enough to hold on."

"I'll hold on," Ann promises, "but can I have one foot in your pocket? It hurts my sore foot."

"All right, stick the sore foot up here, and I'll hang onto your leg."

Roy and Ollie leave Ann and John in the shade of a small persimmon tree while they walk around the melon patch.

"It looks like every seed sprouted." Ollie bends to look close at a plant. "We may need to thin them, but I hate to pull healthy plants."

Roy shakes his head. "If we get rain, that manure I put in the hills will make them grow. If we don't get rain they'll die anyway."

He swings Ann onto his back and trots to the house. Ollie follows, pulling John in the wagon.

"Daddy," Ann says, "that's the most fun I've had all year."

"All year?"

She giggles. "All year."

School has started for the fall semester. Ann's hair is getting long. She usually has a lock of it twisted around one finger.

Ollie is constantly telling her to push it away from her face. "Ann, if you can't keep that hair out of your face and your plate,

I'm gonna cut it short."

"No, you'd bob it off like you used to do Syble and Morene's."

"Then you better learn to braid or tie it back so it's not dragging in your food."

One Saturday morning at breakfast, Ann gets sorghum molasses in her hair. Quickly, she goes to the wash pan and rinses it out, but Ollie notices.

After washing the dishes, Ollie gets her scissors and calls Ann to the porch.

Seeing a towel draped over a chair and her mother with scissors in her hand, Ann runs screaming, "No! You're not gonna cut my hair." Her short legs are no match for Ollie's.

Angry that Ann would dare to run from her, Ollie grabs hold of Ann's hair and whacks off a wide strip. "Now, how do you like that? Get in that chair and sit still or I'll cut it *all* off."

Shaking with sobs, Ann sits while Ollie cuts her hair in a bob style that was stylish when Ollie was in her teens.

"Now, you look cute, and your hair won't be dragging in your plate."

"I hate it! I hate it!" Ann screams, and runs to the barn to hide in the hay.

"Mama, why did you do that to her?" Morene looks toward the barn. "She looks awful."

"It would look better, if she would have sat still."

Morene pauses. "No, it wouldn't. No one wears their hair like that anymore."

Syble comes out onto the porch, looks around at the hair, and frowns. "Every kid at school will laugh at her. I don't blame her for crying."

Ollie pops the towel over the edge of the porch. "No one will laugh at her. She's cute."

"Maybe to you, but not to Ann. Long hair is the style, and I know they'll laugh at her. Don't blame her if she gets in a fight on Monday."

"She better not."

"Blame yourself if she does. She's already shamed by having her hair cut. She won't let anybody rub it in."

"Get in the house and hush."

Ann is still in the barn when Roy comes home. He sends Morene to bring her inside.

"She's on the porch. I couldn't get her to come in."

Roy walks onto the porch. "You're gonna miss dinner if you don't come to the table."

"I don't want any."

"Let me see your haircut."

She raises her head from folded arms resting across her knees. Her chin quivers, and big tears roll from her eyes.

"Do you want me to bring you a plate out here?"

She shakes her head and again rests it on her arms to sob.

Roy goes inside. "Ollie, what were you punishing her for?"

"I wasn't punishing her. I was tired of hair dragging through her plate."

He frowns and shakes his head.

"Stop making such a big deal out of this. Her hair will grow back. Maybe then she'll keep it out of her plate."

"It's a big deal to her, and I agree—it looks awful."

"Roy, stop trying to undermine my authority with these girls."

Morene and Syble get up and go out on the porch with Ann.

Chapter 9
Jobs

After the fall harvest, Roy goes to Little Rock with Mel, a neighbor. They find work at the Roundhouse of the Missouri Pacific Railroad. On weekends, they are always ready to start home for time with their families. One cold Friday, snow is in the forecast, and they decide to wait until Saturday morning to leave. Ollie has lunch ready when Roy arrives home.

They linger at the table after the meal. "Roy, did anything exciting happen on your job last week?"

"Do you remember Sport?"

Ollie nods.

"Last night he stopped by to ask us if we wanted to go for a drive. Red, that boy I wanted to hire, is driving a taxi in Little Rock. He had to deliver something to Camp Robinson, and told Sport to ask if we wanted to ride along. Mel said he was tired and would rather rest, but I went."

"Did you get to see much of the military base?"

Roy shakes his head. "It was dark. He made the delivery to the gate, and we drove off. After that, he drove to the top of a big hill. The area all around was wooded, with no houses. We could see the lights of Little Rock and traffic below us moving around like electric ants going to and from an anthill."

"I'll bet that was pretty."

"It was a beautiful sight. We sat a while, talking about nothing in particular, and then Red said, 'Today's payday, the best day of the week. With your pockets full of money, you men ought to be out having a good time.'"

"I shook my head. 'Our families need the money, or we wouldn't be down here. Every Friday, as soon as I get off work, I write 'for deposit only' on the back of my check and mail it to the bank for deposit into my account. That way, I'm not tempted to spend it on things unnecessary. Sport said he hadn't cashed his yet.'"

Ollie frowns. "Didn't he ask you about money that time you saw him in Conway?"

Roy nods. "Last night, he tried to convince us to get out of the car—to see a better view of the city—but it was terribly cold. I told him that in this kind of weather, I can see all I want from inside the car."

"Did Sport get out?"

Roy laughs. "Not that ole boy. He told him the same thing I did."

"Did you leave then?"

"Red got out by himself, slammed the door and walked off into the woods. He was gone a long time. We were about to freeze inside the car, and I was getting worried about what might have happened to him. Finally, he came back, got in, slammed the door again, and took off spinning the wheels. He took us to the rooming house, and said, 'Another time, men. Another time.'"

"With the weather like it was last night, I expected you'd come home this morning, but I couldn't help worrying about you."

"After I was in bed, I had a hard time falling asleep. I thought of a dozen different things that could have happened, and wondered why he acted so irritated when we wouldn't get out of the taxi. I'm gonna do my best to stay away from that boy from now on."

In the spring, Roy quits his job at the Roundhouse and returns home to plant more crops.

Nell, one of the mares, has a new colt. She has always been a good work horse, and gentle around the children. She is a good mother to her baby, but does not like being away from it. She and the colt whinny to each other throughout the day as Roy plows.

One day, while Roy repairs some equipment, Ollie and the kids take the wagon and go to the store. They only have a few items to purchase and do not think it necessary to tie the mares to a post. When they finish shopping, the wagon and team are gone. A neighbor tells Ollie that he thought it strange when he saw the team trotting down the mountain without a driver.

After he finishes his business, the neighbor takes Ollie and the children home. The wagon and team stand next to the pasture. Nell is nuzzling her colt through the fence.

Morene and Syble love to ride the horses, but seldom get time for pleasure rides. One summer day when Roy has a lot of work planned, the cows break through the rusted barbwire and run away. "Girls, while I repair this fence, put bridles on the mares and go find those cows before they're completely out of range."

Excited, the girls run to the barn before Ollie can come out of the house and differ with Roy. Several hours later, shelling beans on the porch, Ollie watches the lather-streaked horses ridden by two suntanned girls herd the cows back into the pasture.

"Where did you find them?" Roy asks.

The girls exchange glances before Morene answers, "In Wolf Hollow."

"I didn't think about them being that far away. How'd you get them up that mountain?"

Morene pauses. Syble looks at him without cracking a smile. "We followed their tracks, stopped and broke off some long poles, rode in on each side of the cows, and whacked them across the rear a few times. They went back up the same ravine they came down."

"There's not a ravine on that mountainside that's not awful steep. How'd you stay on those mares without saddles?"

"We held onto their manes really tight, or we would have slid right off their rumps."

Ollie raises her voice. "Girls, don't ever go down there again. If the cows run into that hollow, you come home and let Roy go after them."

Syble lets out her breath in a short huff. "The mares carried us up that ravine easier than either could have carried Daddy. He weighs a lot more than we do."

"That's not the point. There are wild animals in Wolf Hollow. I don't want you girls going by yourselves."

Roy pushes at the brim of his straw hat, and wipes his face with a blue handkerchief. "Did you see any wild plums or muscadines?"

The girls shake their heads.

Ollie frowns. "Roy, you can't just go anywhere looking for fruit."

"I think Mel owns most of that area, and I doubt that he'll go there, or mind if we did. I'll ask the next time I see him."

"Don't bother. The government rationed sugar. I'll not be making much jelly until the war's over. We'll have to eat our biscuits with sorghum syrup." Pushing the loose bean hulls down into a bucket, Ollie calls, "Morene, take this bucket of hulls and dump them in the cow trough."

Roy sits on the porch and cuts a piece of tobacco from the twist he has in his bib pocket. "Ollie, if you want me to take that corn to the mill and get it ground, I need to go this afternoon, after the mares rest for a while. Tomorrow, the fields should be dry enough to plow. Syble, do you want to ride Nell and hold onto one sack?"

Syble nods.

Ollie glares at him. "Roy, without a saddle, it'll be hard for her to hold onto a sack of corn or meal, and Nell's awful nervous now that she has that colt."

"I'll strap it around Nell's belly. There's no need to drag that wagon up the mountain. Syble, would you rather ride Maggie?"

"No. I always ride Nell." Syble whispers, "She's got spirit."

Almost through the front door, Ollie turns to face them. "I heard that, young lady, and I'll tell you one more time, I better not hear of you racing that mare."

Syble grins. "I better go help Morene shuck some corn for Nell and Maggie."

After lunch, Roy pushes back his plate. "Syble, I'll put bridles on the mares and get the corn ready. Soon as you help with these dishes and get your shoes on, come on out. We'll go get the corn ground. That cornbread was awful good with those fresh pinto beans. I'd hate for your mama to run out of meal."

Syble brushes her shoulder-length brown hair, fastens a clasp on the right side, pulls on a pair of white anklets, and ties her brown oxfords tight.

Sitting on the porch, Ollie is watching Johnny play when Roy and Syble come into view, on their way home from the mill. Syble is riding behind Roy; with the sack of meal tied across Nell's back. The mare pulls on the lines. Roy drops them, letting her go toward the colt.

Free at last, Nell runs off the road and down a hill. The meal sack, off to one side, tilts her balance. She trips over a small stump, falls, and struggles to get up, before racing to her baby. Other than a skinned nose, she is fine.

"Roy, why was Syble not riding Nell?"

"That mare was acting so nervous, I was afraid she might take off running to her colt. I didn't want Syble on her back if she started galloping down that mountain."

"Those two mares are a great pair. It would be hard to replace one of them."

Roy dismounts. "Ollie, have you checked on Jersey's new calf this afternoon? It had a bad case of scours last night and acted really weak this morning."

"I didn't know it was sick."

"I meant to get some more pills, but forgot. I better go check on it."

By morning, the calf is weaker and cannot stand without help. "We probably let it have too much of Jersey's rich milk. I've heard that a mixture of flour and soot will cure the scours, but I think this one is too far gone."

Syble pulls on Roy's pocket. "Daddy, if I doctor the calf and save it, can it be mine?"

"If you and Morene will work together and nurse it back to health, you two can share it."

"Morene, did you hear Daddy? We can have Jersey's calf if we make it well."

"But it's got the runs. We might get that on us."

Syble frowns. "We can take a bath. Stay in here, Miss Prissy. I'm gonna doctor it, and it'll be *all* mine."

From the firebox of the wood cook stove, she scrapes out black soot and mixes it with a little flour and water inside a tin can. Syble glances at Morene and heads out the door.

Ollie looks up from her sewing. "Syble, keep a fence between you and that cow. She could really hurt you with those horns."

Later that afternoon, Ollie takes a quick look at the clock, puts her sewing away, and goes to the kitchen to start supper. "Girls, what have you done with my kettle?"

They jump up from where they are sitting on the edge of the porch. "Here it is." Syble rushes inside.

"Why did you have it outside?"

"We mixed some warm soapy water and washed all that muck off the calf."

Ollie frowns. "It's cool inside that barn. Now, the calf will probably die for sure."

Syble shakes her head. "No, he won't. We took him out in the sun, gave him the medicine, washed and dried him, and let him sleep in the warm grass all afternoon while we cleaned the stall."

"How did you get that flour and soot down his throat?"

Syble grins, and motions with her hands. "Like a biscuit, I pulled his mouth open. Morene poured the medicine in and rubbed his throat to make him swallow."

"Maybe it will live. I imagine being out in that warm sunshine was good for it. Have you thought about a name?"

They shout "Soot!" and burst out giggling.

Every day Soot improves. Within a week, he is running around the pasture, as healthy as any calf.

Nancy is born in early January. Ollie's mama comes to the house to help Doctor Hart with the delivery. Nancy is a fat baby with black hair about an inch long.

Morene laughs at her. "She looks like an Indian baby with all that black hair."

Syble shakes her head. "No, she looks Chinese. Her skin's yellow, and her fat belly sticks out like a Buddha doll."

Ann pushes her way through to the bed. "I think she looks like an Eskimo."

Ollie, leaning on one elbow, asks, "Johnny, what do you think about her?"

"I don't like her. I wanted a brother."

Grandma pats Johnny on the head and picks up the baby. "Let's not toss her out yet. You might grow to like her." She pulls the blanket back and examines the baby's skin. "Ollie, she is a little yellow. It may be jaundice. We'll need to watch her close for a few days and notify the doctor if she gets worse. After I bathe her, I'll put her near the window where she can get a few minutes of sunshine. I've heard that light helps to cure jaundice."

"What about her eyes? Won't bright sunlight make her eyes weak?"

"I'll put a blindfold on her."

Morene and Syble cook breakfast while Grandma bathes the new baby. Morene lifts a skillet of gravy to pour it into a bowl. Not used to handling the heavy iron skillet, she tips it the wrong way and dumps hot gravy into Syble's boot.

Morene grabs a dipper of water and flings it into the boot.

Screaming, Syble yanks off her boot, lifts the water bucket to the floor and sticks her foot inside. With her foot still in the water, she pulls off her heavy wool sock, and rolls up the leg of her jeans.

Morene wipes up the gravy, looks at Syble with her foot in the water bucket, and gasps. "Syble, get your foot out of that bucket! That's the water we drink."

With tears in her eyes, Syble yells. "What was I supposed to do—run around the house with scalding gravy burning the skin off my foot and find another bucket? When my foot stops hurting, you can scrub and scald the bucket. You're the one that caused it."

Ann takes another bucket from the cabinet. "I'll go draw more water." She rushes out into the cold winter wind.

It is almost time for lunch before Syble will keep her foot out of cold water. Grandma examines the skin. "That thick sock, your blue jeans, and cold water so close at hand, prevented a more serious injury." The rest of the day, Syble goes barefoot inside the house.

"Grandma," Morene says, "I scrubbed the bucket clean, so we won't get some awful disease from her dirty foot."

"My foot was clean—cleaner than yours."

"Now, girls. Quiet. Your mama and the baby need their rest."

That night after the children are asleep, Roy and Ollie sit talking in front of the fireplace. "Ollie, you know I'm gonna have to go away again to find work. I would have looked in the fall, but I didn't want to leave you until after the baby came. Now that I know the two of you are all right, I need to start looking."

"But it's only three months until time to plant crops."

"That's why I need to find something right away. Morene and Syble are old enough to help you with the little ones and anything around the farm, and I've got enough wood cut to last a year or more."

"I worry so when you're gone—about you away on some dangerous construction job, and about the children. What would I have done if you had been gone when John got diphtheria, or when Ann got tetanus?"

"You would have taken them to the doctor, and someone would have made those trips to Greenbrier for you. This is a good community, and we have two levelheaded girls that I'd trust more than a lot of adults. Ollie, I have to do this or we may not have enough to make the mortgage payment."

She sighs and reaches for his hand. "Do you think we'll ever get to a point where you won't have to go away to work?"

"I hope so, but we'll keep doing what we have to. With five children, I don't think going back to California is the answer. At least, the older girls can help with the farm, and we have family and friends nearby to help with emergencies."

"And good neighbors. The worst part of living in White Oak was that one thieving family. I wonder if they still live on that road."

They sit quietly watching flames dance over logs in the fireplace and listening to the wind whistling around loose windows. "It's warm and peaceful with you here beside me, knowing our healthy babies are asleep in their beds. When you're gone, I don't sleep well, and I worry about every noise."

"You had reason to worry in that White Oak Valley, but not here. As long as you and the kids are inside before dark, and you lock the doors to keep out animals, you don't need to worry." He smiles at her in the flickering firelight, and wipes a strand of hair from her forehead. "Just keep listening for those angels."

"My problem is that I don't always know when something is a warning, or if I'm simply worrying." She sighs deep, and rubs his arm. "Are you going to Tennessee?"

"I'll try there first. Mel said they're still working on that big government project."

Two days after the new baby's arrival, Roy boards a bus for Tennessee to look for a paying job. Ollie's mama stays to help for five more days before going home to her own family. Morene and Syble take care of milking, feeding the animals before and after school, and lifting the heavy logs for the fireplace. Ann feeds the chickens, gathers eggs, and brings in kindling and wood for the cook stove.

Good neighbors stop by on their way to the store to ask if Ollie needs them to bring her anything, or if she needs help with chores around the farm. She rarely requests anything, but asks that they come to check on her and the kids if they should ever hear repeated blasts from Roy's shotgun. She assures them, "I won't be out target practicing, but I'd like to know I can count on you if one of the kids gets hurt or sick."

Within a week after Roy leaves, Ollie receives the following letter:

Dear Ollie, girls, and Johnny:

Are you doing all right? Does the baby still look yellow? Take her to see Dr. Hart if she does. Charge his bill. I'll send money when I get my first check.

I'm working in Knoxville for J. A. Jones Construction Company. They're a part of Clinton Engineer Works out of Clinton, Tennessee. As expected, I'm listed as a laborer, the lowest grade job that they have, which means doing the dirty work. I told the supervisor that I could do rough carpenter work, but he said all carpenters, rough and finish, must belong to the Carpenters Union.

I'd like to be in that union, but it costs more than a week's wages to join. One man said a friend of his paid fifty dollars. Maybe I'll apply after we pay the mortgage and stock-up on a few things we need. I'd earn more wages, and the work's not as strenuous, dangerous, and not nearly as dirty—it will be worth the cost.

It's cold out here. They say the temperature is the same as in Arkansas, but when it's this cold at home, I always find something to work on inside the house or barn.

I miss all of you. Write and tell me everything that's going on. Stay safe.

Love,
Roy

Chapter 10
Union Card

In the spring, Roy gets a few days off to come home and plant corn and cotton. He does not plant watermelons, popcorn, peanuts, and sorghum. Several jugs of molasses are left from last year. It is laced with sugar granules, but will melt into syrup when Ollie boils it.

Once the seeds are in the ground, Roy returns to the construction site—Ollie and the girls will plow, hoe and harvest.

Ollie plants a few melons in the garden for their own use. Two rows each of popcorn and peanuts will be enough for snacks on cold winter evenings, especially since Roy plans to stay in Tennessee through the winter.

Morene and Syble haul two wagonloads of manure from the barn and shovel it into garden furrows—a job that Roy always completed. They no longer complain about helping. They know times are hard, and they see Ollie struggling to nurse the baby and keep up with the farm work.

Johnny and Ann have fairer skin than Morene and Syble. They freckle and sunburn easily. Ann is good to wear her bonnet, but he hates wearing his hat. Preparing to go to the store, Syble puts the hat on her little brother. He pulls it off and throws it on the bed. She tries repeatedly, but he refuses.

"All right, don't wear it." She stomps out of the room. "I

hope you sunburn."

That afternoon, clear blisters pop out across his nose. The rest of his face and his arms are red. Syble's tears are almost as numerous as John's. Until he falls asleep that night, she keeps drawing fresh water from the well to place cool washcloths on his face and arms.

Johnny has decided he likes his chubby little sister, and watches her carefully while Ollie plows or hoes the crops. After school is out in the spring, Ann and John share watching the baby while Ollie, Morene, and Syble work the fields.

Ollie has a tough time of pushing down hard enough on the cultivator handles to make the plows dig into some of the hard dry ground. Perspiration drips from her forehead, and her shoulders ache, but she will not quit.

The mail carrier goes along the road and stops at the mailbox. Ollie looks up at the position of the sun. It is not time to prepare the noon meal, but her whole body aches from working the sun-baked ground. *The baby would be crying to nurse, if it were time to go.*

Morene yells, "Mama, can I go get the mail and fix our lunch?"

"I'm going when I get to the end of this row." She sees disappointment on Morene's face, but it is time for a letter from Roy. If she could rush the horses without plowing up corn, she would slap the lines against their backs. "Morene, you and Syble hoe to the end, then come on with Ann, John and Nancy. We'll all work on the meal and rest a while."

Roy's handwriting seems to jump out from other mail. She rips open the letter.

Dear Ollie and kids,

I hope all of you are still doing fine.

Here, the weather is getting hot. Over the weekend, I bought a couple of lightweight shirts at a secondhand store. I'll have to buy at least one pair of overalls soon. Without you here to patch my clothes, I'm starting to look ragged.

One day last week, I worked with the carpenters because they were short-handed and needed some scaffolds built fast. Since then, I've been in a quandary over buying new overalls or applying for a union card. I think the safest thing is to join the union. The carpenters seem to be a happy bunch— laughing and joking as they work.

There are a couple of men here that plainly hate each other—I think it's over a woman. Joe works with me, the other man drives a dump truck. Last week we finished our work in a hole, and it was ready for refilling. Everyone was out except Joe, when his enemy started dumping a load of dirt.

Joe was pressed against the side, and dirt kept pouring in about to bury him alive. Everyone yelled for the driver to stop dumping, but he ignored us. One man, standing nearby, climbed up in the cab, drew back his hammer and yelled. "Stop it, or I'll knock your brains out."

The driver let the bed down. When dirt stopped tumbling into the hole, we jumped in and dug Joe out. I don't know what happened to them. The boss took both men away for a talk, and everyone knows better than to mention the subject.

I'll wait about the union until after crop harvest. You may have to hire someone to help. We don't need to keep the girls out of school too long.

I'm mailing a little present for all of you to share. I hope you enjoy it.

       Love,

       Roy

The present did not arrive the same day as the letter. Two days later, Johnny and Ann are waiting at the mailbox when the postman arrives. "I bet you're waiting for a parcel from your daddy." He hands a small brown paper-wrapped package to Ann. "You should take it inside and let your mama open it. It could be something breakable."

"I will. Thank you." She turns and runs inside with Johnny close behind.

Ollie cuts the string and tears away the tape. Inside is a cellophane-wrapped package of gum. "Kids, there are twenty-four packs of gum in here. If the five of us take one piece each day, it will last almost a month. Nancy is too little to have a whole piece—she'll swallow it. I'll give her a little pinch of mine."

Ollie hears a step on the porch.

Johnny runs to the door. "Come in, Mack! Look what Daddy sent. I'll share mine with you."

The boy and his family live a short distance down the road. He is near Johnny's age. When Ollie is not working in the fields, she welcomes the boy, but will not let Johnny go to Mack's house. His mother is sick, and coughs constantly. The woman might have tuberculosis.

Ollie dyes some feed sacks dark blue and makes Johnny a shirt. She makes Mack one like it, knowing that almost everything his daddy earns goes for medicine.

"I really like this shirt, Miss Glenn." Mack's smile covers his face. "I wish I had britches to match. Mine are about to wear through to my butt." He turns around and pats his behind.

She smiles. With their matching shirts, the two boys look like brothers. Opening the door, she glances back at them. *His pants have already worn through.* Before Mack goes home that evening, Ollie has made matching pants for both of the boys and cautioned her girls not to say anything about them. "They don't look store-bought, but they'll only wear those pants around home."

The boys play for hours without fighting. They use small pieces of wood for cars, trucks, and trains. Tin cans serve as water tanks in their small city constructed skillfully with rocks and sticks.

The only disadvantage is that Nancy gets lonesome. Usually Ann can be persuaded to play with her, especially when Ollie promises to make cookies, but sometimes having good flour is a problem.

Since the war began, it is difficult to find flour without weevils. Ollie thinks it is because the government buys so much of the good wheat for feeding the military. Each time she buys flour at the community store, she has to take it back. Whenever Roy comes home, he tries to bring flour from Conway, and Papa brings it when he goes to town.

One of Ollie's neighbors sends her daughter to borrow a lard can full of flour. She always returns the borrowed amount, but she buys from the community store, and what she returns has weevils in it. At first, Ollie mixes the flour with the pig's slop, but that is expensive feed for pigs. After the second time, she saves the returned flour in a lard can. When the woman asks to borrow again, Ollie gives her the flour that she returned.

Wednesday night before Thanksgiving weekend, after riding from Tennessee to Conway, Roy spends the remaining night in a chair at the Conway bus station. Without breakfast, he hitchhikes home on Thanksgiving morning.

Ollie has roasted two large hens and made cornbread dressing. Apple pies are cooling along with yeast rolls. Syble is mashing potatoes, Morene is beating butter into a bowl of sweet potatoes, Ann is setting the table, and Ollie is stirring gravy when Roy opens the door.

After hugs from the family, he sits with John on one knee and Nancy on the other.

John asks, "Daddy, do you think I could share my dinner with Mack? He said his mama is too sick to cook pies and lots of good things."

Roy looks at Ollie and nods.

She returns the signal. "There's an empty box under our bed. Roy, will you bring it in here and help me pack it?" Before they sit to give thanks, Roy and John deliver a box to Mack's family containing half of the food prepared by Ollie and the girls.

"Ollie, if I'm not too heavy to get out of this chair after eating that good dinner, I'm gonna hitch the mares to the breaking plow and begin turning under the old cotton and corn stalks. If the weather will allow me to work in the fields each time I get a holiday weekend, I'll have it ready to plant again by spring."

Early Sunday morning, Roy, Ollie and the children leave home in the wagon. They stop to visit with Pa Glenn and Fanny, Roy's oldest sister. Fanny insists that the children stay with her while Roy and Ollie go on. Ollie is about to agree when a cousin volunteers to drive Roy to Greenbrier. "Heck, if you'll buy me a dollar's worth of gas, I'll drive you all the way to the bus station in Conway."

"You've got a deal, buddy. Maybe I can catch an earlier bus to Tennessee."

Five-year-old Johnny is the only one that questions. "Daddy, why can't you stay longer?" The older girls have asked that question before.

Roy does not come home at Christmas, but sends presents and writes often. The last of March, Ollie receives a letter telling her he has joined the Carpenters Union.

Dear Ollie and kids:

I finally paid the dues and joined the Carpenters Union. My union card is dated March 16, 1944. You know, I've wanted that card for a long time.

Since all of my tools are at home, I had to buy the ones required for the job—a hammer, handsaw, wrecking bar, tape measure, level and square. I found what I needed at a hardware store and wrote out the payment on that check I put in my wallet for emergencies. I was almost ashamed to use it, with the edges bent and ragged from carrying. I need more tools, but they are not required at the start. I'll buy a few at a time until I have enough.

I like the work and the men. They all try to help me as I'm learning customs and routines.

I miss you all. I'll see you as soon as I can.

Love,
Roy

Long before the Fourth of July, Roy asks for Monday, of the holiday week, off from work. A four-day weekend will give him time to get home and help Ollie with the last plowing before crops are laid by.

On Saturday, Roy starts to the barn to hitch Maggie to the plow. Ollie begins raking leaves away from the house. Mel, their friend and neighbor, stops on the road. "Good to see you, Roy, and you Ollie."

Roy throws up a hand in greeting. "Mel, I finally joined the Carpenters Union. "Should have done that a long time ago, but fifty dollars is a lot of money."

"It is, but you would have saved yourself some hard work

and, in the long-run, come out ahead."

Roy chuckles. "I knew that, but it was still tough for an old dirt farmer like me to let go of that much."

"Roy, I'm going to Hanford, Washington, next month on a carpenter job for the Government. Now that you're in the Carpenters Union, you won't have any trouble getting on. It pays good, better than a private construction contractor does. I have to go to the Employment Office on Monday, and maybe on to Camp Robinson. Go with me and sign up. I can almost guarantee that you'll be glad you did."

Roy frowns, looks down, and scuffs a well-worn work shoe in the gravel. "Jones Construction has been good to let me off every time I've asked, and I promised Ollie I'd get these fields plowed this weekend."

"Talk it over. Pray about it. I'll leave before seven on Monday, if you decide to go."

Ollie has raked around the house until she is out of their sight, but she hears most of the conversation. *Washington State is a long way from Arkansas.*

All day and into the evening, Roy rushes the mare through the field until it is too dark to see the rows clearly.

Wiping hands on her apron, Ollie meets him at the door. "You don't have to kill yourself this weekend. I can finish what you don't get done."

Roy washes his hands then leans over the wash pan, splashing water onto his face. After drying on a flour sack towel, he drags out a chair, sits at the table, and wearily sighs.

"I couldn't make the children wait any longer." Ollie sets a plate in front of him. "They were too hungry, but they'll have pie with us."

"That's all right. I have something to talk to you about. "Mel told me about a carpenter job in Washington State where he's going next month. He wants me to go to Conway with him on Monday to sign up. It'll pay more and have more benefits than working for a private contractor. I'm tempted to go. He's never steered me wrong before."

"You've built a good record with Mr. Jones."

"He said it'll last at least a year. The government bought the whole town. They're building some kind of ammunition plant. Probably something like what they've done in Tennessee, except I think the Army's overseeing more of this project. No telling what they plan to build or do there. All I need to know is that they'll pay me good to do carpenter work."

Ollie folds her arms and closes her eyes. She and Roy sit quiet for a moment.

He starts filling his plate. "This sure looks good."

"I don't get to cook for you often enough."

"That's another thing to consider. Washington is a lot farther away than Tennessee."

Ollie gets up to get a jar of pickles from the cabinet. Before sitting again, she rubs his neck and shoulders. "Maybe they'll give you more time to come home on holidays. Why don't you go with Mel on Monday, get all the details you can, and do what your heart tells you."

"I won't be able to plow all the crops if I go with him."

"I can manage that. The girls have really been good to help."

Monday morning, Roy is waiting when Mel drives his truck into the yard. Ollie worries over the outcome of the trip, but never feels panic. She does laundry, mends Roy's clothes, and prepares a good supper.

Ann and Johnny run to the porch when the truck stops. Ollie wants to do the same, but waits until she hears tires crunching as it pulls back onto the road. Roy tosses Johnny into the air and pats Ann's back.

"Ollie, I'm bound for Washington next month. I'll go to Tennessee tomorrow night and give them my notice on Wednesday. They may let me go right then. If they do, I'll have some time to work on the farm and be with you and the kids. But if they want me to work longer, it'll be more money to pay on the mortgage."

"Tell me about your new job."

Roy sits on the porch, and cuts off a chew of tobacco. "I don't know much more than I did this morning—except that my name is on about a dozen papers that I didn't have time to read. I gathered that we'll be staying in Hanford and will have to get military permission to leave and come back in."

"I wonder if they'll have a store."

"One for the military, but it may not be much more than a place to buy tobacco and a candy bar. They'll feed us—I don't have to worry about groceries. I'll start out making more than I do now, and in six weeks, I'll get a raise. The man told us that winter weather can get bad, fast, so they encourage the workers to take time before October to celebrate Christmas. He was smiling, so I don't know if he was joking or not."

Ollie shakes her head. "He was probably serious. I've heard about some of those northern blizzards. I would hate for you to be traveling in a snowstorm. We can celebrate before you have to leave, before winter sets in."

"I'll need warmer clothes—at least two pair of heavy longjohns, lined leather boots, wool socks, a wool lined cap with ear flaps, gloves and a heavy coat. He said we could buy things at a discount in the military store, but it would be a good idea if we brought the basics with us. With the war going on, they're often short on supplies."

"I doubt that I can find clothes that heavy around here. I'll check in the Sears and Roebuck catalog. Maybe you can find your boots in Tennessee. You need to try those on."

"I will."

"Another thing—when you give your notice, reserve at least one day for business here. I'd like for you to make the mortgage payment before you go. I don't want to drive the wagon all the way over to the Enola bank with Johnny and Nancy, and I don't want to trouble any of the neighbors with keeping them."

Morene opens the screen and steps onto the porch. "Mama, I'm starved. When are we gonna eat?"

"Right now." Ollie jumps up. "It's ready. Start emptying the vegetables into bowls."

After supper, Morene and Syble go to the bedroom to look at the latest catalog that came in the mail. Standing on the porch, Ann and Johnny watch lightning bugs fly across the yard. Ollie peeps through the screen door. "Don't step off the porch. Copperhead snakes might be crawling in the yard."

Roy bounces the baby on his knee. "Ollie, what do you think about letting the kids have a dog? I saw Sam at Greenbrier when we stopped for gas. He has a little black-and-white pup he's trying to give away. He says it'll kill rats and mice. It could sleep in the barn and maybe catch a few of those pesky critters."

"What about chickens? Will it kill my chickens or eat eggs?"

"I asked him that, and he said it never has. It's not quite two years old, but is already full-grown. He has three dogs, and May insists that he get rid of one."

Ollie nods. "All right."

"Ann, you and John come in here. I want to ask you something."

They come running. "Daddy, Johnny almost caught a lightning bug from the porch. If his arm was a little bit longer, he would have got it."

Roy sits grinning until they are quiet. "How would you two like to have a little dog?"

"Can we, Daddy? Can we?"

"Will you feed and take care of it? Everyone older already has too much to do, so if you don't take care of it, we'll have to give it back."

They jump and giggle. "We'll take care of it. We will!"

The next day, Ollie takes Roy to Greenbrier where he finds a man to give him a ride to the Conway bus station. On the way back, Ollie and the kids stop at Roy's brother's to get the dog. Sam puts a little rope halter on it and hands the rope to Ann.

Johnny is down on his knees petting and loving the little pet. They are instant friends. Ann and Johnny agree on the name Pluto.

Afraid that the dog will run away, Johnny begs Ollie to let Pluto sleep under his bed. "No! Don't ask me again. I'll not have a dog bringing fleas and ticks into this house."

Johnny puts a piece of an old blanket on the porch, lays Pluto on it, and sits petting him until bedtime. The dog is still there the next morning.

Ann likes Pluto, but she has to take care of Nancy. Johnny and his friend Mack play with the dog from morning until night. It is not long until Pluto will fetch a stick, and roll over for a piece of biscuit.

Roy leaves for Hanford, Washington in the fall. The next spring Ollie and the older girls prepare the fields for planting. They will plant a corn crop and gardens, but not much cotton. She cannot continue to keep the girls out of school, and she cannot watch Johnny and Nancy while plowing.

Ollie takes a letter to the mailbox and raises the flag. A neighbor comes down the road. A cloud of dust catching up to his rattling truck as he stops.

"Hello, Miz. Glenn. How's Roy doing?"

"Fine. He likes his boss and gets along well with the people he works with."

"That's good. I guess you've heard the bad news buzzing through the Valley."

She draws in her breath. "I haven't been off the farm for several days."

"That nice-looking boy everyone calls Red. You know him?"

Ollie nods. "He asked Roy for work a few times."

"Well, he's in police custody, charged with killing several people, including his pretty little wife. Rumor is that he confessed to killing her and more than twenty others. They've already found parts of her skeleton and clothes. He led them right to her, and told the police he killed her because she was griping about money. The others he killed for money."

Ollie holds to the mailbox. Suddenly, the sun is too hot, and she feels dizzy. "I better get inside and check on the baby. Thanks for stopping, and you have a good day."

The neighbor drives away as Ollie stumbles to the house. Once inside, she splashes water on her face, sits in the rocker, and leans her head back. *Thank You God for warning us and for saving Roy from evil hands.*

Roy works in Washington for over a year, coming back once during that time. Ollie and the girls plant, work, and harvest the crops. In October 1945, Roy comes home before winter snows make roads impassable.

Mack's mother has grown worse. Ollie lets him stay at the house to play with Johnny as much as he wants.

One day Mack's daddy tells his three children to go down the road to the neighbors, to not stop, turn around, or come back to the house. The children hear a gunshot as they are running.

Their mother has died with tuberculosis. Unable to face the pain of life without her, her husband shoots and kills himself. The sheriff takes the children to an orphanage.

Johnny watches as the sheriff drives away with the children in the back seat of his car. Mack's sad face is pressed against the window. "Daddy, why did the sheriff take them away? They didn't do anything bad."

"Son, he's not taking them to jail. He'll take them to a home where they'll stay until someone adopts them."

Johnny sniffs, and alternates between rubbing his eyes and his arms. "Can we adopt Mack?"

Roy wipes at his own eyes, and spits tobacco juice into the yard before answering. "Son, we'd take Mack in a minute, but we can't afford to take all three. And it wouldn't be fair to take him away from his brother and sister."

Although Roy and Ollie try to keep the details of the

situation from Ann and Johnny, the children overhear other people talking. Johnny no longer plays in the dirt pile where he and Mack constructed their make-believe town, and he asks strings of questions about what might happen to his friend.

Roy and Ollie like living in Happy Valley. The farm is close to family and good friends, but when they receive a reasonable offer from a man wanting to buy the place, they decide it would be a good idea to move Johnny. He spends most of his time sitting on the porch petting Pluto, looking down the road, and wishing Mack could come back to play.

Roy and Ollie sell the farm in Happy Valley, and buy one between Greenbrier and the Republican community. The only high school for miles around is at Greenbrier. All of the children will ride the bus and go to the same school when Johnny starts in the fall. Ollie likes knowing that the older girls will be on the bus to look out for Ann and John.

Chapter 11
The Willis Place

The new farm, called the Willis Place after a previous owner, only has a few clear acres for farming. Most of the land is fenced pasture. The house is not much different from the one in Happy Valley, except it has a sleeping loft. Johnny likes the loft; the girls get the bedroom. Roy and Ollie set up a bed in the living room where they can tend the fireplace in the winter.

While moving, Pluto rides next to John in the wagon, eyes and ears alert for everything they approach and pass. That night, Johnny makes Pluto a bed on the porch, ties his rope to a post, and talks to him through the window. After a couple of days, Johnny takes him off the rope. The next morning, Pluto is gone. Johnny is frantic that some wild animal came out of the woods and carried off his dog.

Roy consoles him. "No, John, I'm sure that during the night, your dog decided he wanted to go back to his old home. I'm going over there Monday to get another load of my farm equipment. Pluto can ride back with me."

"Daddy."

"What, son?"

"Do you think the sheriff might have Pluto?"

"No, the sheriff didn't take him. Pluto got confused and tried to go home."

Monday, Roy and Ollie are working in the barn. After school, Ann drops her books on the porch and rushes to ask about Pluto.

"Sis, I'm sorry." Roy shakes his head. "That woman at our old place said Pluto was dead when she found him. He might have been hit by a car before stumbling back to the yard."

Ann's face scrunches into a frown. "No! No, he didn't." Trying to stifle a sob, she turns away and sails a small rock off the toe of her shoe. "I was hoping that boy was just being mean and hateful."

Ollie rubs her apron. Roy wipes his face on a crumpled handkerchief before asking, "What boy?"

"The one whose parents bought our farm in Happy Valley. Today, at school, I asked if he'd seen Pluto. He said, 'Yeah, that dumb little dog came back barking at me, but you can forget about him. I knocked him in the head with a hammer.'"

Johnny does not believe Ann's story about Pluto's fate. "That boy wouldn't do that. He couldn't be that mean." Before and after school, he calls and looks for his dog. For days, his conversations turn to talk about Pluto.

Roy and Ollie sit on the porch, watching Johnny walk the borders of the yard, calling, and looking into the woods.

"He's lost without that dog." Ollie puts a hand to her heart, as if she could soothe her son's pain. "I wouldn't mind having one big enough to be a guard dog. We're isolated from the main road, and with all these woods around, no telling what kind of animals will wander in."

"I'll check with my brothers. Maybe they'll know of someone that has one they want to get rid of."

Ollie leans her head against Roy's shoulder. "This place is

pretty with all the big trees and that spring next to the yard. I hope we can make a living here, without you having to go away again."

He pats her leg. "We'll plant corn on the cleared fields, and raise cattle on the rest. With our savings and what we got from the place in Happy Valley, we're free of mortgage payments." With a big grin, he slaps his own leg. *"Free of mortgage payments*—I can hardly believe it. I'll get a good pair of work mules and clear off more pastureland. You can hoe your garden, but I hope you never have to plow another field."

"You'll need work mules on a farm like this, but the mares are so gentle, and the kids love them."

"I know, but we can't keep horses *and* mules."

The spring runs across one edge of the cow lot and along one side of the backyard. It holds dozens of crawdads. When Johnny is not in school, he spends almost every waking hour at the spring. With a bent straight-pin on one end of a string tied onto a small stick pole, John catches crawdads from the stream. They clamp the pin to get a worm John has threaded onto it.

At first, Johnny feeds his catch to the chickens, but fears he will hook all the crawfish. He starts tossing them back to catch again and again.

The mules that Roy trades for are big and strong, but they are not saddle-broke, and Roy does not trust them on the highway with his family in the wagon. He rises early Sunday morning and walks to Soda Valley to see his pa. He brings back a big red dog that his brother Sam gave him. It is still a pup, but looks full-grown. "John, he's your responsibility. You have to know, before you start liking him too much, that if he starts chasing chickens or cows, we'll have to get rid of him."

Down on his knees, patting and loving the new dog, Johnny asks, "How would you do that? I bet he'd come right back to me."

Roy's voice is gruff. "I bet he won't. Son, you're a farm boy." He pauses to spit. "You have to know this—when a dog chases animals that people depend on for a living, he can't stay around. If he runs after the mules, they'll kill him, real quick."

Johnny jerks his head up. "What do you mean?"

"You know what I mean." Roy pulls a blue handkerchief from his back pocket and wipes his mouth. "Keep that rope on him for a few days. Walk him near the chickens with a switch in your hand. If he tries to chase one, whack him with the switch. Do the same if he barks, or runs toward the cows or mules."

Frowning, Johnny shakes his head slowly. "I don't want to whip him. I want him to like me."

"John, if you want him to live, you have to teach him to respect your commands."

The next day, Johnny goes inside for a drink and does not tie Red to the clothesline post. He has hardly put his lips to the dipper when he hears barks and chickens squawking. He runs outside, grabs the rope, and yanks. The big stocky dog is having fun making the chickens run. John's shoes slide on the grass as the muscular dog pulls him along in the chase.

"Come here, Red!" John yells in his meanest voice, and slaps the dog on the hip, hurting his hand more than the dog. After breaking a strong switch, he walks Red back and forth near the chickens.

When the cows come into the lot for feed and milking, John parades Red near them with the same switch in his hand. It only takes the dog two barks and two switchings before he walks silently beside the pen.

Another day of work is done. The children, tucked into bed, sleep peacefully. Roy and Ollie sit on the porch, talking. Moonlight glistens on the dewdrops forming on the grass. Inside the woods, night birds call, and from the spring, the deep croaks of bullfrogs reverberate.

Roy folds his pocketknife, and pushes aside a box of wood shavings for the cook stove. "Ollie, Pa didn't look well when I visited last week." He turns to spit into the yard. "He asked about you and the kids, and wanted to know how we like our new place. He sure hated to hear that we sold the mares, and said he's afraid he won't get to see John growing up, since we live so far away."

Ollie rubs the top of his hand. "Even though Fanny cooks and takes care of the home place, he misses your ma. She was such a good lady."

"Next Sunday, I'm gonna take John with me when I go to see Pa."

"Roy, it's probably seven or eight miles over there, and he's only six and a half years old. That's too far for him to walk."

"We'll stop and rest when he gets tired or I'll carry him on my back. Pa's not doing well, and he always asks about John."

"What about the girls?"

"Nancy's too little. The others can go if they want, but they'll have to walk."

Late Sunday afternoon, Roy trudges home with a tired little boy on his back.

Ollie shakes her head as he approaches the porch. "I told you he was too young for such a long walk."

"He walked most of the way. I'm glad I took him. Pa was so happy to see him. He could hardly eat for playing with John." Roy lowers his head. "Pa won't last much longer."

Roy's pa, William Barton Glenn, dies on April 1, 1946. His sons and daughters lay him to rest beside his wife, Nancy Jane (Battles) Glenn in the Thorn Cemetery at Greenbrier.

Morene has met a young man, Jarrell Smith. They are making plans for marriage. She promises Ollie that she will go back to school and finish her senior year of high school. Jarrell rents a house in the Republican community, and they get married at the end of Morene's junior year.

Ollie and Nancy cry when Morene leaves. After Nancy was old enough to drink milk from a cup, Morene took care of her more than Ollie. Each morning, she dressed Nancy and combed her hair. At mealtime, she served her plate, buttered her bread, and wiped her face. Before bedtime, she bathed and helped her into a nightgown, and chased away monsters when Nancy had bad dreams.

Nancy tells Jarrell he cannot take Morene. Jarrell promises to bring Morene back to visit and to let Nancy come to their house. He keeps his promise. Soon, she likes him almost as much as she likes her sister.

With Morene gone, Syble is in charge when Roy and Ollie are away. It is not long until they plan a trip to Conway on the bus and leave Syble to watch the younger children. Before walking to the highway to catch the bus, Ollie calls Ann, John, and Nancy. "All of you have to mind Syble. If you'll behave, we'll bring back candy for you."

Late in the afternoon, Roy and Ollie return with several packages. John and Ann run onto the porch to meet them. Ollie gasps. "What happened to your faces?"

Ann puts her hands on her hips and looks back at her older sister. "Syble poked us with the broom."

"Syble, you poked them in the face with the broom? You could have put their eyes out with those broom straws."

"They wouldn't mind me. I was sweeping the floor and they kept getting in the trash."

Ann glares at Syble. "She was sweeping out my paper dolls, and John's toys."

Syble frowns and exhales with a huff. "Old scraps cut out of the catalog and some pieces of wood with wheels drawn on them."

Ollie shakes her head and drops an armload of packages onto the porch. "Syble, we can't afford expensive store-bought paper dolls and toys. These kids have to make their own. You had no right to destroy their playthings."

"I knew you'd take up for them. This house looks like a trash dump with all that junk strewn around."

"You cut out paper dolls and laid your toys around when you were their age. Let them have their time for play." Ollie squints, and grits her teeth. "And you better not ever again poke one of the kids in the face with a broom."

While in town, Roy heard that the John Lane farm—the farm that belonged to Ollie's grandparents when she was a girl—is for sale. He goes to check on it and comes back full of enthusiasm. "Ollie, if we could sell this place, I think we could manage to buy that farm. With a hundred eighty acres, we could farm and raise cattle. It has two barns. One of them is a big hip-roof for storing more hay than we could ever haul in a season, rooms for corn and grain storage, and a long manger with troughs on two sides where we could separate the cows from mules and horses. The land has two ever-running springs, one on the southeast corner and one on the southwest. The house needs some paint and maintenance, but it's quite a farm."

"Oh, Roy! But what if we sell this place, and someone buys *that* one before we can make the deal?"

"I talked to the land agent about that—He said we can make an offer contingent on selling this place within a specified time. If our place doesn't sell, we don't have an obligation to buy that one."

"I love that place. I spent some of the happiest days of my childhood with my grandpa and grandma. Did you look inside the house?"

"He spent more time showing me the farm, but I think the house will shine after a little cleaning and some paint. It needs a new roof, but we could patch it for a while. It's a big house. That hall is wide enough to make two rooms."

She would love to live there, but is afraid. What if they get in over their heads, lose everything? Dr. Williams said to expect the new baby in August, and Ollie has had trouble with strep throat. She can finally hear, but thought for a long time that she had gone deaf. *What if I get that again, or one of the children becomes sick?* She puts a hand against her abdomen. They cannot afford more doctor bills.

Roy puts his hands on her shoulders and bends a little to look at her face. "Ollie, you're worrying again. You don't have chills running up your neck, do you?"

She smiles. "No, I don't feel any special warnings."

"Then, stop worrying. We'll do the best we can with what we have. Remember the story of the talents. Don't you believe God helps those that help themselves? Let's go look at it tomorrow, and get the agent to look at this place and set a price."

After seeing the farm again, it is hard for Ollie to wait on a buyer. She insists that they get everything ready. "I wish we had a tank for dipping the cattle, but since we don't, let's spray them. Maybe some strong spray will keep ticks away. At least it will get rid of flies. Grandpa's place has been vacant for months—we don't want to take any pests with us."

Within a short time, the land agent brings a family from Texas to look at the Willis place. They make an offer; Roy and Ollie accept. They sign papers, and Ollie starts packing dishes.

Chapter 12
New Home and New Baby

August 3, 1946, Roy and Ollie move their family to the John Lane farm. This is where Ollie's mama grew up, and where she came to stay for several days with her ma before Ollie was born. *I was born in this house, right here in this room, and this is where our new baby will be born."*

Syble has already swept the ceilings, and walls, and helped Ollie scrub all the wood floors with lye water. With a wet cloth, Ollie rubs at a smudge on the door. "I wish we could have painted before moving, but maybe we can do that in the spring."

She walks down the hallway where maroon paint is beginning to crack. *I'll get some cream-colored paint to lighten these walls.* The floors are bare wood. *Eventually, I'll cover the floors with pretty linoleum.* Vandals have carved crude letters into the kitchen door and ripped wallpaper from the walls: *Syble and I will repaper the walls and patch that door, but it can wait until after the baby comes.*

Jarrell, Morene's husband, helps Roy carry in Ollie's white Hoosier cabinet, and the cook stove that she rubbed down yesterday with stove black. Turquoise and cream-colored doors on the warming and cooking ovens stand out against the shiny black.

The yard is a jungle of weeds as high as Roy's head, taller in the barnyard where the ground is rich with manure. "Ollie, I'll mow these down as soon as I can bring my mowing machine over. Until then, keep John and Nancy inside. They might step on a copperhead, and all of you, stay away from that old gray building behind the house."

"That used to be Grandpa's smokehouse. There's a cellar underneath."

"The floor of the smokehouse is rotten and the cellar's full of water. Anyone going in might fall through and meet the same fate as those rats and a rabbit that's down there."

John runs to Roy. "Can we get the rabbit out?"

"Son, that rabbit's dead and stinkin'. I figure it fell in from the cellar window and couldn't get out. The same thing might happen to you or your sisters if you step on that rotten floor. The window is almost level with the ground outside, and the door is missing. After mowing these weeds, I'm gonna drain that cellar."

Roy shovels where the ground has caved in on a drainage ditch. After his many hours of hard work in the August sun, water starts to trickle into the ditch. A few shovels of dirt later, water gushes into the ditch and down the hill. The next morning, the water has drained from the cellar.

He removes the dead animals, trash, and a layer of mud. Roy takes off the nuts threaded onto bolts holding the smokehouse on top of the cellar walls. Jarrell helps pry and prop the building up with lumber. They wrap a heavy chain around it, harness the mules, and drag the creaking structure about forty feet to the southeast. Propped on rocks for leveling, it will continue as a smokehouse after some repair to the floor.

Jarrell helps build a form with steel rods inside, to hold the wet cement for a cellar top they plan to pour. Roy makes several trips to North Cadron Creek with the mules and wagon to shovel sand. When he has stockpiled enough of the gritty material, Jarrell comes back to help mix and pour the cement into the form for a thick concrete top.

Roy builds a new entry door above the steep cellar steps; a door for the small window; a wide bench for sitting, or laying the children on stormy nights; and shelves across the north side for Ollie to store canned fruits and vegetables.

The sturdy rock-and-concrete cellar is a great improvement over the dirt-covered, log-supported dugouts where they have hunkered many times from threatening storm clouds. "Ollie, unless you have to go in the cellar to escape a storm, stay out of there until after the baby comes. Those steps are steep. I'm afraid you might fall and hurt yourself."

"Hold onto me so I can bend and look at my new shelves."

Roy kills several snakes after mowing the yard and barn lot; some are copperheads. The next day, he brings home a shepherd dog. It is a pretty mixture of black and tan, carries his head high and proud, and loves the kids from the start. "Arthur gave him to me. He says Pooch will clear out the snakes."

"Did you ask your brother if the dog kills chickens or eats eggs?"

"I didn't ask, but I'd give up every chicken we have to get rid of these snakes."

Ollie frowns. "A farm has to have chickens."

"Children come first, don't you think?"

"Of course, but—"

"No buts. One of the kids is bound to get bit if we don't get rid of the snakes."

All of the kids like Pooch, especially Nancy. "Roy, Nancy is hugging and petting that dog every chance she gets. I'm almost as afraid of tick bites as I am of the snakes."

"I haven't seen any ticks on him."

"But he's bound to get them, the way he runs over the farm."

"As soon as I get an extra minute, I'll trim his long hair and rub tick dip on him."

"Whew, I remember that smell. Maybe the kids won't want to pet him with that stinky stuff on his body."

The new house has a long porch across the front with concrete steps. At ground level, a concrete pad extends more than twice the width of the other steps. Each evening, after the day's work is done and supper dishes are washed, the family sits on the porch, talking and enjoying any cool breeze that might stir.

On one such evening, three-year-old Nancy quietly slides from the porch to the top step, to the second, third, and is about to put her foot down again on her way to pet the dogs that are resting in the yard a few feet beyond. Pooch springs toward her, his teeth bared. With a yelp and a deep growl, Red follows.

Frightened, Nancy scrambles toward the top step. Pooch snatches a copperhead snake just inches from where Nancy's foot had been, and shakes it violently. Red tries to grab the snake, and causes both dogs to get bit.

Ollie screams, "Get in the house, kids! Get in the house. They could sling that up here."

Nancy's cries almost drown Ollie's commands.

Ollie grabs her arm. "What's wrong? What's wrong? Where do you hurt? Did the snake bite you?"

Nancy slumps to the floor, gasping for breath between sobs.

Ollie grabs one foot and then the other, looking for marks. "Roy, come here." She holds her protruding stomach and backs away to lean against the wall.

Nancy lets out another howl as Roy comes through the door. He stops. "What's wrong?"

"Look at her feet and legs. See if that snake bit her." Ollie slides along the wall, into a bedroom, and sits on the edge of a bed.

"Ann, hold that lamp down here," Roy orders. "Nancy, hush. Nothing's wrong with you."

Her chin quivers, she sniffs and wipes her eyes on her sleeve.

"Do you hurt somewhere?"

She shakes her head.

"Then why are you crying?"

"Pooch almost bit me."

Roy laughs, and picks her up. "No, he didn't. He bit the snake that was gonna bite you. Pooch likes you."

Smiling, she wipes at another tear. "I like him too."

"Ollie, are you all right?"

"It'll take me a few minutes to calm down. The way she was screaming, I thought the snake bit her."

"With the two of you screaming, I thought it bit all of you."

"Stop joking. That gave me a real scare."

The snake lies scattered across the yard. Whimpering, both dogs crawl under the smokehouse. The next day, their heads are swollen to the size of water buckets. Ollie watches Roy and Nancy slide pans of water and food into the shade near the dogs.

Roy rubs Nancy's back and speaks softly. "They're not moving. They may die from the snakebites. We'll have to wait and see."

The dogs stay under the smokehouse for several days, only moving to take a lap or two from the water pan. Occasionally, a faint moan escapes one of them.

Eventually, they recover. Red never bothered snakes before; now he and Pooch roam the meadows, searching and killing every one they find.

Ollie sees Pooch coming out of the henhouse, and goes to check on the eggs. All she finds are broken shells. She approaches Roy where he is replacing a rotten board on the back of the house, "Roy, that new dog's eating eggs." She holds out a broken shell as evidence. "What are you gonna do about it?"

He stands from a squatting position and rubs a sore knee. "We'll fix some eggs filled with hot pepper, but I bet he's smart enough to leave those alone. We need eggs, but more than that, we need to get rid of snakes. I'll try to break him. If that doesn't work, I'll tear down the nests and build some higher on the wall."

Ollie shakes her head. "If he gets Red started, we'll have to get rid of both dogs. Red's so big that, if he stood on his back feet, his head would be way up there. I wouldn't be able to see the eggs in nests that high. I bet your brother knew that dog would suck eggs."

Roy bangs the hammer against a nail in the wall. "What if he did? What if I knew it? We'll do without eggs, or we'll buy them. He's already saved Nancy from a copperhead."

"I want rid of the snakes as bad as you do." She walks

away, but stops at the porch steps. "Syble took my letter to Mama and Papa up to the mailbox. I asked them to come stay with us until after the baby comes. It'll be here before the end of the month."

"Do you think they'll come?"

Ollie frowns at him for a moment. "I know Mama will come. She's helped with five others, hasn't she?"

He takes a deep breath and lets it out. "Ollie, I'm a little distracted. This board's not fitting like I meant for it to." He hooks the hammer's claw under the board and rips it from the wall.

Ollie climbs the steps.

A few days later, Mama and Papa come walking slowly down the road from the highway, where they got off the bus. Sweat drips from their foreheads. Papa, as round as Santa Claus, breathes heavy and walks with a slight limp. He carries a canvas bag in each hand. Mama, looking very thin and fragile, walks softly, lifting her feet high like a deer.

Ollie wants to rush out to greet them as they walk toward the house, but at nine months pregnant, she cannot rush anywhere. "Oh, Mama, Papa, if I'd known when you were coming, I would have sent Roy to get you in the wagon. It's a full mile from the highway, and today's so hot. You might have had a heat stroke."

Papa sits on the edge of the porch, slaps John on the shoulder, and says, "Son, go get us a drink, if you will."

John runs around the house and comes back with the dipper and a bucket half full of water.

Mama, holding onto Ann, climbs the steps and sits in a rocker. "Ollie, I see you waited for me. I wanted to run down here when I got off that bus, but want and putter along is all I could do. That is the longest mile I ever walked."

"I'm glad you came, but I hate that you walked that far."

Morene and Jarrell come to visit in the late afternoon. Ann, John and Nancy go home with them. Two days later, Roy goes to Greenbrier to get Dr. Williams. The doctor delivers another girl for Ollie and Roy—Patty Evelyn. She is a good baby, long and not as fat as Ollie's other babies. Nancy is fascinated with little Patty. John ignores her at first, but never says he does not like her. She adds more work for Syble and Ann, but they love her.

Roy keeps the mules busy that winter, dragging trees, pulling stumps, building terraces to stop erosion from the hillsides, and getting fields ready to plant in the spring. One morning, he goes out to harness them for a day of work, and they run from him. Each time he gets close to one to put the bridle on, it kicks up its heels and runs away. After a few tries, he goes into the house and loads the shotgun with birdshot.

"Roy, if you're not careful, you'll kill those mules, or blind one."

"If I don't show them who's boss, they'll be trying to kill me."

They are still running around kicking up their heels when he returns to the lot. One turns its back to him and kicks. He shoots it in the rump, reloads, and shoots it again. After a couple of shots each, the mules stand trembling while he puts the bridles on. After that incident, he keeps a long stick beside the gate. When he goes to the mules with bridles, he takes the stick in one hand—they stand quivering, never again attempting to kick him or to run away.

Ollie reads in the newspaper that an eighty acre farm, that joins theirs on the northeast corner, is delinquent on taxes and will be sold at auction if the taxes are not paid by a certain date. Roy hitchhikes to the courthouse in Conway and pays the taxes. The previous owner was Ollie's cousin. Ollie sends the notice from the paper to her cousin, along with a letter stating an offer for the property, and a check for the offered amount with "paid in full" marked on the bottom. Her cousin accepts the offer.

Jarrell and Morene want to buy the eighty-acre farm and build a house on it. Jarrell learned construction while working for the WPA. Soon he and Morene have a two-bedroom house within walking distance of Roy and Ollie's home.

Roy and Ollie can hardly wait for planting time to get seeds in the ground for crops and gardens. A farm like this is what they always wanted. After planting all that Roy thinks he will be able to cultivate, Ollie talks him into planting one more field: "I've always wanted a piano for the children. If we plant a field, promising the kids that the proceeds will be for their piano, they'll be eager to help work it." She is right. Everyone, even four-year-old Nancy, wants to help hoe. The crops sprout and grow like Roy and Ollie's dreams.

Nancy sits in the shade with Patty and John while Roy, Ollie, Syble and Ann build haystacks on the high sides of the meadows. Roy peddles watermelons, cantaloupes and garden vegetables around Greenbrier. Then hot summer winds blow, and the sky is void of rain clouds. Ollie's garden dies. The piano field withers along with the others. Cotton bolls shrink in the sun.

Sitting on the porch, katydids screeching in the pecan tree, Roy says, "Ollie, you know I'm gonna have to go north again to find work. There's no use sitting around here. We'll get a little corn for feeding the animals, but the cotton crop is nearly ruined, and we still owe over two thousand on this farm."

"I know, but I hated to say it."

"Since we don't have a lot of cattle, I think they'll be fine in that big pasture. They can scrounge around and find enough grass to survive. The springs are still running freely. Everyone that I've talked to about this place says they've never known those springs to run dry. I'll get some feed ground for the milk cows. The manger is full of hay. When that's gone, rake more out of the loft. I'll try my best to get home for Christmas. Then, I'll open gates to let the cattle into the haystacks. I don't want you or the kids in the pasture with that bull."

"What about the mules?"

He shakes his head. "I wish we still had those gentle mares. I'm gonna fasten the mules out of the barn lot so you or the kids won't ever have to be near them. They have water and plenty of grass in that pasture. Don't go in there for *any* reason."

"I can walk to the highway and catch a bus, but that's a long way to carry Patty. It's longer still for Nancy's short legs to walk. I'll hate not getting to go to see Mama and Papa."

"I may try to get rid of those mules before I go. John has been asking about trading them for horses. He should have a horse he can ride. My brother, Bonny, has a mare and a gelding for sale. The mare is the one his boy, Thurman, rode the last time he was down here. She looked strong and healthy. They're both broke to the saddle and harness. Thurman said they're gentle. Before the week's out, I'll ride over to Guy and talk to Bonny and Thurman."

"You said you'll have to go north to look for work. I hope

that doesn't mean as far away as Washington or North Dakota like in the past."

"I'll catch the bus into Conway tomorrow and check with the unemployment office to see if there are any jobs around here. If not, I'll have to go north. I hear things are booming around Kansas City."

The next day, Nancy comes running into the house, screaming. "Mother! The mules kicked Pooch and chased Red. While they were chasing Red, Pooch crawled into the cow pasture, but he's not moving. Red ran under the gate before they could kick him."

Ollie frowns and takes a deep breath. "It's too bad Roy didn't trade them yesterday." She kneels on one knee, and pulls Nancy close. "Honey, pooch is probably dead. They would kick you the same way if you get in their pasture. Those mules are mean. They've already killed a calf that got on the wrong side of the fence. We can't do anything to help Pooch. Roy will check on him when he comes home."

John wants to go to the dog. "Maybe he's not dead. I could put him in the shade."

"No, you'll have to wait until your daddy gets home. Those mules might be tempted to jump the fence and kick you."

Roy and John bury Pooch under a shady tree in the cow pasture. The next day, Roy hitches the mules to the wagon and goes to look for gentle horses. John sees him coming down the road with a black horse and a brown mare pulling the wagon.

"Mother, he got them! He got Lucky and Tony. The one on the right is Lucky. She's the one Thurman let me ride."

Ollie is almost as excited as John. She has been afraid of those mules since Roy traded for them.

Without Pooch, Red is lonesome. He stays on the front porch until Ollie runs him off. On the second day, she catches him coming out of the chicken house, and hits him with a pan she has taken to gather the eggs. He runs across the field with his tail tucked under. She never sees him again.

Chapter 13
Another Try

Morene and Jarrell pick up supplies for Ollie in town. If she needs fabric or something special, she and the children ride to Conway with them. Sometimes Morene takes Ann, John, and Nancy to the movies. John particularly likes the westerns with Gene Autry and Johnny Mack Brown.

Syble, now sixteen, takes care of feeding the cattle while Roy is working in Kansas City. John likes to feed the horses, but Ollie will not let him ride while Roy is away. On Saturdays and after school, Syble hitches the horses to the wagon. She, Ollie, and John gather the corn while Ann stays at the house to take care of Patty and Nancy.

After the corn is stored in the barn, Syble and Ollie cut up an oak tree that Roy and Ollie sawed down before he left. With the axe and a one-man-saw, they work several afternoons to cut the branches. Cutting and splitting the large trunk will wait until Roy gets home. John stacks the wood in the wagon and piles the brush that is not large enough to save for the stoves.

Ollie repairs the cotton sacks and begins picking cotton and pulling the unopened bolls. Syble empties the sacks before they get as full as they would if Roy were home. John has a small sack to pull, and Nancy carries a pillowcase.

John tosses a worm at Nancy. "Those white fuzzy worms will sting if you touch one, and the black and yellow spiders with webs stretched across the rows are getting ready to jump on anything that shakes their web."

Nancy is doing nothing but squealing—entertaining Johnny and keeping him from working. Ollie sends her to the house to stay with Ann and the baby. When the mixture of cotton and unopened bolls fill the wagon, Syble and Ollie shovel it into an empty corncrib. Roy will take it to the gin when he comes home.

Syble is not lazy; she works hard and rarely complains, but she does not like school. The Home Economics teacher comes to talk with Ollie. "Syble is as smart as any student that I have, she's a good cook, and could probably take over and run a household without any trouble, but she's stubborn. She won't try to learn sewing, saying she'll buy her clothes ready-made."

The school bus stops on the highway, a mile from the farm. It is a pleasant walk when the warm sun falls on the children's shoulders, cattle graze in nearby pastures, and spring wildflowers or autumn leaves decorate the landscape. In the winter, when rain, snow, and icy winds blow out of the north, the children come home almost frozen.

Lottie, Roy's sister, lives across the highway from the bus stop. When the children arrive early, she welcomes them inside to warm before the bus comes. Still, Ollie worries that they will get wet and spend a chilly day at school in damp clothes.

Lottie has two girls near Syble's age. They are equally bold. Syble spends as much time with the girls as Ollie will allow. They walk or catch a ride with a friend to functions they want to attend. Ollie knows they are mischievous, but counts on Elfleda, the oldest, to keep Syble and Laquida out of trouble.

One Saturday night, Syble asks to spend the night at Lottie's, but Ollie refuses. Syble reasons and begs. Ollie cannot give her a good reason for denying the request, except, "I think you need to stay home tonight."

Though Ollie feels guilty about making the demand, intuition tells her it is the right thing to do. In the night, Ollie hears someone in the hall. She gets up and finds Syble fully dressed with clothes packed in a suitcase.

"Where are you planning to go?"

"I'm tired of being stuck on this farm, working all the time, and not being able to go anywhere."

"Where do you think you can go and not have to work? Work is a fact of life unless you're lucky enough to be born rich."

"I'm gonna get married."

"Married!

"You hardly know that boy. He's only been here a few times."

"He asked me to marry him and I said 'yes.'"

"You're not old enough to get married without my consent. Put that suitcase down and get back in bed. You're not going anywhere tonight."

Syble takes a step toward the door, but stops when Ollie steps in front of her. "I'm as strong as you. I could run out of here and you couldn't stop me."

"I'll stop you. Getting married is something to think about and plan for a long time. It's not a game."

"Morene was only seventeen—you let her get married. I'll be seventeen in March."

"She thought it over for a long time, and she married a young man ready to settle down and make a home. You want to marry a boy with no ambition other than having a good time. Finish school, and then if you still think you love him and want to get married, I'll not disagree."

Syble goes to the bedroom, slams the suitcase down and kicks it under the bed. Ollie lies awake the rest of the night. Later she discovers that Laquida and her boyfriend intended to leave with Syble and Thurston. The four of them were planning to go to St. Louis, get married, and find jobs—they thought the rest would be one long party.

Lottie and her girls are going to Texas over the Christmas break with Lottie's son Glen. They invite Syble to go. Ollie gives her consent.

Ollie has finished most of the washing, and it is hanging on the line, drying in the breeze. The wringer washer and a washtub three-quarters full of rinse water sits in the smokehouse. Outside, a black cast-iron wash-pot, half-full of bubbling water, stands over smoldering coals where Ollie does a final rinse on dish towels and anything that might still have lingering germs after going through the washing machine.

Syble walks to the smokehouse door as Ollie comes out. "Mama, I've got the itch."

"Oh my goodness."

Nancy comes running toward Syble.

Ollie commands, "Stay back, Nancy. You can't touch her. She's caught the itch."

Motioning for Syble to come inside the small gray building, Ollie asks, "Did you know they had that before you went with them?"

Syble nods. "Yes, but I wanted to go."

"Well, now you have to stay by yourself until you get rid of it. I can't take a chance on the other kids catching the itch. Strip off your clothes while I go in the house and get medicine."

Ollie dunks Syble's undergarments in bleach water, puts her jeans, blouses, and dresses into the boiling wash-pot. Her wool coat hangs on the line until Ollie can press it with hot irons.

Syble covers herself, including her scalp and hair, with the stinking mixture Ollie gives her, and then puts on a clean flannel gown. Ollie quarantines her to a bedroom until the itch is gone. Everything she took with her or brought back from the trip is bleached, boiled, ironed, or burned. After Ollie declares her well, Syble takes a bath and washes her hair with lye soap.

Ollie brings Syble's clean clothes and places them on a chair beside the tub. "Was going to Texas worth getting the itch?"

Syble grins. "Yes, but now that I've been there, I wouldn't want to go again if I knew I'd get that."

Roy comes home in the spring, ready to plant, but April showers make everything soggy. Tree limbs drip water from budding leaves. Standing on the front porch, Ollie hears water gushing along Pea Vine Creek.

"I wish I'd worked another couple of weeks," says Roy, "but the worst state of affairs seems to be a farmer's luck."

He goes into the woods and comes back dripping wet with a handful of green hickory limbs. Sitting on the porch, he takes out his pocketknife and makes hickory whistles for all the kids.

John and Nancy run through the house blowing whistles until Ollie thinks she is going to scream.

Roy chuckles. "It's better than crying. At least they're happy."

She frowns. "I can't even send them outside, because it's raining, but if it keeps up much longer, I may send you all to the barn."

"Kids, bring those whistles out to the front porch."

The mailman drives into the yard, and Roy walks out in the rain to take a large package. It contains peach, nectarine, apple and pear trees that Ollie ordered from a catalog. Some of the bushes have pink buds and tiny leaves pushing through the thin bark of small branches. Roy and John measure, dig holes, and plant the young trees in the wet soil south of the house.

Ollie pulls a jacket over her arms and goes to check on the progress.

Roy leans on the post-hole-diggers. "What do you think?"

"They're pretty, lined up on the terraces like that. They'll be beautiful with blooms in a few years, and especially when they're loaded with fruit."

Roy lifts the diggers from a hole. "John, think of the pies we'll get if these grow."

"Yeah, Daddy, and with all these trees, we should have bushels of peaches and apples to sell in town."

"I hope so. By then, you'll be big enough to help deliver them. In fact, I think you need to help me peddle melons and vegetables this summer."

John grins and stands straighter. "I'll make a good salesman. Much better than a bean sheller—I hate sitting all day shelling beans and peas, or shucking and silking corn."

Ollie grins. "I thought you liked that."

"Nah, that's girl work."

Roy chuckles. "It's too bad we don't have a truck. I'm sure we could sell more melons and vegetables in Conway where not so many people have gardens."

In the spring, when the ground is dry enough to run the wagon through the field, Roy and John haul manure from the barn, and put the rich fertilizer in each round hill prepared for watermelon seed.

At the dinner table, John asks, "Daddy, if it doesn't rain, all of our work will be wasted, won't it?"

"If it doesn't rain at all. But watermelons ripen in July. We usually get plenty of rain through June. Those rains will make melons, early gardens, and corn. If we don't get rains through July, our corn will be sorry but cotton will be ruined—it does most of the growing in July."

"When I'm grown, I'll do something besides farming— something more dependable."

Ollie hangs lace curtains for decoration and does not worry about shades for privacy—the closest neighbor lives a half mile down the road. One night Syble comes home from a date, and places her nightgown on the bed. The lights from her boyfriend's car have faded far into the black night.

She pulls off her dress and tosses it onto a chair. Reaching for the tail of her slip, she sees a man's face and hands pressed against the window. She screams, "Daddy!"

Roy jumps up, grabs his shotgun, runs to her room and then out into the night searching. All he finds is a man's footprints under the window.

Ollie buys canvas shades for the bedrooms. Even with the shades pulled, the girls are afraid to undress with the lamps turned on. Nancy wakes in the night with nightmares of monsters peeping through the windows.

Roy and Ollie plant corn, cotton, several acres of watermelons, and large gardens. After the crops are laid-by, Roy hangs a swing in the walnut tree. He cuts notches on the ends of a short board to make a seat for the swing. It is not long until Ann and John are standing on the board, pumping their legs to make the swing go higher and higher.

Ollie steps onto the porch. "Roy, you've created something to get one of those kids hurt. If Nancy walks in front of that board, she could be killed."

Roy shakes his head. "She knows better than to walk in front of the swing."

"Well, make them sit down. What if it breaks? Or one of them falls out?"

"Ollie, let them have some fun. That's a strong rope and they're big kids. They won't fall out."

The watermelons are almost ready for market, and the corn, higher than Roy's head, is developing well. The children pick and shell bushels of peas and beans. Ollie cans peas, beans, tomatoes, corn, soup and berries until all her jars are full.

The cotton is green and growing. Roy beams with pride, until he walks through the field and discovers boll weevils. Adult weevils are on the squares. Cutting open some of the newly formed bolls reveals larva gorging themselves inside.

From the porch where she is shelling beans, Ollie watches Roy's long strides coming back to the house. "Ollie, we've got boll weevils in the cotton."

"Oh, no. What can we do? We can't afford a crop duster."

"Get me two thin meal sacks. I've heard they come out at night to do the most damage. At least the dew will help the poison cling to the plants. I'm gonna mix some arsenic with flour and dust the fields tonight."

"No, Roy. Let the cotton die. You'll get that poison all over yourself. You don't even know that will kill them, but I'm sure it won't be good for you to breathe."

"Get me another meal sack that I can tie over my nose and mouth."

"Even with a sack over your head, you couldn't help breathing some of it."

"Find the meal sacks and fix me a mask. I'm going to town to get poison."

At dusk, when dew starts to collect on the leaves, Roy stretches the mask across his face and ties it tight, lifts a broom handle behind his neck and across his shoulders with a sack of poison on each end of the stick. He starts down the middle between two rows, shaking the sacks as he walks. Before midnight, he has dusted over half of the field and used all of his poison.

Ollie has two tubs of warm water and clean clothes waiting for him in the smokehouse. "Maybe you didn't inhale any of it but every part of your body that's not covered is white. All the kids except John are asleep, so step out of those clothes here on the lawn. Wash your face and arms in this pan, get in that tub and soap-up, then you can rinse in the second one."

The next day, he finds some dead weevils. "John, come on. Let's go to the store for more poison. I'll dust the rest of the field tonight, and do it again in two or three weeks."

Syble has gone to the mailbox; Ann and Nancy sit on the back porch with pans full of beans with soft yellow hulls. "Ann, look at these pink ones. They'd make a pretty necklace if they would stay this color when they dry."

"But they won't. I don't like this kind of bean. They taste bitter to me. They should be called bitter beans instead of butter."

"I don't like to eat them either, but I kinda like shelling them. They're so pretty—like jewels in a pan."

Ollie is washing jars for the beans when a loud noise comes from the kerosene refrigerator. Flames shoot from underneath. "Ann, take Patty and Nancy to the yard. Quick! Get out of here!

Beating at the flames with a damp towel, Ollie keeps yelling, "Oh, Lord help me. Lord help me." When the flames are extinguished, she resumes washing jars. She is canning beans before Roy and John get back from the store.

A man comes to work on the refrigerator, but Ollie is afraid it will catch on fire again. "Kids, if it flames when you're in here, don't try to fight it—just get outside. It could blow up and kill you."

John frowns. "Then the house and everything we have would burn."

"I'd rather have a pile of ashes than a dead child."

He shakes his head and grins at his daddy. "Mother, you didn't run out and leave it."

"That's different. You do as I say."

Roy rubs his neck. "Maybe we'll get electricity down this road before too long. Then we can get an electric refrigerator."

"Oh, I wish we could. Have you heard anyone say anything about it?"

"No, but they've run lines east of Greenbrier. I'll go ask at the power company the next time I'm in town. In the meantime, stop worrying. Let's talk about the cattle."

"It's easy for you to say, 'Don't worry.' You didn't see the fire."

He looks at her for a moment. "Ollie, if we keep all the heifers and sell the bull calves, we'll eventually have a good herd of cattle. We have plenty of pasture, ample water, and hay in the barn and in haystacks. I believe there's more money in cattle than in row crops.

She frowns and twists her apron. "I hope we can find something that's profitable, so you don't have to go away to work every winter."

Roy pushes back his chair. "We have a good crop of sorghum. I checked on it this morning. It's ready to strip and take to the mill. Jarrell said we can use his truck to haul it, and they'll come over on Saturday to help strip the leaves. Tomorrow I'll fasten long handles on our butcher knives. We have four and Jarrell said they have a couple."

"We'll only need five. Ann needs to stay with Patty, Nancy

and John."

"I'll build a brush arbor beside those sassafras bushes where they can stay in the shade. That way Ann can help."

"I'm not sure she's strong enough, or if it's safe for her to be swinging that big knife."

"If you'll cook food that she can warm up tomorrow, she can work in the morning then come in to fix lunch and keep Patty here to take a nap in the afternoon."

"We can try, but stripping sorghum is a man's job. I don't think I can keep at it all day."

"Do what you can. Take several water breaks with the kids."

"We'll have enough molasses to last us and Jarrell and Morene for a couple of years. And those tops, ground with corn, will make mighty fine cow feed."

"We need to figure how many jars of molasses we can use, and sell the rest. It will start tasting strong after two years. Depending on the price, we might only want to keep enough to last a year."

Morene comes to the brush-arbor for a drink as Ollie rests in the shade. "Mama, I have something to tell you."

Ollie catches her breath. The look on Morene's face tells her she will not like the news. "What's wrong?"

"Nothing's wrong—I hope. Jarrell wants to sell our farm and move to Little Rock. He thinks we'll do better if we work for someone else. Farming is too uncertain, and I don't want to be left alone while he goes away every winter to work because a drought has destroyed our crops."

Ollie looks down, and scratches a stick in the dirt. She takes a deep breath and swallows before speaking. "I understand,

and I don't blame you. We might do the same if we didn't have young children. Still, thinking of you being that far away breaks my heart. This is worse than when you got married. Then, you were close by."

"We'll come home often."

"I hope so. Little Rock is too far away to come home every week, but don't forget about us."

"I won't do that."

Chapter 14
Model A

Syble graduates from high school and finds a job in Conway. She and a friend rent a furnished apartment. She has money to spend, and enjoys her independence.

Ollie goes to the porch where Roy sits smoking his pipe. The children are in bed. All is quiet except a few crickets and a tree frog. She sits on a step looking at the star-filled sky. "Roy, I worry about Syble living in town. She's always lived in the country. I'm afraid she might be persuaded in the wrong direction."

Roy shakes his head. "Not her. She wants to have fun, but she's smart."

"Ollie, while I was in town, I heard some men talking about a woman, over on the mountain north of the Cadron. She has a Model A for sale. They say it looks and runs good, and she's got a good price on it."

"We don't need a little car like that with all of these kids. I thought you wanted a truck."

"I do, but if it's as good as it sounds, we'll drive it a while and trade it for a truck when we sell the crops. I'm gonna walk over and look at it."

Ollie shakes her head and frowns. "Roy, its three or four miles over there. That's a long walk for looking."

"I walk more than that behind a plow."

Ollie is placing hot jars of beans under a towel when she hears a car. She goes to the back porch.

Roy is driving the Model A.

Ann, Johnny, Nancy and Patty rush into the yard ahead of Ollie. Johnny runs to the car and opens the trunk. "Look at the rumble seat." He lifts Patty inside. "This is where we'll sit when Mother and Daddy go to town or to see Grandma and Grandpa."

Nancy, looking for a place to put her foot to climb in, squeals, "Johnny, help me get in."

Ann steps in with no trouble. "I'll feel stupid riding back here."

Johnny opens the passenger door. "Mother, get in. Let Daddy take you for a ride."

Ollie laughs, "Johnny, you sound like a salesman. Roy, when you go peddling, you need to take him. I think he's a natural." She backs away. "Take the kids for a ride. I'm not sure if I closed the damper on the stove."

"I'll go check. Get in." Johnny runs toward the house.

Roy turns the car and waits for Johnny to hop in before starting up the road.

"Ollie, look at those kids. They're having a good time."

"I should have put Patty in here between us. She could fall out."

"She's in the middle with Nancy. The older kids watch out for her. Relax and enjoy a short ride with me."

They smile. Glancing at the children, she pats his shoulder.

Stopping the car, he asks, "Did you enjoy the ride?"

With a grin, she bows slightly. "Immensely."

Roy chuckles. "While you fix supper, I want to check on this year's melon crop." His facial expression changes to a frown. "Crows are starting to peck those close to the woods."

He has tried to shoot the crows, but they always fly away before he gets close enough. Before daylight the next morning, as Ollie goes to milk, he hides between a persimmon bush and a cedar tree at the edge of the field. Dozens of crows fly in, settling in nearby trees. Soon one drifts down and pecks at a large melon.

Ollie climbs into the barn loft. Peeping through a crack, she can barely see Roy.

He aims and fires. Suddenly, the pink sky explodes with a black cloud of noisy birds. He walks to his target, lifts it by a wing tip, drapes the crow atop a fence post, and walks to the barn to get a hatchet and some wire.

"Ollie, the melon has peck marks on top, but they don't go all the way through the thick rind. I think it's ripe, though. Somehow, those critters seem to know that. And they'll always pick the biggest—ones that I could sell for the most money."

With the hatchet, he cuts a tall, sturdy sapling, trims it, and attaches the crow to the top with wire, and then he wires the pole to a fence post. Standing back, he watches the blue-black wings flapping in the breeze.

Johnny can hardly eat his breakfast for wanting to go see the crow. "I bet they'll stay out of our patch for a while. Daddy, you need to shoot another one and hang it beside the corn field."

Nancy waves her hand. "And another to hang in the peanut patch."

Roy grins at her. "Birds are not bothering them yet, but they will this fall when we get the peanuts in shocks. Maybe then I'll try to shoot another crow."

John scoots his chair away from the table. "Daddy, are the melons ready to sell?"

"Some are. Late this afternoon, let's pick a sack of beans, a bushel of tomatoes, and enough watermelons to fill that rumble seat. Tomorrow we'll take them to Greenbrier."

"All right. I bet we sell every bean, tomato and melon."

When they come home, Johnny is beaming. "Mother, I sold them all. I knocked on doors and told the women what we were selling. Daddy weighed beans and tomatoes, and carried the melons. Look! We have a sack full of money."

On Sunday afternoon, the family gets in the Model A and heads for Mama and Papa's. At thirteen, Ann is not thrilled about anyone seeing her in a rumble seat, and scoots down when they pass houses. The other children giggle all the way. After Patty falls asleep, Nancy and John sit upright, letting the wind blow their hair.

"Roy, what do you think Eldridge will say about our car?"

"I think he'll like it. Maybe he'll be at your Papa's so he can look it over. I was surprised that we could haul so many melons in the rumble seat. Tomorrow, John wants to take a load to Conway."

Eldridge, his wife Osie, and four of their children are sitting on the porch with Mama and Papa. Eldridge steps down, and is walking across the yard, before the car stops under an oak tree. "Hey, it's about time you got some wheels. I like it." He looks under the hood, at the tires, and even crawls underneath. "I think you made a good deal. Roy, you can easily sell it for more than you paid."

Ollie visits with her brother Earl and his family, and stops to visit at her sister Bertha's. The sun is hanging low in the west when Roy pulls the car off the highway onto the dirt road leading home. "Ollie, if you and Ann will milk the cows, John and I will start loading melons."

"We can do that, but I don't want Johnny lifting those heavy watermelons. Let him gather cantaloupes, and you caution him about watching for snakes under those vines. They'll be hard to see at this time of day."

Ollie and the girls get out of the car and start for the house. "Ann go on inside and scald the milk pails. I'll be back in a little while." She grabs a garden hoe that she keeps leaning against the chicken house — in case a snake crawls into a nest.

Roy is loading melons and does not notice her. Neither does John as he tiptoes over the vines with his bare feet.

Frowning, she grips the hoe handle. "John, where are your shoes?"

He jumps at the sound of her voice, and draws in a breath. "In the car. I didn't want to get them dusty and dirty. I polished them this morning."

"I don't like the idea of you and Roy out here at this time of day. Copperheads will be crawling out of their cool shades looking for bugs and mice. Take this hoe and rake back the vines before you stick your hands under those leaves."

"Ah, that'll take too much time. We have to hurry."

"Do what I say or go to the house."

He takes the hoe, pulls at a vine, and jumps back with a scream. A copperhead is wrapped around a big cantaloupe.

Roy rushes over and kills the snake. "Get in the car, both of you. We'll finish this in the morning when it's cooler. We need to get those cows milked."

He is up early the next morning, loading watermelons while Ollie milks the cows. The rumble seat of the Model A is filled before John wakes.

"Why didn't you wake me? I wanted to help."

"Well, son." Roy smiles at him. "I didn't want you in those vines after finding that snake last evening. I'm sure there's one or more of those critters still in that patch."

John leans his head back to look at his daddy's face. "What about you? You could get bit, same as me."

"That's true, but my work shoes are thick leather, and my skin's a lot tougher than yours."

Johnny shakes his head and looks down. "I wish we still had Pooch and Red. They would've torn that snake apart. Daddy, when we come back from town, can we go see Uncle Arthur and Uncle Sam? One of them might have another dog that will kill snakes."

"If we sell the melons in time, we might do that."

It is late afternoon when Ollie sees a blue truck stop in the yard. She pulls off her soiled apron, straightens her dress collar, and starts toward the front door. Pausing in front of the hall mirror, she hears Johnny yelling.

"Mother, come look at our new truck."

She lifts Patty as Nancy and Ann run out the door.

Ollie takes a deep breath and frowns. "Roy, I thought you were gonna wait until we sell the fall crops."

"I was, but we stopped to look, and he gave us a lot more for the car than I paid. We got a good deal, and now we can haul twice as many melons to town."

"Mother, look inside at the nice seat. It's comfortable, and there's room for three or four people in the front. Ann can ride in the cab with you and Daddy and not get her hair messed up."

Ollie grins. "You don't have to sell me on it, Johnny. Your daddy's already bought it."

"Mother, we really needed a truck. Now that Jarrell and Morene have moved to Little Rock, we don't have anyone to haul things for us. In the fall, we have bull calves to take to the sale barn and loads of corn to take to the feed mill for grinding. And if we make cotton, Daddy will need a truck to take it to the gin in Conway. Farmers have to have trucks."

"Johnny, I may have to keep you home. No telling what you might talk your daddy into buying."

"I help him *sell*. We ran out of melons today, or we could have sold twice that many. With the truck, we'll have more tomorrow."

"I was only teasing. I know you're a big help. What kind of truck is this?"

"A 1936 Chevrolet." Roy holds out an envelope. "Here are the papers. You need to put them in a safe place."

"Mother, we went by Uncle Sam's. He didn't have a dog to give us, but he liked our truck. He said he'll check around and see if he can find us a good dog. Uncle Arthur wasn't home, but I only saw one dog at his house. It was old."

Roy takes hold of John's shoulder. "Son, go put on your work clothes and stack some of that split wood on the porch for the cook stove. Hurry along. I have some business to talk over with your mama."

Ollie twists her apron and gives Roy a worried look. "How are we gonna pay for this truck? We need to save money to live through the winter and plant crops next spring."

"I'll have the truck paid for by the time we sell all the melons. I told you, he gave a good trade-in on the car. Tomorrow, I'll take a bushel of tomatoes and anything else you have in the garden that you don't want to can. John's right—we need a truck."

"I've canned enough butterbeans. There's probably a bushel of those that you can take. I'll help you load melons and cantaloupes. I don't want John in the patch. He's not cautious enough."

"He's a good salesman, though. He tells those housewives all about the melons. The women are sold on the produce before they see what's in the truck."

"I want to go to town with you one day this week to get some fabric. I need to get started making school clothes. Nancy won't be six until January, but I think she's ready to go. If they'll let her enroll, I'm gonna send her."

"She'll do well, but Patty will be lonely without her."

It is almost milking time when Roy and John get home the next day. John brings a bag of change and plops it down on the table. "Mother, the truck's empty. We sold all the beans, tomatoes, cantaloupes and all but one watermelon."

"Did one get busted?"

"No. Daddy gave it away." John lets the screen slam as he goes outside to talk to the girls.

Ollie looks puzzled. "Did you run into one of your brothers in town?"

Wearily, Roy sits at the table and leans back. "No. We stopped on the side of a residential street. The women saw our truck and came out of the houses. As a woman would buy a melon, she and her kids would go inside their house. I kept watching one little boy standing alone beside a tree. He was terribly skinny, barefoot, ragged, and his hair was much too long." Roy takes a handkerchief from his pocket and wipes his face.

"I cut a sample melon and handed out small pieces to all the kids that came near. Even though I knew he didn't come up to get any, I asked him if he liked the watermelon.

"'I ain't got no money,' he said." Roy leans back in his chair.

"Well, I need somebody to take one of these melons and sample it. Then the next time I come through here, let me know how good it was. Could you do that for me? I gave out some sample pieces today, but all the kids left without letting me know if it was good or not.

"A smile seemed to cover his whole face, and he said, 'Yes, sir. I be glad to do that for you.'

"I chose a melon, that I thought he could carry without dropping it, and handed it to him."

Ollie leans her head to one side. "Do you think he'll come back to tell you if it was good?"

"If he sees us, he'll come by. But that wasn't why I gave it to him."

"I know." She smiles a sad smile, and brushes at a thread clinging to her dress. "What did Johnny think of that?"

"When we got in the truck and drove away, he said, 'We'd make more money if you'd stop giving away melons.'"

"I said, Son, do you remember how that little boy looked?" Roy pushes his chair back.

"If anything ever happens, so that you get to looking as pitiful as that boy, I hope some kind person will give you something good to eat."

"What did he say to that?"

"He was quiet for a long time, and then he said. 'I'm glad you gave him that melon. He did look hungry.'"

Roy lifts a towel and looks at the hot jars underneath. "Ollie, why don't we get a propane gas tank, and replace that wood-burning stove? Then when I'm gone off to work, you won't have to worry about getting wood split for the cook stove. It'll make adjusting the heat under that pressure cooker a lot easier and safer too."

"If you think we can afford it. The girls have wanted a gas stove for years."

"I don't know about affording it, but as much as you have to can, I think it's a necessity."

"The last time she was home, Syble said that same thing."

"I hope she comes home this weekend. I'm thinking she might ride the afternoon bus. Maybe she'll stay tonight, tomorrow night, and go home Sunday afternoon."

He takes his hat from a hook on the wall, before turning back to Ollie. "Dan's horses were in the corn again this morning. They destroyed a large area, some eaten, some trampled. I put them in the barn before John and I went to town."

"You should have told me. What if Dan had come by looking for them, and I didn't know they were in the barn?"

"I meant to tell you, but got busy and forgot. Anyway, I'm glad he didn't."

"Isn't this the third time they've been in the corn?"

Roy nods. "And last time I told him he'd have to pay damages if it happened again. He's had plenty of time to fix his fence. I hate to have problems with neighbors, but I didn't plant that corn for his horses."

He leans his head back and sniffs. "Is that fried chicken, I smell?"

Ollie smiles. "I want to have a good supper for Syble if she comes in tonight."

He looks around the kitchen. "And is that a peach cobbler, all set to go in the oven?"

She nods. "The potatoes are ready to mash. I've already cut up okra to fry, and sliced the tomatoes."

"What about gravy and biscuits?"

"We'll have those."

"John, you and Ann come on. We need to get the milking

done. If Syble's coming tonight, she'll be here within an hour."

Syble walks into the yard as Roy comes out of the barn with a pail of milk. "Hey, there. Your mama was counting on you coming home this weekend. She fried a chicken with all the trimmings like a Sunday dinner."

Syble grins and drops her suitcase to give her daddy a hug. "I'm glad she thought about me. I'm starving."

"If you can take this milk to the house, I'll give the cows some hay and be along soon. John and Ann have already gone inside."

The children enjoy having Syble at home, and cling to her until she can hardly help Ollie with Saturday's chores.

Sunday morning, Roy pushes back his breakfast plate. "Ollie, I haven't heard a thing from Dan about those horses."

"Do you think you should go tell him that you have them?"

"No. I think he knows where they are. He's probably watching the pasture and thinking he'll take them if I turn them out with my horses."

"Well, what are you gonna do with them? You can't continue to keep them in the barn and feed them hay."

"I'll go talk to the sheriff if he doesn't come by before Monday."

Sunday afternoon while the family sits on the porch talking, Dan and his wife stop in front of the house, but do not attempt to get out of the truck. Roy and Ollie walk out to speak to them. Ollie notices the rifle propped up against the seat between the two.

"Mr. Glenn, I'm looking for my horses. Have you seen them?"

"Yes, I got them out of my cornfield on Friday morning.

You took your time in coming to ask about them."

"Well, I've been kind of busy."

"You should have been busy fixing fence. I told you if those horses got in my corn again that you'd have to pay to get them back." Roy hooks his right thumb on his back pocket.

Dan looks at him with a scowl. "I know you've got a gun in that pocket."

Before Roy can answer, Dan grabs for the rifle, but his wife holds onto the gun, shouting, "No, Dan! No!"

Ollie yells, "Get in the house, kids! Get in the house! He's got a gun!"

Rushing around to the wife's side of the truck, Syble reaches through the window, grabs the gun by the barrel and holds on.

By the time Ollie runs the younger children inside, Roy has Dan by the shirt, pulled partway through the truck window. She hears Roy say, "And don't come back on my farm unless the sheriff comes with you." He shoves Dan back into the truck.

Dan grabs the steering wheel and steps on the gas. Syble releases her hold on the gun only seconds before the truck roars down the road.

Later that afternoon, Syble packs her suitcase, preparing to meet the bus going to Conway.

Roy hugs her. "Sis, do you want me to drive you to the highway?"

"No, you've got feeding and milking to do. It's a nice day, and this old case is not heavy."

"All right then. I'm a little uneasy about leaving. I half-way expect Dan to come after those horses."

Nervous, Syble walks along the road, looking ahead as well as right and left. She pauses at the curve. Dan has pulled his truck off the road under some trees. The gun barrel sticks out the window.

Turning, Syble runs home and to the barn where Roy and Ollie are preparing to milk. "Daddy, Dan's parked in the woods beside the road. I could see that rifle barrel. I bet he thinks you'll be driving me to the bus and he'll shoot us and just drive off."

"Let me finish milking these cows. Ollie get the kids inside. I'll go west and double back to the highway to avoid passing him. We'll talk to the sheriff before I take you to your apartment."

The sheriff brings Dan to get his horses, and sees that he pays Roy for damages. Roy never has any more trouble with the young man and his horses.

The next time Syble comes home, she is driving her boyfriend's car. Dust coats the black car, so she and Ann decide to wash it. They draw two buckets of water from the well, dump laundry washing powders into the buckets, and begin to scrub with rags.

Ollie sits under the walnut tree shelling beans and delighting in the fun they are having.

The washing powders will not dissolve in the cold water and smear across the car. Syble pours a kettle of hot water into each bucket, and stirs with a large spoon until she creates a thick foam that is difficult to rinse away. Ann draws bucket after bucket of water to slosh over the car, before the girls dry it with towels.

Syble stands back to look. "I wish we had some car polish. It looks a little dull. Those washing powders were strong; I think they washed off all his polish."

"Mother has some of that red furniture polish. It makes the furniture shine. I bet it would make his car glisten like new."

"Ann, that's a good idea. Go get it while I put these buckets away."

With scraps of soft flannel, they rub the red-oil polish on every inch of the car, except the headlights and windows.

"Look at it sparkle." Ann stands gazing at the achievement. "I bet his car has never looked this good. Syble, he'll think you took it to the dealer for polish. I wish I could see his face when he sees it."

"I better get going. Since this is the first time I've driven, I don't want to be getting into town after dark."

Ollie, coming to the well for a bucket of water to wash the shelled beans, gasps, "Surely you're teasing. He didn't just let you drive off in his car and you not know how to drive."

Syble laughs. "He showed me how to start, stop, and change gears. I drove it through Conway a couple of times with him beside me."

Ollie draws in a breath and shakes her head. "Well, get going, and don't drive too fast."

The next time Syble comes to visit, Ollie asks, "What did your boyfriend think of the wash and polish job on his car?"

Syble laughs. "He didn't say anything. He didn't have to. By the time I got to the highway on that dirt road, dust was stuck in that oily furniture polish, and that car looked like a mud ball."

Chapter 15
School

Ollie makes Nancy some pretty dresses to wear to school. For days in advance, school is all she wants to talk about. The day before she is supposed to go, she tells Ollie she wants to wait until she is older.

Ollie stares at the sad look on her face. "You don't need to be bigger. What made you change your mind?"

"I'm afraid I might wet my pants. Ann and Johnny said I can't go whenever I want to. They said I have to ask the teacher, and if she says no, I'll have to sit down and wait until recess."

"Don't worry about that—she'll let you go if you need to."

"But Johnny said one boy in his first grade class wet his pants and all the kids laughed at him. He said they'll never, ever forget it."

"He shouldn't be telling you stuff to scare you. You don't ever wet your pants at home."

"But I don't have to wait for recess."

Before walking to catch the bus the next morning, Nancy is still worrying about wetting her pants.

That afternoon when Nancy gets home, Ollie asks, "Did you have a good time at school?"

"No. I don't like school."

Ollie draws in her breath and asks softly, "Did you wet your pants?"

"No, but I almost did."

"Tell me about it."

"This morning, Johnny told me to go every recess and to not drink any water or milk at lunchtime. Ann took me to my room, told the teacher my name, and left. I didn't know what to do, so I just stood there. The teacher pointed at me and said, 'Sit down.' I sat down. Then she looked at me and almost yelled, 'Not in the floor. In a chair.' A chair was close to me so I crawled up in it. The teacher looked mad when she said, 'Not there—that's mine. Sit in that one.' It was a little chair. I didn't have to climb. I sat right down."

Nancy lowers her head and is quiet.

"Tell me what else you did."

She takes a deep breath. "The teacher showed us the bathroom and told us to ask her when we need to go. I waited until recess, and ran fast. When the bell rang we went back to our room."

"What else?"

"She showed us boxes under the windows. Every boy and girl has one. She put our names on them. When we colored a paper, she told us to put it in our box, but I couldn't find mine. The way she wrote my name didn't look right, and I didn't want my picture to get lost, so I folded it and put it in my pocket. She looked in the box, didn't see my paper and said, 'Nancy, where is your paper?' She didn't look happy when I took it out of my pocket. She slapped her hand against the side of the box and said, 'this is where you're supposed to put it.' I sat there looking at her until she said real loud, 'Put it in here.'"

"Did you eat your lunch?"

"It wasn't good like you cook, but I ate my pie and some of

the beans. When I started to leave, the lunchroom lady made me go back. She said I have to eat more food and drink all my milk."

"Did you?"

"I couldn't. I felt like I was gonna throw up. I kept trying to leave, but she wouldn't let me. I knocked the milk over in my tray and spilt most of it. Then I started crying. All the kids my size were gone and the big kids were coming in before she let me go. Then the bell rang before I could go pee."

"What did you do after lunch?"

"The teacher told us to write our names on a paper and draw a picture. I wrote my name and then went up to her desk and asked if I could go outdoors. She said, 'No, go sit down and draw your picture.' I got scared I was gonna wet my pants and went to ask her again. She said, 'No, you just came in. You'll have to wait until recess.' I was about to cry, and was rubbing my eyes. She came to my chair and asked if I needed to go to the restroom. I nodded and she said, 'All right.'"

"What did she say when you came back?"

"She said, 'Next time you need to go to the restroom, say that. Don't say you need to go outdoors.'"

Ollie grins. "Tomorrow will be better."

"Do I have to go? I'd rather stay home with you and Patty. I don't think that teacher likes me. Johnny said, when he was in that grade, she whipped him for coloring a rabbit wrong. She might whip me if I get something wrong."

Ollie wipes a curl from her forehead. "She won't whip you. Tomorrow will be better, you'll see. Come to the kitchen. I'll give you some peaches with sugar and cream on top."

The children miss the bus one morning. They walk home,

and Roy drives them to school in the truck.

"Roy, why did you stand outside talking to the kids so long before you took them to school?"

"I told them not to mention this to you, because I've already talked to Nancy. So don't bring it up. I'm sure she won't do it again."

"Well, what is it? What did she do?"

"They were halfway to the highway when Ann saw the bus top the hill over by Herring's Store. Ann and John started to run and yelled for Nancy to do the same, but her short legs couldn't keep up with them. They were way ahead of her when she stopped. Ann yelled at her again, and Nancy yelled back, 'We can't catch that damn bus.'"

"Nancy said *damn*?"

Roy chuckles and nods.

"It's not funny. You have to be more careful what you say around these kids. I heard you say that word yesterday when you mashed your finger."

"Ann and John had her scared half to death by the time they walked home. I talked to her about it. I'm sure she won't say it again, and I told them not to say anything to you, so don't mention it."

"Roy, she needs punished for talking like that."

"She was punished by the time the kids told me. I don't want you to bring it up. All right?"

"All right, but I would have handled it differently."

"I'm sure of that. By the time you stopped grumbling, she would really want to cuss."

Ollie frowns, tosses a dishtowel onto the cabinet, and goes to the stove to check on a bubbling pot.

Each day Ollie asks Nancy about school. Usually she doesn't have much to say, but Ollie understands that she does not like school, she is afraid of her teacher, and really dislikes the lunchroom lady that tries to make her drink her milk.

The children rush into the house one afternoon. Bending with laughter, Johnny teases Nancy, "One side of your hair looks like a witches' broom."

Nancy's chin quivers—tears ready to overflow. Blond ringlets curl around one side of her face, but the other side hangs straight, part of it moving with static electricity from little fingers raking through it.

Ollie gives Johnny an angry look and waves toward the bedroom. "Nancy, come here." She repositions a barrette, pulling the straight hair away from Nancy's face. "What happened?"

"A boy turned over a vase and sloshed water on my hair. Johnny and kids on the bus laughed at me."

"It doesn't look bad. Boys just like to tease girls." She pats Nancy on the back. "Go change into your play clothes. Patty's been waiting all day to play with you."

Johnny comes into the kitchen, looking for a snack. "I was only teasing. I didn't mean to make her cry."

"She's not very happy with school. Do you ever see her at recess?"

"Sure, we have the same playground. She usually hangs around the First Grade porch. I tried to get her to ride the merry-go-round, but she said it's too fast and the slide's too high."

Nancy seems happier the next day when she comes home. "Did you have a good day at school?" Ollie asks.

Nancy nods. "I got to play after lunch."

"Did you drink all your milk?"

"No, I have a new friend. He likes milk, and said he wished he could have more. When the lunchroom lady wasn't looking, I took his empty bottle and set my full bottle on his tray. He even ate my black-eyed peas. I hate black-eyed peas."

"I hope you're not giving him all your lunch."

"I ate the potatoes and my pie."

"You need to eat as many of the vegetables as you can."

"Before the big kids came outside, I got on the merry-go-round and pushed it a little with my foot, and I climbed the tall ladder for the slide."

"How did you like the slide?"

"I didn't go down. It was too high."

Chapter 16
Electricity

Roy comes home from town and announces, "Ollie I heard that the power company is gonna bring electric lines out here. The wires will go down the section line instead of right in front of our house. I went over to Arkansas Power and Light to find out for sure. A man in the office said they should be through here this winter."

"I don't understand why they don't run them down the side of the existing road. Will it cost us a lot to bring the lines over to our house?"

"They're running them on the section line to keep from zigzagging back and forth. We won't have to pay anything more to get it brought to our house—apart from a five-dollar deposit and then our electric bill once a month. Some more news is that the county has plans to run a new road along the section line. I don't know when they'll start that, but I'm glad. It will eliminate a lot of dust. As more and more people get cars, this road in front of our house could get so dusty in the summer that we can't sit on the porch."

"Roy, I can hardly believe that we're finally gonna get electric lights! And, when we sell the crops, an electric refrigerator."

"And maybe an electric radio. Our old battery model has so much static that I can hardly hear the weather report."

She smiles and looks toward the old radio. "Today, at noon I was trying to listen to my Judy and Jane story, but I couldn't hear the words for the static. Finally, I had to turn it off."

"We'll have to get someone to wire the house for electricity."

"Oh, I didn't think of that. How much do you think that will cost?"

"I don't know. I'll get Tom Spears to give me an estimate— he does that kind of work. If it's not too expensive, I'll tell him to get started as soon as he can."

On February 22, 1949, Roy pays the five-dollar deposit required by Arkansas Power and Light Company to connect the electric lines. The children are delighted, especially Ann. In the winter, it is dark by the time she gets her chores completed. She is fourteen, conscientious about her homework, and likes to read, but it was difficult to see clearly in the light of the old kerosene lamps.

Ann milks two or three cows morning and evening, and helps run the cream separator. Roy and Ollie milk three or more cows each. Johnny does his best to keep pace with Ann. Selling cream is another way of bringing in a little money for the family to live on.

All of the children advance to the next grade in school. Nancy and John are proud that school is out for the summer, even though they know many chores wait for them.

Johnny approaches Ollie. "Mother, what do you think caused this lump on the side of my neck?"

"It's probably a swollen gland. Does it hurt?"

"No. It's not sore at all."

"Rub some olive oil on it every night before you go to bed. There's a little bottle in the cabinet. If it doesn't go away after a while, we'll go ask Dr. Williams about it."

The lump does not go away. Dr. Williams gives him salve to rub on it. John starts the fourth grade, and wants to forget about the knot on his neck, but Roy and Ollie take him back to see the doctor.

The doctor examines the knot. "It's growing, but slowly. I want you to go see a doctor in Little Rock. I think it may be a tumor."

Roy takes John to the recommended doctor. Dr. Williams was correct—John has a tumor and it must be removed. Roy and Ollie have no health insurance, and only enough money in the bank for living through the winter and planting crops in the spring.

The doctor tells Roy that he will admit John to the University Hospital. There will be no charge for the surgery and hospital stay. Student doctors will observe and participate, but the surgeon will be one of the instructors. Roy agrees, and the doctor schedules the operation. Roy and John go home to tell Ollie.

Someone must stay at home to take care of the animals and the other children. Ollie cannot drive, and Roy cannot cook.

The next week, Roy takes John to the hospital.

Ollie has never prayed harder. She knows of cases where a doctor's diagnosis was simply a tumor, but it turned out to be cancer. She remembers her Aunt Jane suffering with cancer, and Roy's ma before she died.

The day of the surgery, Ollie tries to stay busy, but she cannot keep her mind on work and keeps making mistakes. She burns a pot of beans, spills a bucket of water on the kitchen floor, and forgets to fasten the gate when turning the cows out to pasture.

Before Ann and Nancy get home from school, Patty yells, "Mother! The cows are in the yard, and that mean bull is making lots of noise."

Ollie draws in her breath. *Oh, Dear Lord, help me. I have to put them back in the lot, but how will I do it by myself?* "Patty, stay in the house! Don't go outside for any reason."

"But I'm scared. Can't I go with you?"

"No, the cows might run over you. Crawl under your bed and stay there until I come inside. Hurry! I've got to get those cows before they scatter."

Patty scoots under her bed, but a worried little face peeps from under the bedspread.

While the bull is on the north side of the yard, Ollie grabs a garden hoe and rushes along the south side to the barn. She opens the gate that leads to the long manger full of hay. Roy keeps it closed when pasture grass is plentiful, but during bad winter weather, he opens that gate to allow the cows to eat.

Ollie goes to the milking stalls and dumps ground feed into the troughs. Taking the feed bucket, she walks to the gate where the cattle escaped and beats on the side of the bucket.

The milk cows come running, their heavy bags jiggling from side to side as they rush to get the feed. Ollie closes the stall gates. Most of the others follow to the manger and quickly plunge their noses into the hay.

Lee, the big whiteface bull, and a few calves linger in the yard, eating late-blooming flowers and nibbling at shrubbery. Ollie takes an armload of hay, dumps it on the ground inside the lot, backs away, and rushes around the barn to come out another gate. A cow runs to the hay; calves follow.

After snapping off a large rosebud, the bull sniffs a marigold, jerks his head away in disgust, and saunters into the lot. Ollie runs to slam the gate and secure the chain behind him. With the loud clank of the gate, Lee kicks up his heels, turns toward Ollie, snorts, and paws the ground.

Ollie breathes a sigh of relief. "Snort all you want, you old devil. Now it's fastened." She has already closed the gate that leads to the manger. In the morning, when the bull leaves the lot to go to the spring for water, she will drive cows and calves away from the hay and out into the pasture.

Going inside, Ollie calls, "Patty, you can come out now. That mean bull is in the cow lot. I have to scald the milk pails and start milking while the cows are in the stalls. Nancy and Ann will be here soon. They're coming down the road."

After Johnny's surgery, Syble—now married and living in Little Rock—drives to the farm to tell Ollie that the operation was successful. The lump was a tumor—not cancer. Roy stays at the hospital with John.

Johnny likes his fourth grade teacher, and does not fall behind in his schoolwork because of the hospital stay. Nancy enjoys the second grade, and has gained enough courage to go down the slide and ride the merry-go-round. One day when Nancy comes home, she is unusually quiet. Ollie demands to know what happened at school to make her so sad.

"Do you know what the outside of my class building looks like?"

"Yes, it's light gray asbestos siding."

"I don't know what it's called, but it made a good place for me and Barbara to draw pictures with pieces of black rock. We drew Christmas trees, angels, candy canes and lots of stuff. Other kids told us they were pretty, but I guess Miss Bertha Lee didn't think so. She told us to get a bucket of water and some rags and wash the pictures off the wall. The bell rang before we were finished, and Santa Claus came to our room to give out candy. We couldn't hide. He saw us before we saw him. Santa asked us what we were doing. Barbara told him, but I kept scrubbing."

"What did he say?"

"He said he was sure we wouldn't do it again, and gave us candy canes."

"Did you get all the marks off the wall?"

Nancy nods. "It was cleaner than before. Other kids had already marked on it."

"I hope you learned a lesson and you don't ever mark on walls again."

Nancy nods, bows her head, and walks away.

Once a week, Nancy's class goes to the music room. The music teacher's daughter, Saundra, is in Nancy's class. That winter, Saundra gets strep throat. It turns into rheumatic fever, and Saundra dies.

The music teacher is on leave for the rest of the school term.

Nancy's second grade teacher tells the class that Saundra has gone away and will not be coming back. Nancy overhears kids on the bus talking about her friend's death, and asks questions. Ollie gives simple answers and tries to distract the child, but before Ollie realizes that Nancy is listening, a woman at the grocery store goes into intense detail. Nancy hears every word.

For months afterward, every time she or one of the other children gets a cold and sore throat, Nancy asks if it could be strep throat and rheumatic fever.

While selling watermelons the summer before, Johnny met Mr. McCray. He drives a truck to Little Rock every morning to sell eggs and produce. John likes him, and goes to his store to talk to him when he is in Greenbrier.

"John, I'll buy rabbits for a quarter each, if you'll bring them gutted and wrapped in newspaper. I can sell every one you catch. Many nationalities of people shop at the Farmers Market. They like the meat, and they keep the skins—so don't skin the rabbits."

"I'll start building traps when I get home."

Rabbits have been eating greens from Ollie's garden, and chewing the sweet bark off trees in the orchard. Roy and John have already wrapped sacks around the fruit tree trunks to keep rabbits from killing the trees.

"Daddy, will you help me build the traps?"

"Sure, I'd like to get rid of all the rabbits around here."

"If I can sell enough, I'll buy a calf in the spring. Then she'll grow into a cow and have calves. By the time I graduate, I'll have a whole herd."

Ann wants to help, so they look around in the barn and under the manger where Roy stores scrap lumber. They make six traps, place thin slices of turnip or apple inside, and set them in the orchard, the plum thicket, and under the edge of the boysenberry bushes.

John turns to Ollie. "Mother, will you set your alarm and wake us up an hour before milking time, so we can run the traps and clean the rabbits?"

"I'll do that, but I won't keep calling. You'll have to get up."

The next morning is very cold, but they jump out of bed when Ollie calls. "Hurry, Ann," urges John. "Get your coat. I bet we've got one in every trap."

Ann knots a scarf under her chin. "I hope so. Six rabbits will be a dollar and a half."

From the kitchen window, Ollie watches them place four rabbits on one corner of the cellar and hears them planning for their business.

"John, I'll go get newspapers while you start gutting the first one. I'll be right back." Ann returns to the house, "Mother, the three traps baited with apple had rabbits inside. We only caught one with turnip pieces."

Ann rushes outside with the papers. "John, where are we gonna get apples to bait the traps? Mother canned all of ours."

"I guess we'll have to buy one. We'll get a dollar for these. An apple will probably cost a nickel. I'll ask Mr. McCray to save me all the bad apples and shriveled carrots he has left in his produce truck."

"What will you do with them during the day?"

"If they're not so rotten they stink, I bet Miss Fern will let me keep them in the closet."

No matter how cold the weather, Ann and John run the traps and prepare the rabbits as Mr. McCray requested. John gets off the school bus at Greenbrier, and delivers the newspaper-wrapped bundle. With money jingling in his pockets, he walks to school and stores his shriveled rabbit bait in the cloakroom.

By spring, he and Ann have each saved enough money to buy a calf.

While milking one evening, Roy tells them he has two cows with new calves. "Kids, those cows could easily raise two calves. If you want, you can go to the sale with me and buy your calves. You have to remember, it's your gamble. If the calf dies, you've lost your money. It can easily happen; I've lost several calves through the years with scours. We can buy scour pills, but they won't always save an animal. On the other hand, if it lives, you'll have a cow next year. Whether the calf lives or dies, I won't be responsible."

They buy the calves and bring them home. The first night, Roy's cow kicks Johnny's calf and kills it. Johnny runs out of the barn, crying.

"John, I told you it was a gamble, and if the calf died, I would not be responsible. But in Old Testament law, if one man's animal killed another's, he had to pay for what his animal did. That same principal is law today. Your calf didn't get sick and die, my cow killed it, so legally I'm obligated to give you my calf."

Within a few days, Ann's calf dies with the scours. She expects Roy to give her one to replace it. "Ann, my cow didn't kill your calf. I told you before you bought it that I'm not responsible if it gets sick and dies."

"But you gave Johnny one."

"I didn't give him a calf. I paid for the damages done by my cow."

Ann thinks it is unfair, but she and John continue to trap and sell rabbits. She is determined to buy another calf.

Eldridge and his family come to the house on a Saturday night before leaving for Kansas City. Ollie and Ann cook a fried chicken supper, with peach cobbler for dessert. All of the kids play games in the yard. While running, Ann falls and jams her arm against the ground. The adults think it is a sprain, but when she gets up the next morning, it is badly swollen, hurting her to the point of tears.

Roy and Eldridge are gone. Ollie looks at the arm and makes a sling for it out of a piece of old sheet. "Ann, you'll have to get off the school bus tomorrow and go to the doctor at Greenbrier. In the meantime, I'll fix some Epsom Salts for you to soak it."

"Can't you go with me?"

"Do you want me to take you to Greenbrier in the wagon?"

Ann shakes her head. "You could ride the school bus."

"How would I get home? I can't hang around school or a store all day with Patty. I know you hate going by yourself to see the doctor, but you must. I can't drive Roy's truck, Patty is too little to walk, and I can't carry her that far. Tell the doctor to charge it. Roy will pay him when he gets home."

Ann comes home after school, her arm hurting badly. "Mother, when I got to the doctor's, he was walking to his car with his black bag. I showed him my arm and told him I thought it was broken. He rubbed and mashed on it and said, 'Well, I think it may be broken, but I have an emergency now. Come back later, and I'll take you to Conway to get an X-ray, and set it if necessary.' I walked on to school. I'd have no way to get home after the bus left in the afternoon."

Ann spends an agonizing night. The next morning, she gets off the bus and again goes to the doctor's house. He takes her to Conway for an X-ray and puts her arm in a cast. One bone is broken.

Morene combed and curled Nancy's hair before she married.

Syble took over the job, and then Ann curled it after Syble left. With her broken arm, Ann can barely take care of her own hair.

She struggles to wind the curlers, and gets Nancy to snap them closed. "Nancy, you better learn how to curl your own hair, or Mother will be after you with her scissors. She used to keep Morene and Syble's hair cut short, and she bobbed my hair off when I was your age. I had to go to school looking like Lular."

"Who's Lular?"

"A blind woman who let her husband cut her hair. It was bobbed off, with gaps in places. He told her it looked good, and she couldn't see that it didn't. But I knew my hair looked awful."

"Did kids tease you?"

"Only one, to my face. I yanked a wad out of her head, and she never teased me again."

Listening from the kitchen, Ollie walks to the living room door. "Your hair didn't have gaps. You looked cute."

Ann glares at her. "You're the only one that thought so. I hated it."

"I never noticed it dragging in your plate after that."

"No, and I don't remember you braiding or curling my hair. Cut it off was your answer."

"You were old enough to keep it out of your plate when I cut it. I'll cut Nancy's, too, if she doesn't keep it neat and sanitary." Ollie turns back to the kitchen.

"See what I mean?"

Nancy nods. "Show me how to curl it."

"It's easy with these new curlers Syble bought for us. You hold a strand of damp hair, clamp the bar over the end, twist it around and around, and snap the little red roller onto the end."

"I can do that."

Afterward, Nancy curls her own hair, except on picture day or for some special occasion. Then, Ann curls and combs it.

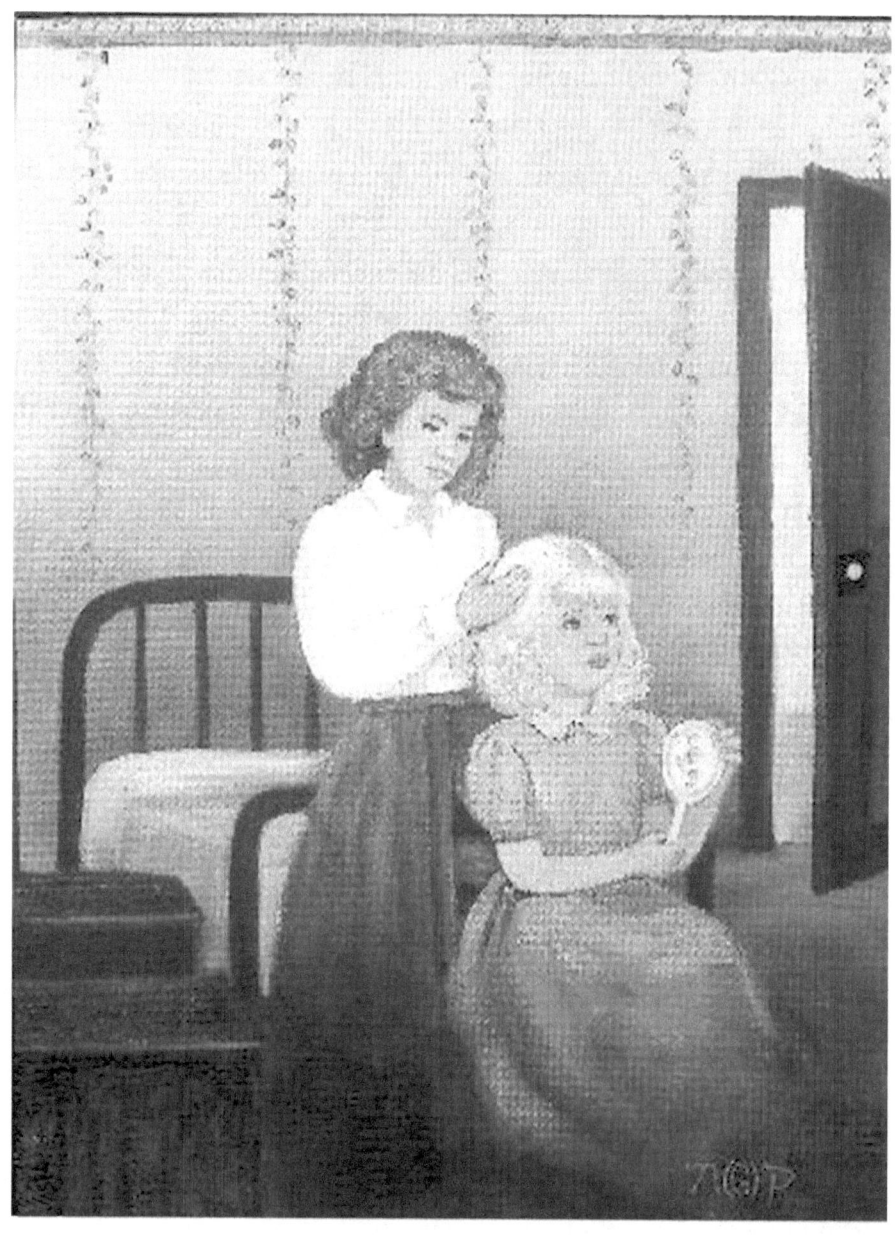

Chapter 17
Hope and Despair

As in other years, while the ground is still cold in early spring, Roy and John prepare the melon patch. "John, if we can plant a few seed in paper cups or cans, and let them grow in a sunny window until after the threat of frost, we might be the first to have melons to sell. Having some before the Fourth of July will assure us of selling them all at a good price."

Ollie adjusts her glasses to stare at Roy. "Paper cups will leak. I don't want soggy cups molding on the window sills."

"Daddy, what if we set them outside in old tubs and buckets like Mother does her tomato plants? Then if it turns cold we can cover them or put them in the smokehouse."

"That's a good idea, John, but I think your Mother has already planted tomatoes or flowers in all of our old tubs and buckets."

"I bet we could find some at the dump."

Roy laughs. "Son, I don't think I want to go scrounging around in a junkyard."

Ann frowns at Johnny. "I'd hate for someone to say they saw you digging around out there."

"All right, forget the dump. Mother, save the newspapers. We can make some paper hats and stake them over the plants on cold nights."

Still frowning, Ann asks, "Johnny, how did you think of

that? Newspapers will blow away."

"Not if you fix them right. You can buy little cones to go over plants to protect them from frost."

Ann looks at her daddy.

"He's right, but I don't know what keeps them from blowing away. John, your idea sounds good. Maybe we ought to start cutting some stakes. I guess we could use a small tack to fasten the hat to the stick."

Roy and Johnny plant one row of melons early. The weather is warm most of the time. The night that the weather forecast calls for frost, they take the paper hats to the field, drive the stakes into the ground, and rake dirt around the bottom of the paper. Most of them stay in place, protecting the tender plants from frost.

The paper hat row does produce melons by the Fourth of July. They sell quickly, and for a little more than they bring later in the month. As long as melons are in the patch, Roy and John are on the streets of Conway, knocking on doors, asking, "Would you like to buy a watermelon? We have some fine ones, juicy and red, picked fresh this morning."

One evening at supper, Johnny tells Ollie about a man in town that bought a melon. Roy pushes back his chair and grins.

Almost yelling, Johnny begins, "Mother, there's a man that stays at Miss Joseph's boarding house. Daddy parks our truck nearby, where we usually sell melons. That man comes by almost every time, thumping, looking and taking up Daddy's time, but he never buys one. He dresses nice, like a banker or somebody real important, but he's too stingy to buy anything from us."

"Do you know him, Roy?"

Roy shakes his head.

"Mother, when he started thumping today, Daddy asked him if he wanted to buy one. 'They sound a little green to me,' he said."

"Daddy said, 'I'll plug it so you can tell. If it's green, I'll give you another one. I guarantee my melons.'

'"All right,' he said and pointed to one. Daddy plugged it and showed him the plug.

'"It's got too much green rind; it'll have a white streak down the middle.'

'"No, it won't,'" Daddy said. '"This kind of melon has a thick rind, so they can be transported. I'll cut it and show you it has a red middle.' He ran the knife through it—inside was bright red."

Ollie grins. "Did he pay for it?"

Getting excited, Johnny yells, "The man kind of grunted, 'I can't take it; I can't carry two halves.'

"Daddy said, 'My son will carry half of it for you.' The man hesitated, and turned to go."

Johnny hops off his chair and leans forward. "Daddy said, 'Mister, you're gonna pay for this melon or you're gonna wear it home.' He reached in his pocket and handed Daddy the money."

"Roy, surely you wouldn't have hit him with that melon."

Roy nods. "I might have wound up in jail, but I would have done what I said. I wanted to, even after he paid. He struts down the sidewalk in his fancy suit, showing his gold pocket watch, and looking down his nose at farmers like me. You bet, I wanted to hit him with that melon. Not only hit him, I wanted to grind it in."

Drought becomes severe in July and August. Cotton dries up in the field before the bolls are fully developed. The corn makes short stubby ears with small grains. Pasture grass withers. One cutting of hay in the spring is not enough to feed the cattle through the winter. Roy and Ollie know they will have to sell some if dry weather continues.

John likes to ride Lucky into the pasture to get the cows and bring them into the corral before milking time. Ollie sits on the front porch with her lap full of mending as John follows the cattle into the pen. The big whiteface bull, Old Lee, bellows, lowers his head, and turns toward the horse.

Roy yells, "John, get that mare outta here!"

John turns Lucky and gallops out of the lot.

Roy walks to the corral fence, keeping his distance from the bull, and climbs over into the pasture. He cuts a long sapling, strips it down to a limber pole, and motions for John to bring him the mare. Once on Lucky, Roy rides up to the bull and whips him right and left, all around the corral. The bull tries to get away from the long green pole, but Roy keeps whipping. When the bull cowers in a corner behind some frightened cows, Roy gives the mare back to John and starts walking across the lot.

Seeing Roy without the horse or a weapon, the bull regains his courage. Lowering his big curly head, Old Lee bellows and charges toward Roy.

Caught in the middle of the pen, Roy picks up a rock about the size of a baseball. As the bull advances, he throws the rock and hits Lee between the eyes. Old Lee reels back and forth. Blood drips from his nose as he staggers to lean against the sturdy oak fence. He stands for a long time with his head down. When he finally moves, it is with slow deliberate steps to a corner where he awkwardly plops his enormous body down for the night.

"John, put Lucky in the horse pasture. We need to get started milking."

Ollie is not feeling well, so she does not go to help milk, but John is still excited about the incident with the bull when he comes in for supper.

"Mother, did you see Daddy throw that rock?"

"Yes, and I thought sure that bull was gonna stomp him."

"Daddy, you should have been a baseball pitcher. Did you ever try out for a baseball team?"

"I thought about it, but I didn't have money for a special uniform, or the time to go to all the games."

"Where did you learn to throw like that?"

"Your Uncle Coy and I used to have contests with throwing rocks. We didn't have BB guns or money for bullets, so when we were young we hunted rabbits with rocks."

Johnny laughs. "With rocks! Are you kidding?"

Roy is not smiling. "I'm serious."

"Wow! Did you ever kill one?"

"Several times. Rabbits were thick along Blackfork Creek. We had plenty of targets."

Ollie passes him the bread plate. "I hope you didn't kill that bull, but I was starting for the shotgun when you threw that rock."

"I thought I *had* killed him for a minute, when he was reeling back and forth with blood coming out his nose."

Pastures across Arkansas, Oklahoma, Texas and New Mexico are drying up, bringing the price of cattle extremely low. The drought forces Roy to sell many of the cattle they have accumulated.

Nancy and Patty hear Roy and Ollie talking and worrying about the lack of rain, and see the fear on their faces. One summer night, they slip out into the moonlit yard, turn their faces toward heaven and pray for rain. Focused on their prayers, they do not hear Ollie call until she comes outside.

"What are you doing out here? You could step on a copperhead snake. Snakes crawl around on warm summer nights looking for bugs and mice."

The girls do not reply.

"Answer me! What are you doing out here?"

Nancy shies away, unwilling to tell why they are in the yard, but four-year old Patty is not embarrassed. "We were praying to God to make it rain on the fields."

Ollie takes a deep breath. "Well, you can pray inside."

Before the drought became severe, Ollie knew she was expecting and worried about the expense of another child. Now, her middle is rapidly expanding. *Could I be carrying two? Roy is a twin.*

That night, after the children are in bed, Ollie asks, "Roy, how will we manage if we have twins?"

With a deep sigh, he turns to look at her in the shadows of the front porch. "We'll manage the way we always have—the best we can."

Early in the pregnancy, Ollie tells Morene and Syble that she is expecting. They are concerned about her health. She will not tell Nancy and Patty—Roy can tell John if he wants to, but Ann needs to know first.

While the younger children are outside, Ollie blurts out, "Ann, I'm going to have another baby around the first of the year."

"Why do you want another one?" Ann shakes her head. "You can barely feed and buy clothes for the ones you have." She slams the pan of peeled and washed potatoes onto the stove.

Ollie can feel her face getting hot. "We didn't plan it."

"Don't start explaining to me. I know babies are not dropped off by storks." She leaves the kitchen, and goes to do her homework.

What will she say if it turns out to be twins?

Ollie goes to see Dr. Williams. He confirms that she is pregnant, but explains that she has two or more tumors. "I'm not a surgeon, but I know they can't be removed until after the baby's born."

Ollie's world is spinning. She clenches her teeth and holds onto the table, her heart beating fast. *And I was worried about the expense.* Tears brim, and her hand shakes as she places it on her abdomen. "Doctor, how dangerous is this for the baby?"

"That depends on how fast the tumors grow. If they grow too fast, they can crowd the fetus. In that case, you'll need to go to Little Rock and have it surgically removed, or if the heartbeat is strong and you make it to the eighth month we can induce labor."

She sits, breathing quick and shallow.

"Ollie, I don't think you have to worry about two tumors. I've never seen a tumor grow to more than the size of a normal baby. Come in every month, so we can closely monitor the growth."

With previous pregnancies, Ollie delivered large babies, but did not gain a lot of excess weight or get stretch marks as many women do. This time she becomes unusually large. Doctor Williams tells her the tumors are growing rapidly.

Before Patty was born, Ollie got strep throat and temporarily lost her hearing. This time the sore throat keeps coming back. The doctor does not want to give her a strong antibiotic for fear it will harm the baby. Again, the infection goes into her ears and she loses her hearing.

Morene and Syble want Ollie to come to Little Rock, stay with them and take it easy, but she refuses. Roy takes her back to the doctor. Dr. Williams swabs her throat with medicine and tells her to rest.

"Doctor, I have four children at home, and I can't even rest at night when they're all asleep. My legs ache, my back hurts, my ears and my throat hurts."

Dr. Williams holds a bottle of dark colored liquid. "Ollie, swab your throat with this medicine three times a day, and lay down for at least ten minutes every hour. Don't go out in the rain or the cold for any reason."

He pats her on the shoulder. "Stop feeling guilty for not working every minute. If you had a crying baby, you'd sit and rock it. So consider your resting time as rocking the child. Your baby needs you to rest."

In bed that night, Ollie rolls from right to left, trying to get comfortable. *I'm larger at five months than I should be at nine with a normal pregnancy, sick with strep throat, and ear infections. I've lost my hearing, these tumors could be cancerous, and we may lose the farm because of drought—how can I rest and not worry?*

Roy needs to go away to find work but Ollie is not able to run the farm as she did in years past. One day when he comes to the house, she is not there. He goes looking for her and finds her in the hayloft, standing dangerously close to the large door used for tossing hay into the barn. He pulls her away from the door.

"Ollie what are you doing out here? You shouldn't have climbed that steep ladder, and you shouldn't be standing so close to that door. It's a long way to the ground."

Seeing the tears streaming down her face, he takes her in his arms and holds her.

"Roy, I'm so afraid of what's to come."

She cannot hear him unless he yells. She puts her fingers to his lips. "Don't talk. One of the kids might hear. I don't want them to know I'm crying."

Chapter 18
Two Hearts

In November, Ollie is so big that Dr. Williams sends her to see a specialist. That doctor insists that she remain in Little Rock near the hospital, even though the baby is not due until the middle of January.

"Mrs. Glenn, the hormones that help the baby to grow are also making those tumors grow rapidly. We may need to take the baby early. I don't want it squeezed too tight in there, and I don't want to expose it to an X-ray. Its heartbeat is good and strong. We'll monitor that often."

Ollie and Patty stay in Little Rock with Morene and Jarrell. Roy goes home to care for the farm animals, and to stay with Nancy, John and Ann. They must go to school.

Staying in the small apartment is uncomfortable for Ollie and Patty. Ollie refuses to take the bedroom, insisting that she and Patty will be fine on the fold out couch, but the couch is hard. She cannot find a place where her back does not hurt.

The first two days, Morene entertains Patty with soft songs and quiet games, but the three-year-old is accustomed to vigorous play and talking loud so her mother can hear. On the farm, Ollie would sit on the porch watching Patty run in the big yard, pulling her doll in the noisy little wagon without bothering anyone.

Morene and Jarrell live on a corner lot with heavy street

traffic. Ollie will not let Patty go outside. Morene keeps telling the little girl to sit down and be quiet. "Patty, you need to whisper, or the woman that owns this building will tell us we have to move. Children are not allowed to live here." The third day, Patty begins to whine that she wants to go home. Ollie manages to hide her own tears until bedtime.

In December, the doctor decides to induce labor. Roy goes back to Little Rock to be with Ollie at the hospital. He takes Ann, John, Nancy, and Patty to wait with Ollie's brother John and his wife, Jo.

At the hospital, the doctor explains the situation. "Ollie, you and the baby have a better chance if we take it now. At eight months, it is fully developed and can survive outside the womb."

A nurse gives the shot to induce labor. Another nurse separates Ollie's hand from Roy's, and wheels her away to a room with bright lights overhead. Pain comes hard and fast.

The doctor, listening with his stethoscope, says, "There is one, and another one is over here."

"That's the tumors?"

"No, heartbeats. You have twins."

"Twins! Doctor Williams didn't say anything about twins."

"This is the first time I've heard separate heartbeats. Their hearts must have been beating together."

Ollie draws in her breath. "Does that mean they'll be smaller and have less chance for survival?"

"I don't think so. These heartbeats are strong."

Six previous babies were born at home, with Mama at her side. *Lord, how can we care for two premature babies? God, we need lots of help.*

Coming to check blood pressure, a nurse humming 'Silent Night' interrupts Ollie's prayer.

The small babies are easier to deliver than her large full-term babies were. It is December 1950, a week before Christmas, when Ollie hears the doctor say, "Baby A is a healthy girl. Baby B is a healthy girl."

Roy is in the waiting room with Morene and Syble. Ollie sighs and relaxes after her labor. I wonder *what Roy will say when the doctor tells him he has twins?*

Syble and Morene help Ollie and Roy decide on the names— Robbie and Bobbie.

After a few days, the doctor releases Ollie and the babies from the hospital. Syble offers to take them to her apartment. She does not have close neighbors.

Ollie smiles. "I'd like to stay with you a while. I think we've about worn out our welcome at Morene's. Patty finds it hard to be quiet all day."

They stay until after Christmas, with Syble working nights at the Westinghouse plant. While Ollie and the little girls are there, Syble sleeps very little. She rocks babies, makes formula, does laundry, and cooks.

Syble's husband works days. At night, he goes into his bedroom and Ollie does not see him until morning.

One night, Ollie has chills and fever, and calls for help as both babies cry with colic. He does not respond to her pleas. Ollie suspects that he has slipped out. A few weeks later, Syble catches him with another woman. She files for a divorce.

Patty loves the twins, and sits for hours watching every move the tiny babies make. She does not have to be quiet in Syble's apartment, when they are awake.

Before the doctor releases Ollie to go home, he sits directly in front of her, looking into her eyes, and talks loud enough for her to hear. "Mrs. Glenn, you need to start building yourself up so I can remove those tumors, but the babies will have a better chance if you nurse them for six weeks. Keep alternating your milk with the formula—nurse one baby and give the other formula, and then switch them for the next feeding. After six weeks, put them on formula alone."

He pats her arm. "These babies will make it just fine. Your milk will help them, but they need extra vitamins, and so do you. You have a large abdomen because of the tumors, but you are far too thin to be nursing two babies. I want you back in here within six months to get those tumors removed."

He gives her sample vitamins for the babies and some for herself. She continues to give them to the twins, but because of the expense, never buys more vitamins for herself.

Roy and Ollie move their bed and the crib for the twins into the living room where the room is warmed night and day by the wood heater. After being away for so long, Ollie is happy to be home, and happy to bring two babies with her.

Shocked to find a new electric radio, Ollie asks, "Roy, with money so short, why did you buy that?"

"The kids bought it. One of the neighbors had a field of cotton that didn't make much except dried bolls. He said if the kids and I wanted to pick the bolls, he would be glad to get them off the field. I asked Ann and John. They wanted to do it, so we gathered it one Saturday, then I took it to the gin the next week."

"What about Nancy?"

"She helped as much as she could. We picked up some

walnuts, and I sold those, too. The kids all said they wanted to buy a radio if the cotton brought enough. I couldn't think of anything the whole family would enjoy more." He runs his hand over the shiny black plastic case, and touches a finger to the gold expanded metal across the front.

"We've been listening to stories after supper—programs we could never pick up on that old battery radio. We didn't have money to buy Christmas presents, so I guess they bought their own. One of the first things we heard when we turned it on was 'Rudolph the Red Nosed Reindeer.' Nancy liked that."

The babies share a crib. Ollie has taken a strip of an old sheet and wrapped it around the middle bars of the crib to separate them. Little Patty spends many hours peeping through the bars and asking, "When can I play with them?"

Bobbie, the youngest and smallest twin, stirs in the crib and whines. When she cries, she gasps for breath and gets pale. Someone rushes to console her, afraid that she might stop breathing or not get enough oxygen to her heart. The family is not as quick to respond to Robbie's cries, but when she cries, Bobbie gets upset. Neither one is neglected.

Sometimes in the evening, Roy rocks the babies, one in each arm. Soft and low, he sings slow lonesome songs like 'May I Sleep in Your Barn Tonight Mister.'

Ollie is weak from the strep infections, giving birth to the twins, and problems caused by the tumors. Not being able to hear grates on her nerves, as do financial worries. Still she cares for the twins, cooks, and reclaims her authority of running the household.

For the two months Ollie was in Little Rock, Ann cooked, cleaned, did laundry, helped milk morning and night, took care of Nancy, and went to school every day. Now, there is friction between Ann and her mother. Ollie is strict: she does not request—she demands. Ann has proved that she can run the house, and resents Ollie's commands.

Nancy comes home from school with a big smile. "Mother, today the teacher told us about an art contest with prizes. What do you think would be good for me to draw?"

"I don't know. Whatever you want. Go on now, and be quiet before you wake the twins."

Nancy takes a deep breath and walks into the kitchen where Ann sits at the table with her history book.

Ann glares at Nancy and raises her voice so that Ollie hears. "Why did you ask her? She doesn't have time to help you."

Ollie watches as Nancy leans against the table, staring down at the paper about the contest.

"Who usually helps when you have a problem with homework?" Ann asks.

"You do."

"Then why didn't you ask me to help with your picture?"

"Will you? I have to do it at school, but I don't know what to draw."

"What do you do best?"

Nancy shrugs. "Flowers and birds, I guess."

"Most of the girls will draw flowers and birds. You need to choose something different. Do you know how to draw winter trees?"

Nancy shakes her head.

"Come over here and I'll show you." Ann tears a clean page from her notebook. "First you have to draw the background of mountains or hills—like this. Next shade in a few light clouds, then start with a tree trunk and lots of limbs, then another tree and another until you have several. It's not hard. Take some of these scrap papers and practice drawing on the back."

Ollie calls from the living room, "Girls, get your clothes changed. It's time to get your work done."

Ann grabs Nancy's arm. "Tomorrow, don't tell anyone what you plan to draw. If you do, someone might copy. Your picture needs to be different for the judges to take notice of it."

Ann goes to the bedroom and gives the door a hard shove.

Several days pass before the teacher announces the winners of the art contest. Only the first and second place winners get a prize, but Nancy places. Her name is listed with the winners.

At supper, she tells Ann "Thanks for helping. Miss Doris said I should be proud because the other winners were older. She hung all the pictures from our class. There were lots of birds and flowers."

Roy and Ollie are broke. The drought and added expense of the twins has left them wondering what to do. February winds rattle doors and whistle around windows as Ollie sits beside the pot-bellied stove with a huge pile of mending. *We'll have to make do with what we have until the crops come in, or until Roy finds work.*

All of them need clothes. Last fall, before Ollie went to Little Rock, she bought new socks and underwear for the children.

Now, the heels of Nancy's socks have large ridges where she has tried to repair them herself. Ollie clips the knotted threads, and darns the socks. *She can wear these a few more times.* Ann has done a good job of repairing her own. John's thicker socks only have a few small holes.

"Nancy, how did you get such a tear in your blue jeans? That was your best pair."

"While I was washing dishes, I accidently stuck a butcher knife in my leg."

"A butcher knife. That must have been a bad cut—this is as wide as the knife blade. Let me see your leg."

Nancy pulls up her dress and shows the scar on her thigh.

"Did Ann or your Daddy doctor it?"

Nancy shakes her head. "I didn't tell them."

"Why not?"

She takes a deep breath, looks away, and utters a few words.

"Speak louder. I can't understand you."

"I didn't want them to gripe at me for not being careful." Nancy shrugs. "I was pretty tired, and I guess I wasn't paying enough attention to what I was doing."

"Why were you so tired?"

"Before Daddy came home, we were burning small strips across our field to backfire against a big fire that was burning towards Republican."

Ollie frowns. "Start at the beginning and tell me about the fire."

Nancy takes another deep breath. "It was burning when we came home from school, with the wind blowing toward our farm. Ann and John were afraid it would come across and burn our fields—maybe our house and barns.

"They drew a tub of water and carried it to the field. I carried the tow-sacks and box of matches. They would set a small strip on fire, then we would beat it out as fast as we could before they set another long row to blazing. We burned a wide band across the pasture before a man came running across the field, yelling for us to stop."

Nancy grins. "He was waving his arms and yelling, 'What do you kids think you're doing? I've got a big fire coming toward my farm on one side, and you're setting one on the other.'"

Ollie frowns. "What did Ann and John say to him?"

Nancy shrugs. "They told him what we were doing, but he didn't like it much. John said, 'Oh, well, we've probably got enough burned to keep it away from our house."

"What did your daddy say about your firebreak?"

"He said it was a smart idea, and that guy should have asked us to help him burn one on the other side of his house."

"After you stuck the knife in your leg, did it bleed much?"

Nancy nods. "I finished the dishes before I noticed the blood on my jeans and in my sock. Then I wrapped and tied my leg with a white rag, and washed my socks and jeans."

"You didn't put any iodine or medicine on it?"

"I put some Merthiolate on it. The next morning I put a little lard around the edges to help get the dried bandage unstuck from my leg."

"Did you go to school that day?"

Nancy nods again. "I wrapped another white cloth around it and threw the old one in the wood stove to burn while Ann, Daddy and Johnny were gone to milk. My jeans were dry on the clothesline, so I put them on and went to school."

"If you ever hurt yourself again while I'm gone, you need to tell somebody. You could have gotten an infection."

Ollie's hearing has not returned. When she goes back to the doctor in Little Rock, he sends her to an ear, nose and throat specialist. The specialist tells her the strep bacteria killed the nerves in her ears, and suggests that she try a hearing aid.

Hearing aids do not help. Ollie returns home sad and discouraged. She cannot hear the babies laugh or cry unless they are right against her ear. In the daytime, Patty lets her know when they cry, if she does not see them. During the night, Ollie rises several times to place her hand on their backs and feel for crying vibrations.

Ollie does not have a phone, but the Little Rock doctor calls Morene to tell her that he has heard of a newer, stronger type of hearing aid, called a Body Aid. He wants Ollie to try it. She can hear with it, but it is far too expensive; they have no money, and she still needs surgery to remove the tumors.

On a cool drizzly morning in late spring, Roy and Ollie sit talking beside the wood heater in the living room. The older children are at school. The twins are sleeping, and Patty sits under the crib, whispering to the stuffed yellow dog that Syble gave her for Christmas.

"Ollie," Roy leans forward, elbows on knees, "you should have Morene call the doctor's office and schedule that surgery. The doctor wanted you to have it within six months."

She rubs her stomach. "I know, but the tumors don't seem to be growing since the twins were born, at least not very fast. Unless they start growing fast again, I want to wait until the babies are big enough to eat solid food and drink from a cup."

"You're talking about months from now."

"If we don't have another drought year, maybe I can get a hearing aid in the fall. Not being able to hear bothers me more than the tumors."

Roy sits silent, looking off into the distance. After some time, he speaks. "Ollie, As soon as the water recedes from that terrible flood they have in Kansas City, I'll go up there and try to work through the summer and into the winter. Maybe we can buy you a hearing aid and have a little left."

"What about all the watermelons, potatoes, and truck patch crops we've planted? I can't peddle them."

"John can put a 'Watermelons for sale' sign near the highway, and I'll tell Mr. McCray to keep an eye out for a market. He might even bring a truck out for the vegetables if you and the kids pick them. If not, can them or feed them to the pigs."

"Ollie, that flood in Kansas and Missouri should open lots of maintenance and clean-up jobs for the railroads. Maybe some carpentry work. The railroads usually pay good wages. I'm gonna look there first."

Shortly after Roy leaves, Ollie and the children dig potatoes and store them in the barn. Ollie cans until all of her jars are full of vegetables and fruit.

Mr. McCray brings a truck one afternoon; he and John load it with potatoes, corn, beans, tomatoes, and late peaches. He looks at the melon patch and comes to talk to Ollie and pay her for the fruit and vegetables. "Mrs. Glenn, you have a fine field of watermelons. I'll buy some of them, but it looks like you've got eight or nine acres. That's far more than I can handle. I'll pass the word around, though. What you need are a couple of semi-trucks to take them."

When the melons ripen, John and the girls make a sign: "Watermelons, buy one or a truckload. One mile on left." John takes one of the biggest melons from the patch, cuts it in half, and places one-half in the little wagon. He and Ann take turns pulling uphill; Nancy pulls on the downhill slopes on the way to the highway, where they place the half melon on top of a post with the sign nailed underneath.

When a large truck turns onto the lane from the county road, Ollie tells John, "Those melons are too large for us to lift. If these men want a load, they'll have to carry them."

Ollie has on a faded cotton dress splotched with tomato stain. Glancing in the hall mirror, she smoothes her dress. Two swipes of a brush through her light brown hair will have to do; a man is approaching the porch.

The man smiles and speaks.

"You'll have to talk loud. I've lost my hearing."

Raising his voice only a little the man continues to talk.

Still unable to hear, Ollie turns a puzzled face toward John. He restates everything the man says while they are agreeing on melon price. Then, in a louder voice, the man proceeds to convince Ollie that he is a Mason. He flashes a Mason ring, and yells, "A Mason won't cheat you. I'll count the melons and pay you for everyone. You and the boy don't need to get out in this heat. Just point me to the patch."

"All right, but don't drive into the patch and ruin the vines. Park at the edge, take one section at a time, and take the small ones too. The price I'm giving you is for all sizes. It would be much more if you only take the big melons."

"Yes, ma'am. I'll do as you say. You can trust me."

The man goes to the truck, and the driver starts toward the patch.

"Mother, I'm gonna go count the melons as they put them in the truck."

"No, John. I'm afraid you'll get over there and lift melons too large for a boy your age. They can carry them."

The melon patch is not in sight of the house, so John and Ollie cannot see the men loading the truck. When they come back, the truck bed is covered by a heavy tarp. The Mason pays Ollie for what he claims he took.

Ollie is disappointed; she expected much more. That afternoon, John and Nancy take the little wagon and walk with Ollie to get a couple of melons to eat. Nearing the patch, they stop in disbelief. Deep tire tracks, torn vines, and crushed melons, trail through the patch. The self-proclaimed Mason drove into the field and only took melons over fifty pounds.

Chapter 19
Places to Work and Places to Play

Roy comes home in December. "Ollie, I'd like for you to have that surgery. Patty and I can help with the twins while the other kids are in school. We have enough to pay off our loan and plant crops in the spring. We'll get the hearing aid later."

She finally relents and goes to have the tumors removed. The twins and Patty stay with Morene for a week until the doctor releases Ollie.

The children are eager to tell Ollie about a plan they have to get a bicycle. All the children are saving pictures of the blue horse trademark from Bluehorse notebook paper. They hope to win a bicycle, the top prize in a contest advertised on the label.

At first, almost every kid at school saves the labels, but most become discouraged and give up. Ann and John's friends give them the ones they have saved. When others learn that John has a box full, they save labels for him.

The school store sells Bluehorse paper, so almost everyone uses it. Eventually they have thousands of the pictures neatly cut from wrappers. Using the box that Roy's work shoes came in, John packs it to the brim with the labels showing the head of a blue horse. He mails them to the company along with an entry form. The children eagerly wait for the arrival of a bicycle.

A parcel comes in the mail from the Bluehorse Company. Disappointment is evident on the faces of the children. The box, about the size of the one sent to the company, is lightweight. They did not win a bicycle.

The package contains a football, a large bump on one of the seams. Greenbrier School does not have a football team, and the children have no idea how to play with the thing. It will not bounce, and they cannot throw it straight.

Syble has remarried, and her second husband, J.B., played football at Conway High School. Seeing the ball, he laughs. "Kids, they sent you a dud."

Morene reads in the paper that the Little Rock Police Department is having an auction sale of impounded items. She tells Ann and John about it. They give her some of their rabbit money, and ask her to bid on a bicycle if she sees a good one they can afford.

Morene buys a Latonia brand, twenty-six-inch bicycle for eight dollars. Except for needing new tires and tubes, it is in good shape. In no time, Ann and John are riding it.

Roy and John plant acres of watermelons, sweet corn, and a patch of tomatoes for market. "Ollie, summer droughts have about destroyed us. Maybe we can survive with these early crops. The peach trees are loaded. Unless a storm gets them, we should have bushels to sell, after you can all you want."

In June, the first peaches begin to ripen. Roy and John pick bushels. Ollie and the girls peel and can. Roy and John leave for Conway with baskets of the sweet fruit.

When the sweet corn is ready, they fill the truck bed full and take it to town. It brings a good price. "Roy, sell all that sweet corn; we need the money. I'll can the field corn. It's easier to cut off the cob, and I can always add a little sugar to it."

The tomatoes are starting to turn pink, but the sky shows no promise of rain. "Ollie, I think we better pull the tomatoes that are turning. We can spread them out to ripen in the barn and on the floor of that old gray house on the hill. The weatherman said the temperature will be near one hundred today. I'd hate for them to blister in this heat."

"I agree. Gather up the buckets. Nancy and Patty can keep the twins in the shade while Ann and John help us." Soon, tomatoes cover every open space in the corn and grain bins, as well as the floors of an old empty weathered gray house on the property.

Within a few days, Roy and John pack the ripened tomatoes in the truck and sell them in town. All of the tomatoes left on the vines, from marble size on up, are turning red and blistering where the midday sun hits them. Ann, Ollie, and Nancy pick and can them.

Roy and John sell the melons as fast as they can; those left in the patch that are not shaded in the high grass are blistering. They sell truck-beds full of them to grocery stores and markets. By the middle of July, everything is drying up. Roy and Ollie are glad they did not plant cotton.

Roy reads in the paper that the county is starting to build several new roads along the section lines. He applies for a job and gets it. "Ollie that man asked me how long I could work. I told him, I'd stay as long as he had a job for me. 'But you have a farm.' He said. 'I need somebody to work into the fall. I don't want someone quitting to go harvest crops.' I said, all my crops have dried-up in the field, but I have a wife and six hungry kids at home. I won't quit. I'll be here as long as there's work. He said, 'All right. You've got a job.'"

"Roy, why did you say that? We're short on money, but we're not starving."

"That's just an expression for needy. We might soon be hungry, without any money coming in."

The summer is very hot. Roy comes home every day with his clothes stiff with sweat and dirt from the construction. He always wears a hat, and long sleeves rolled up to his elbows, but his face, neck, and exposed arms tan to a dark brown.

He buys a stick of bologna for his lunch. Ollie fries quarter-inch slabs to go in his sandwiches. Before the stick is gone, he tells her, "I brought home a pound of sausage. I'm getting real tired of dog sandwiches."

Nancy and Patty frown at each other.

Roy laughs loud and hearty. "What's the matter girls?"

Nancy squints along with the frown and looks up at him. "Daddy, you don't really eat dog meat sandwiches do you?"

"No, Sis. That's slang for bologna."

"Bologna." Their faces brighten. "If you're tired of it, can we have some? We love bologna."

He takes the stick from the refrigerator and slices pieces for all the kids.

Despite the heat, dirt, and hard work, Roy likes his job. He comes home tired, but full of funny tales about things that happen during the day.

"Roy, do you men work, or tell jokes and pull tricks on one another all day?"

His expression turns serious. "Most of the men have been

farmers like me. You could never find a harder working crew. None of us would do anything to hurt another, but we like to laugh and we do plenty of it. Laughter makes the work seem easy and the day go fast."

The next day, Roy brings his lunch home. "Ollie, the women on the road where we worked today fed us. They set tables under a shade tree and laid out a feast like a church potluck. I can tell you for sure, they'll have a good road when we're finished."

"That was nice of them. Was this the first time that's happened?"

"A few times people brought us iced tea or sent kids out with cookies when we sat down in a shade for lunch, but never like today. Early this morning, they sent word to the boss that they wanted to feed us."

"I'll give this sandwich to the pig. I'd be afraid to eat it after it's been out in this heat all day."

"My crew will probably work on our road next month. Will you brew us some iced tea and bake a few dozen cookies?"

"I can do that. Let me know when they'll be here, and I'll have it ready. Can the crew sit in the shade of the walnut tree to eat? The girls can take it out. Since I can't hear, I'd be embarrassed to try and talk to them."

"Sure, that'll be fine."

Roy always has numerous jobs to do around the farm on Saturdays. Johnny usually helps, but today Roy is repairing barn stalls. When he goes to the house for a drink, Ollie asks, "Roy what is Johnny doing down at the spring? I've seen him and his friends make several trips back and forth to the barn and tool shed."

"Oh, they're building a little clubhouse."

"Have you been down there to make sure they're not putting together something dangerous?"

"Let them be boys. They'll be fine. The spring is a fine place for them to play. They can swing on the muscadine vines, have water fights, and climb trees without bothering anyone."

"If one of them falls out of a tree, we'll have his parents suing us to pay for the doctor bills, or maybe worse."

"Ollie, you always think the worst. Boys climb trees. That's a fact of life. I bet you climbed a few when you were a girl."

"That's not the point here. We can't afford to have someone drag us to court. When I was a kid, people weren't so eager to run to a lawyer."

The next morning, Ollie walks down to the spring to look at the clubhouse. Boards stretch across tree limbs to form the floor of a tree house. "Tear it down, Johnny. You're not going to build some trap in a tree for a kid to fall off of and break an arm, a leg, or maybe his neck."

"Mother, it's sturdy. Look!" He jumps up and down. "When we get the walls nailed on, no one can fall off. The ladder will come up inside the house. I'll get Daddy to help, so you'll know it's sturdy."

"Take it down."

Johnny throws up his hands. "It's already nailed into the tree."

"I mean it. Tear it down!" She turns and walks away.

Roy goes to the spring to help Johnny dismantle the tree house. They are gone all afternoon.

"Roy, what took you so long at the spring? That thing couldn't have had that many nails in it."

"Since you made him tear down his clubhouse, I helped him build a flying jenny."

"Surely you didn't. Those things are as dangerous as falling out of a tree."

"Ollie, you think everything is dangerous. Your Papa built one for you, didn't he?"

"Yes, but that doesn't mean it was safe. Papa was a lot like a kid himself."

"Pa helped build one for us. We had hours of fun with it. On Sunday afternoons, every kid that lived on the Soda Valley Road came to ride on it."

"What's a flying jenny?" Nancy asks.

Johnny begins to explain. "It's sort of like a merry-go-round. We cut down a tall tree, and Daddy whittled a spindle on the tree stump while I bored a hole in the center of the tree, and then we lifted the tree and set the hole over the spindle. We can ride on the ends of the tree when someone pushes it around and around."

"What's a spindle?"

Ollie frowns. "Never mind, Nancy, you and Patty are not to go down there."

"Why can't *we* play on it, too?"

Roy shakes his head. "Nancy, I'll take you girls on Sunday afternoons, but don't go by yourselves."

"Roy, you're gonna keep on with these contraptions and get one of these kids hurt."

All summer while Roy works for the county, Johnny rides up and down the road with three other boys that live within a mile of the farm. He comes home for lunch, packs cookies in a sack for sharing, and is off to play until time for Roy to come home.

Nancy complains that it is not fair that she has to stay home and watch the twins while John gets to ride his bicycle and play with other kids. "I'll be glad when school starts, so I can have friends."

Ollie frowns at her. "It's not that hard to watch them. I have to make school clothes for you girls. I can't sew and keep my eyes on the little ones. I can't hear them cry, and Ann has other work, so you have to watch them."

One hot afternoon while the twins are taking a nap, Nancy and Patty play on the front porch so they can hear if the twins wake up crying. They see John coming down the road, pushing his bicycle. Nancy runs inside, taps Ollie on the shoulder, and points out a window.

"He's probably got a flat tire. I can't hear what you're saying, so go out on the porch and be quiet before you wake the twins."

John is limping. Ollie puts her sewing aside and goes to the back porch where he always comes inside. Nancy and Patty run in crying and screaming loud enough for her to hear. "Johnny had a bike wreck. A handlebar stuck in his side and his guts are coming out."

Rushing into the yard, she looks at his side. "Son, that's not your guts. It's fat tissue. But you've bruised yourself pretty bad." She pours peroxide on the wound, wraps a wide strip of white sheet around his middle, and forbids him to ride the bike until the gash heals.

His side is sore for several days, causing him to stay at home, and allowing him time to think of more ideas for having fun.

John wants to buy a goat. At the supper table, he tells the family all the fun things he could do if he had a goat. "I could ride it, and hook it to my wagon and let it pull me around. If it's a nanny, we could milk it. Goat milk is supposed to be real healthy—I bet the twins would like it."

Roy leans back with a grin. "Son, I'm not sure that you could do all those things, but if that's what you want to spend your money on, I'll take you to the sale with me next week, and we'll look for one."

On sale night, Roy rushes to clean up after work. He and John are home before midnight with a goat. "Mother, I bought her for eleven dollars. Her name is Gilbert, and we can milk her. She's got a bag full of milk now."

While Roy is at work the next day, John, Ann, Nancy, and Patty take Gilbert for a walk. She is too small for John and Nancy to ride, and Patty is afraid of her. Soon they run back to the house.

Johnny yells. "Mother! Gilbert jerked loose from my hand and ate a bunch of poison pokeberries. Have you got something to make her throw them up?"

"Son, if you ate them, I'd be worried, but a goat's stomach is different from a human's. Goats can eat almost anything without getting sick."

They put Gilbert in the cow lot and come inside to rest. Roy is driving in from work when the cows start coming to the barn for milking. The goat, probably raised with cows, goes running out to meet them. The cows are frightened and run into the pasture. The bull, irritated by the ugly creature, lowers his head to fight. Gilbert runs to the gate, and John takes her out into the yard.

"Daddy, what am I gonna do with her? The bull will kill her if I put her in with the cows."

"You'll have to tie her up." Roy looks at the goat. "John have you milked her today?"

"Early this morning."

"Goats have to be milked twice a day, just like cows. You had better get at it. We have cows to milk pretty soon."

"I'll let her go dry. I don't like the milk, and the girls didn't, either."

"You can't stop suddenly without causing her a lot of pain. Her bag looks like it's about to pop. Take a little less each time.

Taper it off slowly for about a month. You can give the milk to the pigs. They'll like it."

"You mean I have to milk her twice a day? Even when I don't want the milk?"

"That's right. She's your responsibility, and it would be a sin to let her suffer."

John milks Gilbert, and ties her on a long rope where she can eat grass and find shade to rest. The next morning when he goes to check on her, she has chewed herself free of the rope. Gilbert is in Ollie's late garden. She has eaten almost a whole row of young beans that Ollie watered from the well.

John works for hours making a little harness for Gilbert so she can pull his Radio Flyer wagon. She does not mind the harness, but will have no part of pulling that rattling red thing behind her. She kicks and runs away, knocking it sideways and scratching the red paint while dragging it. John unhooks the wagon, but leaves the harness on her.

That night, Johnny loops a chain around the silver leaf maple tree and hooks the chain to Gilbert's harness. "Well, I bet you don't chew this in two and get into Mother's bean patch."

Every minute that Nancy and Patty are not watching the twins, they spend decorating the cellar for a playhouse. Jesus pictures from a McNutt Funeral Home calendar hang along the edges of the fruit shelves. Cardboard boxes, padded with rags and covered with worn towels, hold sleepy-eyed dolls. Two small aprons hang on tacks driven into the shelves. Tiny dishes, old perfume bottles, and milk-glass cold-cream jars sit along the shelf that will soon hold late potatoes.

"Mother, come see our playhouse. It's so pretty."

Ollie smiles as she looks around the cellar. "It's very nice. I like your pictures."

The next morning as John leaves the house to check on Gilbert, Ollie goes to hang dishtowels on the clothesline.

Patty scampers into the cellar. She almost falls getting back out. With wide frightened eyes, she runs to John pointing. "Something's down there!"

Squinting to look into the dark, John hears Gilbert bleat and rushes down the steps. "You stupid goat! I should hang you on a pole over a fire." He drags Gilbert up the steps.

Ollie goes into the cellar, Patty holding to her dress tail. Nancy is close behind.

"Oh, no!" Nancy wails. "Gilbert's ruined everything."

Every picture is on the floor—chewed, torn, and wet with urine and goat poop. Aprons and doll dresses are gnawed and damp with goat slobber. Dishes, bottles, and jars lie on the floor, some cracked and chipped.

Ollie comes out of the cellar with a frown on her face. John has removed the harness and fastened the chain tight around Gilbert's neck.

"Son, you should have named that thing Houdini instead of Gilbert."

"Mother, what am I gonna do with her?"

"I have two suggestions. You can take her back to the sale, or I can put her in that cellar inside quart jars."

Roy and John take Gilbert back to the livestock sale at Conway. John gets four dollars for her. The next night at supper, John shakes his head as Nancy and Patty complain about their torn doll dresses and cracked dishes.

"I thought a goat would be fun for all of us. I should have listened when Uncle Eldridge told me that 'goat' is just another name for trouble. She was certainly trouble, and I lost seven dollars on her sale."

Saturday at lunch, Roy says, "Ann, would you and John like to go fishing at Pea Vine Creek this afternoon?"

"Yes!" They answer in unison.

"Can I go too?" Nancy asks.

Smiling, he looks at her. "It's a long way to walk."

Ollie remarks, "Nancy, it's too far. You need to stay here and play with Patty."

"No. I can walk. I always have to stay home."

"Let her go, Ollie."

"She can't walk as fast as the rest of you, today is so hot, and she might step on a snake."

Roy looks at Ollie, tilting his head back and a little to the side. "And the sky might fall before we get back. She can keep up. She just might catch our supper." He winks at Nancy.

"All right, Nancy, but you have to wear long pants and rub coal oil on your legs to keep off chiggers. You're gonna get awful hot walking through those weeds."

"I can do it." Smiling, she runs to put on blue jeans, socks, and shoes.

It is almost milking time when Nancy comes running inside. "I did it, Mother! I caught the biggest fish! I need a pan for it. Come see, before it's cut up. Daddy said it's about the biggest perch he's ever seen."

Ollie walks out to the cellar where Roy has placed the fish beside those caught by John and Ann. "My goodness—that *is* a big fish."

"I told you! And I kept up with Daddy when we were walking."

"And you caught that all by yourself?"

"Yep. Daddy told me what to do, and I caught my fish from under a big log."

That night they feast on fried potatoes, purple hull peas, corn cakes and fish.

Corn cakes

1 ¼ cups yellow cornmeal

¾ cups flour

1 teaspoon salt

3 teaspoons baking powder

1 egg

1 cup cream style corn

1 small onion chopped fine

1 small bell pepper chopped fine

Mix all ingredients, drop from a teaspoon into hot oil, and fry until brown.

Chapter 20
Pigs, People and a Park

Springtime brings hope with wildflowers trailing lavender blossoms along every fencerow and road ditch. Memories of drought, boll weevils, and crop failures fade in the magnificent beauty of the half-acre peach orchard, its pink blossoms ruffling in the breeze. Decorating the landscape are apple, pear, peach, wild cherry, plum, and mulberry trees. For weeks, the splendor of blossoming fruit trees and berry thickets lift everyone's spirits.

With six children to clothe and feed, Roy and Ollie cannot lessen efforts to earn a living. "Ollie, Bonny's got a sow that he wants to sell. She raised a large litter of pigs last spring. What do you think about us trying to raise a brood?"

"Oh, Roy, one or two hogs for our own use causes enough stink. Think what it would be like with a whole pen full. Besides, sows are mean. I don't want these little girls anywhere near one."

"I wouldn't put it near the house. I was thinking about building a hog-wire fence in the woods below the spring. The horses would still have the upper part, with the pigs getting the runoff. We wouldn't have to carry water, and Bonny said pig feed is about the cheapest you can buy."

"The pen would be almost a quarter of a mile from the house. I can't leave these babies and go that far to feed the pigs if you have to go off to work."

"Nancy and Patty are big enough to carry feed. Pig short is not heavy until you mix water with it. They can dip water from the spring and mix it down there."

"*Pig short*—what is that?"

"Bonny said it's mostly made from wheat, but some brands have corn by-products mixed in. It smells good—almost like cereal." He laughs. "I bet it would taste good with a little sugar and cream."

"I think I'll stick with oatmeal for my cereal." She frowns. "Roy, I'm really afraid for the girls to get near an old sow."

"Nancy's tall enough to dump a bucket over the fence. You know those two would never climb into the pen."

"Nancy wouldn't, but Patty might if she thought she could catch a baby pig to play with. She's too bold sometimes."

"She won't; not after I tell her what that sow would do if she touches one of the pigs."

"Well, you better build a strong fence around that pen."

Roy and John build a large pen of sturdy hog-wire with spring water running through the south side. "Ollie, the pigs can drink clean clear water from the north end where it first runs into the pen over a bed of rock, and they can wallow in the south end. They have plenty of shade, and acorns to eat."

"When are you going to get the sow?"

"Right after lunch. We're finished here."

She turns. "I'll go put the food on the table."

"Wait. Ride back to the house in the truck with John and me."

Ollie is sitting on the porch reading the weekly *Log Cabin Democrat* when the truck comes slowly down the road, easing over every familiar rough spot. The truck is still rolling when John jumps out and runs to open the pasture gate. In the same easy pace, Roy continues to the spring while John fastens the gate and runs to the house.

"Mother, we got her! Uncle Bonny said she'd be having pigs by next week. Daddy's afraid moving her will make her have them too early, but Uncle Bonny said he thought they would be all right even if they were born tonight. I gotta go help Daddy unload her. She's huge, with fourteen milk teats—seven on each side. Last year she had sixteen piglets, but only fourteen lived. Come down and see her."

Ollie follows John to the spring where Roy has maneuvered the truck into a ditch, leaving the truck bed almost level with the pen. He opens the sideboard exit and lowers the tailgate. The big white sow waddles into the pen and goes directly to the spring to drink.

Walking close to the fence, Ollie studies the big hog's every move. "She doesn't act wild."

John runs along the fence watching the large animal. "She's not, Mother. I petted her. She's a Yorkshire. I read about them in a book. They have large litters, and are good mothers."

Ollie gives him a frightened look. "Don't you tell Patty and Nancy. I want them to be afraid of her. She'll get more aggressive when she has those babies."

"Son, get that bucket of slop your mama brought down. We need to keep feed in there all the time."

The big sow lumbers over and begins to chomp on the potato peelings and other scraps dumped into the trough. When the food is gone, she walks around the pen, munching acorns and sloshing through the spring. At last, she goes into the house Roy and John built for her and flops down in the pile of hay.

"Daddy, I bet she likes it here better than that hot muddy pen where she was before. It didn't have much shade."

"I hope the move didn't stress her too much. John, you need to bring a bucket of that feed down here and show Nancy and Patty how to mix it like Bonny showed you. Tell them not to put their hands inside the fence. She could bite a little hand off as quickly as chomping through an ear of corn. They can name her, if they want, but make sure they know that she's not a pet."

In a few days, the sow that Patty names Dolly has seventeen piglets. One is born dead; another dies the first day. Patty and Nancy hear Roy say that another will probably die because the sow only has fourteen milk teats.

Nancy asks, "Daddy, can I have one and feed it on a baby bottle?"

"I don't want to start that. You wouldn't want to get rid of it after you make it a pet. Dolly might be able to raise fifteen."

It is Nancy and Patty's afternoon job to take feed to Dolly and her babies. At first, they enjoy going to see the little pink pigs, and they always take time to splash in the spring, and swing on the muscadine vines. As the pigs grow larger and the summer gets hotter, the path seems to grow longer.

The gentle horses will not bother the girls, but Nancy still remembers seeing the mules kick and kill their dog. She is not convinced that Lucky and Tony will not try to kick her and Patty. Usually, they go to feed the pigs in the middle of the afternoon when Roy has the horses in the field, but one hot afternoon they linger until Roy and the horses return to the barn.

Nancy and Patty grab the feed buckets and rush down the path to the pigpen. After dumping the feed, they are on the way to the house, when the thirsty horses start down the trail toward the spring.

Ollie, looking out the kitchen window, sees Nancy point then run into a clump of bushes near the path. Within seconds, the girls run to another thicket. When the horses pass, the girls take a shortcut across the pasture, running, then tiptoeing and hopping. After climbing the fence into the orchard, they stop and Nancy begins pulling burs from the seat of Patty's pants.

Johnny yells, "What are you girls doing?"

"Patty sat down in a sandbur patch."

John laughs and teases while they continue pulling stickers.

Back at the house, Nancy explains, "Mother, we ran into a clump of bushes to hide from the horses. When we looked up, a big black snake was hanging right over our heads."

"Yeah," Patty adds, "it was hanging on a branch shaking its tongue at us."

"Is that when you ran into the sandburs?"

"That's when we ran to more bushes to stay away from the horses."

"Go a little earlier tomorrow, and you won't have to worry about the horses or snakes in the bushes. For now, drag a washtub into the smokehouse and draw water for a bath. I've got a couple of kettles heating on the stove. If you wait until bedtime to bathe, you'll both be covered with chigger bites."

At supper, Roy laughs with the girls about the snake and sandburs before talking to Ollie about crops. "That field of oats I planted in early spring is ready for the thresher. In the morning I'm gonna run up toward Guy and see if I can get those Bolger boys to bring their combine down and harvest them."

"I hate to see the oats cut down. They're beautiful when a breeze blows over the field. It looks like waves on a large lake."

"They are pretty. I believe a person could get sea-sick by watching that field."

The harvesters dump the oats into a metal-lined room that Roy calls the oat bin. It's in the barn and does not have a door, only a window for climbing through, or for reaching inside and getting a scoop-full to feed the cows. While the twins are taking afternoon naps, Nancy and Patty play in the oats.

When rats start getting into the bin, John shoots some with his BB-gun, and then Roy buries a fifty-gallon drum with the top almost level with the grain and fills the barrel with water. Rats fall into the water and cannot get out. He bans Nancy and Patty from playing in the bin, but they occupy summer hours by jumping from the barn loft into the manger filled with hay, and they tie strings on the shiny green June bugs and make them fly.

John tells them to tie strings on white-faced bumblebees. Bees fly faster and are more fun than June bugs. The girls are skeptical at first, but it is not long until they are knocking bumblebees out of the air with boards. They kill the ones with black faces, and tie strings on the others. Roy would like them to kill all the bumblebees—they bore holes in barn posts.

Ollie comes up to Roy as he watches the girls swatting bees. "I'm afraid one of them will get stung."

"They're cautious."

"I hope so." She shakes her head. "Roy, when do you think you'll need to go to town again?"

"I plan to go tomorrow. Nestled among weeds and grass, several melons escaped sunburn. I hope to sell them. Do you need something from town?"

"I need to buy cloth for school clothes. You can't imagine how I dread that. The sales clerks won't talk loud enough for me to hear. Sometimes they turn their heads and snicker, but I see enough to know what they're doing. It's even worse when I meet someone I know. I want to run and hide. They have to talk so loud for me to understand that everyone nearby stares at us."

"Could Ann buy cloth for you?"

"She'll choose material for her own dresses, but I really need to pick the fabric for the little girls and for John's shirts. I'll take Nancy with me to translate. I can understand her."

"I didn't think you wanted to take the girls to town for fear they'd catch polio."

Ollie frowns and shakes her head. "That does worry me. Did you read in the paper that this year might be another epidemic? I don't remember the numbers from other years, but in 1952, the United States had nearly 60,000 reported cases with more than 3,000 deaths. I'm afraid for Johnny to be out in public with you selling melons, and I don't like to take Nancy to town, but I need help understanding what the clerks are saying."

In town, Nancy holds packages and stays at Ollie's side. She is a shy child, but knows how embarrassed Ollie is about being unable to hear. Nancy will nod, shake her head, hold up fingers to indicate price, and she turns her face toward Ollie and states her words loud and clear. She can also produce a nasty frown, when she thinks a clerk is impolite.

On the way home, they pass the Freewill Baptist Church. "Daddy, will you take us to church next Sunday?"

"You'll have to sit quiet, if you want to go back. Ollie, do you want to go with us?"

"Roy, it wouldn't do me a bit of good to go. I couldn't hear the preacher or the Sunday school teacher. I'll learn a lot more by reading the Bible at home."

Sunday morning, Roy takes all of the children except the twins. Nancy and Patty bring home Bible stories with pictures and sit telling Ollie about their class.

"Roy, what did you think about that church?"

"I liked the class. The preacher gave a good sermon. Everyone was friendly enough, but I couldn't talk to the men for the women asking about you."

"Did you explain that I can't hear?"

He nods. "Yes, I did."

Roy studies the lesson for the next week's class and takes the children back on Sunday.

Nancy and Patty are as excited as they were the week before, but Roy is quiet. They go back for two more weeks, and then Roy says, "Ollie, I'm not going back unless you go. Two women keep pestering me about you coming until I can't carry on a conversation with any of the men."

The next Sunday Ollie goes with them. She hates for the children to miss church because she cannot hear. The small church does not have separate classrooms. Four groups, divided by ages, cluster in corners of the auditorium for Sunday school.

One of the women that pestered Roy sits beside Ollie, repeating everything the teacher says in a loud voice. People in the other groups look her way.

On the way home, Ollie wipes at tears. "Roy, if I could just sit, read my bible and pretend to hear, I would go, but I can't do it with that woman in my face." They do not go back.

Monday, Roy is up most of the night with pain from a decayed tooth. It has been getting worse over the last two weeks. "Eldridge said Heber Springs has a good dentist that's reasonable on his prices. Ollie, get yourself ready, we're both gonna go if we have to sell a milk cow to pay for it."

Ollie worries the entire trip—*what if their old truck cannot make it up the steep mountain, and what if the dentist has to give Roy pain medicine and he can't drive home.* At the top of Heber Mountain, she smiles at the beauty of the view. "What a pretty sight."

The dentist examines their teeth before sitting to talk with them. "Mr. and Mrs. Glenn, you've both let your teeth go far too long. Most of them are past saving. Infected teeth can cause other health issues."

The dentist looks at Ollie, still sitting in the dentist chair. "Mrs. Glenn, infection in these teeth could have affected your ears and maybe your hearing. I can pull Roy's tooth, and relieve his misery for a few weeks, but both of you should think about dentures. It's only a matter of time until you'll have no choice. I know you have a long drive to get here, so if you want me to pull teeth today, I can get started."

Roy shakes his head. "I'd like you to get this decayed tooth out of my head as soon as possible, but I'll think awhile about the dentures. Ollie has more than one hurting her. She'll have to make her own decision."

"All right, Roy, you and your wife swap chairs while she thinks about what she wants to do." He gets a needle and picks up a bottle of medicine. "Roy, do you have to drive home?"

"Yes. Ollie never learned to drive."

"Then I can only give you a local anesthetic and pills to swallow after you get home."

While the dentist is waiting for the shot to take effect, Ollie asks, "Do you really think pulling these bad teeth could help my hearing?"

"I doubt it, but I heard of one instance where a person's hearing returned after getting rid of infected teeth. Anyway, they need to come out."

"We can't pay all of it until the crops are sold, and if there's a drought we might have to wait longer."

"I'll work with you. I know about *farmers luck*."

That day, Ollie gets the molds made for dentures to replace her painfully decayed teeth, and she gets her teeth pulled. It is several days before she gets the new dentures, and she has to return numerous times for the dentist to make adjustments. Her hearing does not improve.

Roy gets molds made, and Johnny goes with him to gets his teeth pulled. The dentist puts the new dentures in his mouth the same day. John walks into the kitchen in front of his daddy while Ollie is preparing soup. "Daddy almost lost his teeth before we got home." Roy smiles. John bursts out laughing.

"Tell me about it, John."

"We were driving home, and Daddy had his window down with his left arm resting across the truck door. Without thinking, he spit out of the window. His teeth came out of his mouth, and he caught them in his left hand. Then he could hardly keep them in his mouth for laughing. He said, 'I think I better keep this window rolled up until I get used to these teeth.'"

When Roy goes to Heber Springs again, he takes Nancy and John with him, and leaves them to play in the park with the mineral springs while he goes to the dentist. Nancy is full of excitement as she tells Ollie and Patty about the trip.

"Mother, Johnny showed me the different springs with mineral water in them. Most of them smelled bad and they taste awful, but people came by and filled jars to take home. One old man told us the water is for curing diseases, but I think it would make me vomit if I had to drink it.

"Lots of old men were sitting on benches in the park. They talked and whittled with pocketknives, but I didn't see any old women sitting around the park. John said he guessed it was because old women don't like to whittle. I like the park. Why do you think old women don't like to go there?"

"It's probably because they have work to do at home. Even when women get old, they still have to cook, clean house, and do laundry."

Nancy frowns. "That's not fair. I wish I'd been born a boy. Johnny gets to go places with Daddy all the time, but I have to stay home and watch the twins or shell beans. He said he's seen those springs several times. Being a girl is not fair."

"I don't disagree, but that's the way it is. A woman's work is never done."

Patty pulls on Roy's sleeve. "Daddy, will you take me to go see the park?"

"Would you stay with John and hold his hand until I come back to get you?"

She has a big grin as her head bobs up and down. "I will."

"All right then, you can go."

The next time Roy goes to the store, he says it is Patty's turn. Nancy runs to her piggy bank for a nickel. "Patty will you buy me something at the store when you spend your money?"

"What do you want?"

Roy yells, "Patty, come on if you're going with me."

Nancy shrugs. "Get me the same thing you get."

Nancy is waiting on the steps when Roy pulls the truck up to unload groceries. "Patty, what did you get me?"

Roy is grinning. John is laughing. "You told me to get you the same thing I got."

"Well, what did you get?"

"An ice cream cone, but it was melting. After I ate mine, yours kept dripping. I had to lick the sides. Daddy stopped to talk to a man after he left the store. When he came back, he told me to eat it before it dripped all over the truck. I didn't plan to eat it—I *had* to."

After school starts in the fall, Nancy and Patty have to feed the pigs later in the day. The weatherman is predicting heavy rain and thunderstorms for late afternoon, so while the twins take a nap, Ollie mixes feed and rushes to the spring. She is almost to the pen when she sees a big gray animal beside the spring. She catches her breath. It looks like the wolves on the wall at Massey's Hardware store.

Setting the feed on the ground, Ollie picks up a rock and throws it at the animal. It takes a step back, but does not run. She yells, "Get. Get out of here." Still it stands and stares. The half-grown pigs stomp in the trough; faintly Ollie hears their squeals. If the wolf is growling, she cannot hear it.

She dumps the feed and again looks toward the spring. The wolf is gone. She remembers the girls telling Roy about a big gray dog that stood watching them from across the spring. Roy told them, "Leave it alone. It's probably somebody's German Shepherd."

That night when Roy comes in for supper, Ollie does not wait for him to take off his jacket before she starts telling him about the wolf. Her voice reveals the fear she felt at the spring.

"Roy, you're gonna have to feed those pigs from now on. That was not a dog the girls saw. It was at the spring this afternoon, and I'm sure it's a big timber wolf. Take the gun tomorrow when you go. Wolves run in packs. They might attack you.."

Roy runs a hand over his face and frowns. "Those pigs need to grow for two months or more. When they go, so does Dolly. I don't have time to take on another job."

On November 21, 1952 Robert Lee McNew, Ollie's papa, dies from a stroke. Roy had planned to leave for Kansas City the weekend of Papa's funeral, but delays his trip until the next week.

Papa is buried in the McNew Cemetery at Centerville where his parents, grandparents, two children and numerous other relatives and friends were laid to rest. William Billy McNew, Papa's grandfather, built the McNew Chapel in 1893. He donated it and three acres of land for the McNew Chapel Cemetery to the Methodist Episcopal Church.

Chapter 21
Faith and Privilege

Lottie, Roy's sister, no longer lives across from the school bus stop. The new family is friendly and welcomes the children to come inside on cold or rainy days. They own a big red dog that barks and runs out when the children walk up, but the people always call him back.

Nancy comes rushing in after school, yelling, "Mother, Johnny almost got killed by that big dog that lives across from the bus stop!"

Johnny comes through the door, letting the screen slam.

Ollie stares at him. "Johnny, are you all right?"

"Yeah." He grins. "He didn't bite me."

Ollie takes hold of his shoulder, and turns him around as she looks for torn clothing. "Well, tell me what happened."

"It was drizzling rain, so we started across the road. It looked like they were gone, including the dog. Anyway, they always say he won't hurt us, so we were gonna stand on the porch out of the rain. I was in front when the dog came around the house, barking. Everyone else ran across the road, but I slipped on the wet gravel in the driveway and fell flat on my back."

"Did you hurt yourself?"

"It knocked the breath out of me. The next thing I knew, that big dog was standing over me, staring down at my face. I couldn't move. After a while, he walked away and lay down on the porch. I got up and went across the road with the other kids."

"Do you think the dog wanted to play?"

"No! He didn't. He was growling and showing teeth while he was standing over me. I can tell you for sure, I won't ever cross that road unless those people are calling to me."

A few days later, Nancy runs in from school, a smile covering her face. "Mother, there's gonna be a book fair in Little Rock. Three students from each class get to go, from the fourth grade up, and it doesn't cost anything. Miss Clarice chose me, and John's teacher chose him."

"That's nice. What is a book fair?"

"I'm not sure. I'll tell you when we get back."

The week of the event, Nancy develops tonsillitis. The weather is cold and rainy. Ollie keeps her home. Thursday, the day of the fair, she doesn't have fever and begs to go.

Ollie shines a flashlight beam into Nancy's throat. Clicking off the light, she shakes her head and frowns. "I wouldn't worry so much if the day was warm and clear, but I'm afraid for you to go out on a cold rainy day like this. Your throat looks raw, and I can tell by the way your voice sounds that it hurts."

Nancy frowns, about to cry. "I'll be inside all the time. It's not fair to make me stay home. I never get to go anywhere, except to school."

"All right. Roy can drive you to the bus stop. Wear your scarf and gloves, and try not to get your feet wet."

The bus has mechanical problems on the way home. The

children sit on the cold bus for hours waiting for repairs. It is near midnight when they return. Nancy has a fever and stays in bed for the next two days, but talks about the trip for weeks.

One spring afternoon, Nancy comes home from school, a mixture of emotions on her face. "Mother, the fourth, fifth, and sixth grade classes are gonna have a program. My teacher picked me to recite a poem, but I'll need a dress with a long full skirt. I have to look like Little Miss Muffet." She takes a deep breath and holds out a storybook picture. "Ann said you don't have money to buy special material for a long dress. Do I need to tell the teacher that I can't do it?"

"Maybe I can remake one of Ann's dresses."

Ann has a white organdy dress with tiny red polka dots that is too small for her. Ollie takes it apart and remakes it to fit Nancy. It looks new, and Nancy is proud to wear it.

Ollie buttons the dress, and ties the sash into a bow. "I won't be going to your program, because I can't hear, but your daddy will take you." She smiles. "Ann did a good job of curling your hair. You really look like that picture."

Someone tells Ollie about a person who recovered his hearing after having a tonsillectomy. Once school is out for the summer, she goes back to Little Rock to ask the doctor if there is a possibility that surgery could help her.

The doctor examines her throat. Then he sits rubbing his chin and staring out the window. "If the nerves are totally dead, surgery won't help, but I wouldn't rule it out. You lost your hearing after having strep throat. Strep is almost always found on infected tonsils. Maybe the nerves are not operating because of the disease."

"What will it cost to have my tonsils taken out?"

"I could do it in my office if it were not for the anesthetic. I can't administer anesthetic *and* perform the operation. Hospital charges and the anesthetist are the expensive parts. Knowing your situation, I'd keep my charges minimal."

"Could you give me a local anesthetic, like a dentist does to pull teeth?"

"This involves a lot more than that. It would be quite painful for you."

"I've had eight children. I would be willing to withstand all that pain at one time if I could regain my hearing."

"I don't doubt that you would, but I'm not sure I can stand seeing you in that much pain."

"Doctor, I'd do almost anything to get my hearing back."

He pats her on the shoulder. "We'll try doing the surgery in my office. My nurse can assist me."

The doctor gives Ollie an antibiotic, and tells her to return in two weeks and plan to stay in Little Rock for a week after the surgery. Roy and Ollie bring Robbie and Bobbie to Morene's. Nancy comes along to help watch the twins.

Early in the morning, Ollie arrives at the doctor's office. He gives her a shot and swabs medicine in her throat. "Mrs. Glenn, hold this pan in your lap, and squeeze it when you think the pain is unbearable. I've never performed a surgery like this without anesthetic, but I'll try to make this as easy for you as I can."

After the operation, Roy brings her back to Morene's.

Morene puts a cold towel on her throat. "Mama, I know that

must have been horrible."

Ollie squeezes her eyes tight and nods.

The next week, Roy knocks on Morene's back door and sticks his head inside. The twins run to him. Picking up a little girl in each arm, he looks at Ollie.

With a sad smile, she shakes her head. "It hasn't helped yet."

"Well, don't let it get you down. Somehow, we'll get you that expensive hearing aid."

Medical bills and farm drought have left Roy and Ollie with very few resources to buy necessities for the children, much less Christmas gifts. The twins decide they want tricycles for Christmas. The older children tell them that Mother and Daddy do not have money for expensive gifts. That does not deter them.

Bobbie says, "Mother and Daddy don't have to buy trikes. Santa Claus will bring them."

Nancy tells her, "Two tricycles cost too much, and will be too heavy for his pack."

"Then we'll share."

"Maybe, but I bet he won't bring something that big."

Bobbie, tiny and frail, puts her hands on her hips, stomps her foot, and declares. "I told you, Santa Claus will bring us a tricycle."

Roy and John search the resale shops, looking for a used tricycle, but cannot find one that is acceptable. Shortly before Christmas, a man brings one to sell in the parking lot of the Conway sale barn. Roy looks it over, decides it is sturdy enough for both little girls, bargains, and buys it. He and John repaint it a bright red and hide it in the barn until Christmas.

On Christmas Eve, John wraps himself in Ollie's hot pink chenille bathrobe—only his hands and eyes are visible. He runs through the living room from the kitchen to the hallway, dropping the tricycle in front of the twins. Two little faces glow. Bobbie begins to shout, "Santa Claus! Santa Claus! It was Santa Claus! I told you Santa Claus would bring us a tricycle."

Chapter 22
Prayer and Broken Arms

"Roy, the almanac shows the signs are fine for planting all above ground crops."

"That's good, because the weatherman said the danger of frost is past and we've got two, maybe three days before we'll get rain. If we work at it, we can get that corn in the ground. Ann will have to miss a couple days of school."

The FHA Spring Convention in Little Rock is a big event for girls in Home Economics classes, and Ann has been looking forward to it for weeks. The teacher encouraged them to wear their Sunday best. It is a time to dress up and feel elegant.

Ann made herself a new dress, ordered high heel shoes from the Sears Roebuck catalog, and practices walking in them on the linoleum floors. She has a little hat with a soft feather draped across the top in the same navy blue color as her shoes and purse.

At supper, Roy begins to plan the next day. "Ann, you're gonna have to miss the next two days of school. We've gotta get that corn in the ground while the weather's clear."

Ann draws in her breath. "Daddy, I can't. Tomorrow is the FHA Convention in Little Rock. I have to go. I spent most of my money on new clothes to wear. This is a special day."

"I can't help it, Ann. If we don't get the corn in the ground now, it could be weeks before the weather is right, and that would put the development of the corn into the drought season. We have to plant tomorrow."

"John can help until I get home."

"He's been running a fever most of the week. I can't put him in the field."

"Mother, can you?"

"Your mother's having problems with her back."

Ann sits staring at the food on her plate. "Daddy, if it rains, can I go?"

Roy shakes his head and smiles a weak smile. "Yes, Ann, if it rains and we can't plant, then you can go."

"Then I'm gonna pray for rain."

Roy gives her a hard look.

At breakfast, Roy says, "I sure would like to get those seeds in the ground before it rains, but it looks like that weatherman may have messed-up again."

The sky is dark gray, with thick clouds and wind blowing from the southwest. Roy pushes his chair away from the table. The ground is still dry.

Ollie looks out the back door. There is not a sprinkle in the dusty path to the barn. Ann needs to start getting ready if she is going to catch the bus. It takes time for a girl to put on a garter belt, nylon hose, slip, and all the other finery.

With a quiver in her voice, Ann asks, "Daddy, can I go?"

"I don't think it'll rain much. These clouds will probably blow over soon."

A few sprinkles splatter the dust in the path leading out from the porch. "Oh, go ahead and get ready. We'll see what it's doing when you're dressed to go."

She has every item of her outfit spread out with precision.

"Mother, are the seams of my hose straight?"

"They look good to me. Get that hatpin, and I'll help you with your hat."

"Mother, do you think Daddy will drive us to the bus stop?"

"I'll suggest it."

It is time to go, but Roy is still looking at the clouds. "I just don't know. We really need to get those seeds in the ground if this blows over." At that moment, torrents of rain fall from the sky.

He shakes his head and plops on an old brown hat. "Okay, get in the truck. I'll drive you to the bus stop."

Within two hours, sunshine and a cool breeze replaces clouds. When the children get home from school, Roy has the horses and planting equipment waiting in the field.

Ann knows the importance of getting seed planted at the right time. She changes into work clothes, and is soon following behind the mare. Late the next day, the fertilized corn waits for rain that is fast approaching from the southwest.

Ollie watches Roy and Ann disappear under the shadow of the barn roof with the horses. Rain cascades across the fields, running off the house and rattling into a washtub placed under the drain to catch rainwater.

Ollie must go back to the doctor in Little Rock. Ann has a summer job and John, Nancy, and Patty do not want to go spend the day waiting. "John, you can stay home and do a few chores, but Nancy and Patty have to go with us."

"Mother, can you leave us in Conway with our cousin, Sammy Dawn?"

"We'll ask her mother if it's all right."

Ollie looks out the truck window as they are about to leave. "Roy, I know your niece will do a good job of watching the girls, and they'll have a good time playing with Sammy Dawn, but intuition tells me we shouldn't leave Patty. She's such a tomboy. Bronnie may have to tie her up to keep her out of those trees." She turns in the seat, looking back. "Roy, let's take Patty with us."

"Ollie, you beat all I've ever seen. Let the girls have a day of fun."

Late that afternoon, Roy and Ollie return to pick up the girls. Patty has a broken arm. Nancy tells them Patty fell over a tub.

"Girls, as we drove away, I imagined Patty with a broken arm. I was worried about her falling out of one of those tall trees in the backyard, or hurting herself playing some tumbling game. But a tub—I never thought of my tomboy falling over a tub."

Patty, face stained with tears, glances sideways at Nancy—neither of them speak. Ollie is sure Patty fell over a tub, but is sure that they were doing something they knew she would not approve of. Pressing the issue will serve no purpose.

Both bones in Patty's arm are broken. Roy and Ollie have another doctor bill that they cannot afford.

The corn did not fully develop before drought began in July. Melons, peaches, early truck patch crops, and a couple of bull calves are all that brought in cash. It will be another rough year.

Eldridge and his family live next to the old Centerville school. It is no longer in use. Students that live in the old district go to Greenbrier or Quitman, but neighborhood children find the vacant gymnasium a great place to play basketball and roller skate.

Sunday afternoon, on their way to visit Mama and Papa, Roy and Ollie drop John off to play basketball with his cousins, Bobby and Wayne. Ollie calls after him, "John, don't you be roller skating in that old gym. I don't want you winding up with a broken arm."

John waves and goes off to find the boys. Roy, Ollie, and the girls drive away.

After a long afternoon of visiting with family, Roy is eager to leave. "Ollie, you need to come on, or we'll be milking after dark." Honking the horn, he pauses outside the old gym.

Without speaking, John runs outside and climbs into the back of the truck with Nancy and Patty.

On the way home, Roy stops on the dirt road beside the pasture fence and gets out of the truck. "John, I want you to drive the rest of the way home. I'm gonna walk across the pasture and herd the cows toward the barn."

John is not old enough to have a driver's license, but he has been driving on the farm for a long time. He gets in the drivers seat, presses down on the gas pedal, and manages to change gears. Although right-handed, he is steering with his left. His right hand is in his lap.

Ollie grabs his right hand and slams it against the wheel. "Get both hands on that wheel before you wreck us with these little girls in here."

John draws in his breath in a loud gasp, and straightens in the seat.

"Don't say a word. I'm already aggravated at you. You

should have walked up to visit with your grandma for a little while, instead of staying to play with those boys all afternoon."

Once in the yard, John puts on the brake, stops the truck without changing gears, and turns off the ignition. The yard is level; he knows the truck will not roll away. Roy and Ann milk the cows while John feeds the pigs.

The next morning, John's right arm has swollen to twice the normal size. He is trying to keep it to himself, but Ollie sees him bathing it in alcohol. "What happened to your arm?"

Squinting with pain, he answers, "I broke it."

"You were skating, after I told you not to."

He nods.

"Roy," she yells. "Come in here and look at John's arm. He says it's broken."

"Son, are you sure? Maybe you sprained it."

"No. It's broken. The bone was sticking out. Bobby pulled on it and set the bone back in place."

"Well, I'll take you to Conway to see if you need a cast on it."

Roy takes him to the doctor and has it X-rayed. The doctor tells them that it is broken. The boys set it perfectly, but it still needs a cast to hold it until the bone heals.

Chapter 23
Making Plans

Ann has been sewing since she became big enough to stand on one foot and operate the treadle sewing machine with the other. She can cook and do housework as well as any woman. She also maintains good grades in spite of her chores before and after school.

The Home Economics teacher nominates Ann as a school representative for the FHA Summer Camp. Ann, thrilled by the nomination, tells Ollie about the letter she has received.

"That's nice. I'm happy for you, but what about your plans to get a summer job and earn money for college? Are you going to give up on college to go to some camp?"

Syble intervenes. "Mother that nomination is a great honor. She can get a job after the camp ends."

"I don't know about that. The good jobs may be taken by that time." Ollie shakes her head. "I never heard of FHA when I was growing up. What is it?"

Syble grins. "I remember that. The letters stand for Future Homemakers of America. It's a nonprofit student organization with family and career preparation as its focus. It wasn't created until 1945. Ann, I think you should go."

Ollie turns away. "Ann, you'll have to work that out for yourself. You don't have much time to earn college money, and we can't afford to send you."

Syble helps Ann buy a swimsuit, shorts, and other clothing she needs for the camp. Ann has a wonderful time, and finds a summer job after the camp is over.

In the fall, Ann enrolls at Arkansas State Teachers College, and rides to school with a neighbor who works in Conway. She has to leave home at six in the morning, and does not return until almost dark.

Again, Roy packs a bag to go find work in Kansas City and earn money for seed and fertilizer. "Ollie, I'll be home in time to plant crops. We have plenty of wood cut to keep you warm until spring. Send Ann or John to get Mr. Rains if you need help. He's a good neighbor."

One night after dark, a car pulls into the yard. The children look to Ollie with wide frightened eyes. Their house is on a private lane, off the county road. They never have visitors after sundown. "John, bring me your daddy's gun. Ann, take the girls to the kitchen."

Standing inside the front door with gun in hand, Ollie flips the switch to turn on the porch light. "John, lock the doors and then help Ann keep the twins quiet."

Ollie cannot hear him call, but quickly unlocks the door when Roy steps into the light. "I'm sure glad it's you." She lets out a long breath. "Unload this gun for me while I stop shaking. I was ready for the worst."

The children in bed, Roy and Ollie sit and talk by the fire. "Roy, I wish you'd stayed a couple of weeks more, and then, maybe—"

"What! You didn't want me to come home?"

"That's not what I meant. I think that maybe we'd have enough to buy me a hearing aid if you'd stayed a little longer."

"After the kids leave for school in the morning, we're going to Little Rock and buy you that hearing aid."

"But what if we don't have enough money to last until the crops produce?"

"Then I'll get a job somewhere else. You've got to have it. You've suffered too long."

The hearing aid is not as good as her natural hearing, but she can hear the children sing, laugh, and cough; and she can carry on a normal conversation without shouting. The children are so used to yelling that it takes them a while to adjust to talking in normal tones.

While Roy was working in Kansas City, Ann stayed up late doing her homework. Now that he is home, Roy insists that Ann close her books and turn off the light at nine. She finishes the college term, but applies for a civil service job, takes the required test, and passes. She works in Little Rock while waiting for notification from the government.

Ann receives notice of a position with the Department of the Navy, and quits her Little Rock job. The little five-foot-two farm girl packs a cardboard suitcase, and gets on a train headed for Washington, D.C. She begins work October 3, 1955.

The twins start first grade in the fall. They like coloring, playing with other children and working puzzles. One day Bobbie comes home with a defiant look. "Mother, why didn't you teach us the ABC's before we started school?"

"That's what you go to school for."

"We need to know them now. The teacher separated the kids that know the ABC's and numbers from the one's that don't. I'm in the dummy class with Robbie."

Ollie frowns. "Did the teacher call it that?"

"No, Nancy did, but the smart kids get to start learning to read, 'cause they know the ABC's. We don't get a book until we can write and say all the letters."

"I have to finish sewing this dress. Get Nancy to teach you. I remember her trying to do that before school started."

Nancy has been listening from the doorway. "I *did* try to teach them, but they didn't want to learn then. I'll help if they'll try, but I have my own homework. If they want to giggle and act silly, they can wait for the teacher."

Before nightfall, they can sing the alphabet song and write some of the letters. They learn fast, but Robbie gets bored and wants to go play.

Bobbie glares at her. "Robbie, you better write your letters. I don't like being in the dummy class. I want a reader book."

Robbie shrugs. "I'll read your book. My hand is tired of writing. I'm gonna go play."

Bobbie's eyes squint with anger. "You won't read my book, 'because I'll be reading it. Nancy, will you help me learn to read?"

"First you have to learn all the letters and how they sound."

Bobbie is serious about learning. Robbie, not wanting to be left behind, picks up her pencil.

In October, after the crops are gathered, Roy goes back to Kansas City to find work. He acquires a temporary job, but it ends in December. With a terrible cold, he hitchhikes home.

Sick and discouraged, Roy sits talking to Ollie over morning coffee. "I'm tired of trying to raise crops in these drought conditions. Let's sell this farm and move to Kansas City. I've spent an awful lot of time there without my family."

"I don't want to raise these kids in a big city. Roy, if it was only the two of us, I'd be packed and ready to go, but there is too much evil in the city to take these children into it."

He shakes his head. "We've got to try something else. I don't like spending so much time away from home. How about raising chickens or starting a dairy?"

"I've been inside your sister's big chicken house. It has an awful odor."

"Cattle stink, too."

"Not like thousands of confined chickens. I'd rather try the dairy business, but where will we get the money? I hate to think of putting another mortgage on our farm."

"I'll try for a long-term loan from the Production Credit Association. We already own a farm that has enough grazing land, year-round water to support a herd of dairy cows, and we have a barn as nice as any in this area. Maybe the dairy cattle and equipment will be enough collateral without mortgaging our house and land. With our original herd included, we should get the loan."

"Most of what we have are beef cattle. We need Holsteins, and some Jerseys for cream content."

"You seem to know a lot about it."

"I've read articles. We'd be good at the dairy business."

"It'll mean milking and feeding every day of the year—rain, snow, sickness or sunshine."

"Any kind of farming is like that. We always have jobs."

"Ollie, there's a piece of equipment that we need, whether we start a dairy or continue farming. I should get one, and start using it before spring rains."

"What's that?

"A tractor. I need to disk the field and sow rye grass seed for winter pastures. In the spring, I'll use it to cultivate corn for feed. I can't get up at four to milk cows and then walk behind a horse-drawn plow the rest of the day."

"How can we afford to buy one now?"

"I'll look around for a used one."

Nancy and Patty like Mr. and Mrs. Rains, the retired couple who moved into a house west of the Glenn farm. The girls gladly walk the long road to take them milk when there is extra. They like to hear Mr. Rains tell about working in the copper mines in Arizona.

Another plus to the visits—the Rains have a television. The girls write to Ann, telling her about the programs they watch with Mrs. Rains. For Christmas, Ann buys the family a Sylvania television. Roy goes to the Sears store in Conway to pick it up.

A few days after Christmas, Roy finds a 1950 John Deere tractor with plows, disk, and brush hog. He signs the sales order on December 29, 1955. "Ollie, I can cut down more bushes in a day with this brush hog than those kids can cut in a year with those grubbing hoes, and I can ride and plow two rows at a time with the tractor instead of just one when walking behind the horses."

Roy receives a notice of denial from the Production Credit loan application he filed in the early spring. "I don't understand. I thought those government loans were supposed to help people like us." He slumps into a chair and plops the mail onto the kitchen table.

Ollie picks up the letter, reads, sighs, and reaches to pat his hand. "There's nothing we can do but continue as usual and try again next year."

Roy stands. "I'm going outside. It's stuffy in here." Ollie follows to the walnut tree where they stand looking across the farm.

They have already planted corn, beans, peas, melons, cantaloupe, tomatoes, and cotton. "Roy, let's plant that sandy strip below the barn in peanuts. If they make, we'll have something to sell in the fall. If they don't, we've only wasted seed and labor."

He spits and pushes back his hat. "That's a good idea. I'm sure peanuts will sell."

"The grass on that sandy ground seems to stay green when other areas turn brown. Maybe there's water close to the surface that will help grow the peanuts."

"It's not even June, and the crops are drying up." He spits again, wipes his mouth, and mumbles something.

"What did you say?"

Roy kicks a dry walnut with the toe of his shoe, sailing it across the yard. "Nothing you'd want to hear. I'm tired. Tired of being away from my family all winter, working so I can buy seed that come up teasing that they might grow into a healthy crop, and then every summer I watch them wither and die." He breathes deep and turns his head away from her.

"I get discouraged too, but we have to keep trying."

"I've been telling myself that for almost thirty years. Friends of mine who moved away to places like Kansas City, Michigan, and California have nice homes and cars. They come home in the evenings to relax with their family, and they get paid vacations so they can travel around every year."

"Those people work in factories, and they don't have eight children, and I remember you saying you wanted a big family."

He kicks another dried walnut. "Ah-h, sometimes I let this farm get me down."

"Would you really want to move John this close to his graduation, and Nancy? She's already talking about boyfriends. How could we control these kids if we drop them into a strange environment? We'd only get to see Morene and Syble once or twice a year." She shakes her head."

"All right. Plan on me going away again this fall."

"Roy, it's hard on us too with you being gone so much of the time. A farm has work for a man. How many women do you know who will plow and harvest the crops? I don't want to stay here because it's easier on me. Think what it would be like with kids in town, roaming the streets after school—and you told me that parts of Kansas City gets rough after dark."

"Forget it. I'll apply for the loan again next year and plan on tilling these hillsides until the twins graduate."

Chapter 24
Fire

On Thursday morning, Roy cuts the field of hay in front of the house. The weather is hot for May, and the hay is dry enough to rake after one day in the sun. The children, out of school for the summer, are busy with various chores. Yesterday, Nancy carried water to the field, today is Patty turn. She prepares a jug of ice water then waits under a pecan tree in the front yard for Roy to turn the horses and stop nearby.

Ollie walks onto the porch to sit in the swing while she hems a dress for one of the twins. She watches as Roy spits out his tobacco, takes a little water from the jug to rinse his mouth, and then drinks eagerly. Water that overflows the top of the jug drizzles down his chin and onto the front of his overalls

"Whew." He breathes deep, takes another drink, and brushes at the water on his chest. "As hot as it is, I'd like to pour the rest of this on me. Girl, I'm glad to see you. I was getting awful thirsty. I thought I was gonna have to leave the horses and come in to fix my own water."

Ollie smiles and adjusts her hearing aid, quietly rejoicing that she can hear them from so far away.

Patty grins. "Daddy, can I rake one round while you drink more water?"

"Sis, I don't think your legs are quite long enough." Once more, he leans his head back and turns up the jug.

"Yes, they are." Before Roy lowers the water jug, Patty scampers onto the rake seat and lifts the lines. The horses take that as a signal to go and start with a jerk of the rake.

Sitting on the edge of the high spring seat, Patty's toes barely reach the axle where the rake tongue attaches. The quick start knocks her off balance and she yells. The horses take this for a command, and increase their speed to a trot. A wheel hits a bump; Patty bounces forward, and falls.

Roy drops the jar and runs after the horses, yelling, "Whoa! Whoa!"

Patty, tumbling inside the rake with hay and briars, somehow slides between the teeth. The horses continue trotting until they get to the end of the field.

Scratched and bruised, Patty stands to brush herself off. Roy grabs the skinny little tomboy in a bear hug and holds on for several seconds.

Ollie's sewing lies in a heap where she dropped it on the porch. She runs across the yard and into the field.

Giggling, Patty pulls a briar from her long ponytail.

Roy and Patty are too far away for Ollie to hear them. Standing near the edge of the field, she looks around, barely remembering how she got there, her mind still seeing Patty tumbling from the rake and rolling inside those long steel teeth.

Roy pats his eager helper on the shoulder before going for the horses. Slowly, Patty walks across the field to get the water jar.

Ollie cannot contain her scolding until Patty reaches the porch. "Didn't you know better than to climb on that rake?"

Patty picks up the jug of water, and angles her path toward the back of the house to avoid Ollie.

"You could have been killed!" Seeing the long scratches oozing blood, Ollie stops complaining. "Come over here and let me look at those cuts."

"Oh, they're not deep. I'll pull the briars out and put some salve on them." She quickens her pace toward the back door.

Syble and her husband are expecting their first child in July. "Mother, will you let Nancy come stay with us for a week or two when we bring the baby home from the hospital?"

"Of course. She hasn't done cooking, but she's not lazy. If you tell her what to do, she can follow directions. I would go help you, but Nancy is too young for me to trust her all day with Patty and the twins while Roy and John are off peddling melons. She might try to cook something and burn the house down."

Syble laughs. "Maybe I should think twice before letting her cook."

"She's cautious enough, but it's easy to be distracted with three younger kids in the house."

Syble has a little girl, Ollie and Roy's first grandchild: Deborah, but her parents call her Debbie. Nancy stays with them for three weeks to help with the housework and taking care of the baby. Ollie only intended for Nancy to stay a week, but five days after Syble came home from the hospital a blood vessel burst in her head causing an awful headache. Her doctor is quite concerned, and wants her to be very cautious for a couple more weeks.

The weather has turned dry with no promise of rain. Hot winds rustle through the fields. Roy looks at the corn and declares, "It's another year to grind nubbins into feed."

Roy and John peddle melons in Conway and sell truckloads, at reduced prices, to grocery stores. In the hot field, the melons are blistering fast. "Ollie, I don't think we'll get much from the cotton. We'll have to pull the unopened bolls for scrap unless we get a rain within the next few days."

Ollie is alone with ten-year-old Patty and the six-year-old twins. She goes outside to feed the dog and notices black smoke and flames on the east side of the farm. "Robbie, go to the barn and get an armload of tow-sacks while I draw water to soak them. Patty, you'll have to stay here with Bobbie. We can't let her breathe that smoke. If it gets close to the house, take her and run for the road. Don't try to fight it."

Patty slips into her shoes. "Robbie's too little to fight fire. Let me go. She can stay with Bobbie."

"No. They might panic and get caught in the fire. Robbie can carry sacks for me."

Ollie grabs three buckets and runs to the well. With wet sacks in the buckets, she and Robbie rush toward the fire.

Flames race across the pasture, roaring to the tops of cedar trees, slapping at the sky as they crackle and pour out black smoke. Blazes zip into the cornfields creating their own winds as they torment the stalks and whip the long leaves. Tough cotton stalks are not consumed as quickly as the corn, but the dry leaves sizzle, and flare up to roast the bolls.

Grabbing wet sacks from the buckets Robbie stands guarding, neighbors and people passing on the road rush to fight the flames. On their way home from town, Roy and John see the fire and run to help. They stay in the fields until long after dark, beating out sparks that pop up in clumps of grass and dead brush. When the fire is finally contained, most of the pasture is nothing but black stubble and gray ash.

Cedar fence posts smoke and smolder, leaning haphazardly against loose wires. The cotton field had not produced much, but bolls that would have brought scrap-cotton prices are now worthless. Corn nubbins that could have been ground into feed are charcoal stubs. Dry Bermuda grass that would have fed the cows until rain brought up new growth disappeared in the flames.

Despite dry weather conditions, a neighbor boy set trash on fire and let the fire get out into the dry grass. Both of his parents were away.

Roy slumps into a kitchen chair after spending the morning

walking over the farm assessing damages. "Ollie, I'll have to sell the cattle. There's nothing in that pasture but dead brush and ash." He slams his right fist into his left palm. "Man, I hate to sell that herd. Cattle prices are way down because of the drought. If it hadn't been for that fire, we could have held them until fall rains sprouted some rye grass."

"Roy, we've got to keep a couple of milk cows." She pulls back a curtain to peek at the girls playing in the yard. "The children need milk."

"I can put two in the horse pasture. These horses won't bother the cows. There's still Bermuda grass near the west spring. Thank goodness, we stopped the flames before they got that far. With these dry conditions, our house and barns would have burned if so many people hadn't come to help fight the fire."

He shakes his head and continues to beat his fist against his palm. "Fire damaged most of the cedar trees suitable for posts. "I'll have to buy posts and new wire, and then spend the rest of the summer rebuilding fence."

Roy asks the neighbor boy's mother to help pay for damages. After she refuses, he contacts a lawyer. When the case goes to court, a friend of the woman tells the judge that Roy's crops and fields were worthless. The man trespassed into the burned fields and pastures and took pictures of drought stricken hillsides. No pictures were shown of the valleys between the hills where there was sufficient pasture grass, and tall stalks of cotton and corn before the fire, and there were no pictures of burned fence posts and blackened trees.

Roy had never sat in court before. His lawyer did not tell him that he should bring witnesses and pictures of damage for his defense. He thought his lawyer was supposed to gather and present evidence in his favor. Since neither Roy nor his lawyer brought evidence to refute what the trespasser presented, the case was dismissed.

Roy returns home more discouraged than ever. "That was a sham—a waste of my time." He sits on the porch, rubbing a scar on his hand where the barbed wire cut him. "I guess it's a good thing we didn't get that loan. We certainly wouldn't have anything to feed dairy cows this year. No pasture, no corn, and no money to buy feed. As soon as I finish replacing fence, I'll have to go away to find work again."

Sitting beside him, Ollie looks at Roy, her lips drawn into a thin line. "I thought those people were Christians. I wonder what they'll say on judgment day when they have to account for bearing false witness in court."

Afraid they will fall out and hurt themselves, Ollie does not like the children to climb trees. She tells the girls it is not ladylike to climb. That does not deter Patty. One afternoon while Roy, John, and Nancy are away, Patty climbs into the silver leaf maple tree to escape the twins, who are chasing her in a game of tag.

Ollie comes to the porch and yells, "Get out of that tree!" Patty looks at her mother instead of at the branch she is reaching for. She falls, with knees bent, preparing to land on her feet, but someone left a metal coffee can under the tree, the kind of can opened by a twist-key. The rim is razor sharp. Patty's big toe comes down on the can, and is almost disconnected.

Blood gushes from the wound.

Ollie runs to her. "Oh, Lord! Oh, Lord, help us!" She wraps a dishtowel around Patty's toe. The blood soaks through, filling her hand. "Robbie, run get Mr. Rains to take her to Conway for stitches."

Robbie, tall and strong for a six year old, takes a shortcut across the meadow with sandals on her feet, never pausing to worry about snakes as she runs to get the neighbor.

"Bobbie, bring me that brown bottle of peroxide from the medicine cabinet, and that sheet I use for bandages." Still holding the cloth against Patty's toe, she pours peroxide over the foot, wipes away dirt with her apron, wraps the sheet tight around and around and ties the ends. She stands, holding Patty's leg high to slow the blood flow while they wait for the neighbor.

Mr. Rains and Robbie come bouncing along the lane in his truck. Roy and John pull in behind them.

Seeing the blood, Roy grabs Patty, puts her in the truck, and takes off for the doctor's office in Conway. Her foot, propped on the dash, she leans back in the seat. John supports her leg and holds a towel around her foot.

Ollie and the twins watch the dust swirl into a cloud behind the truck. "I wish we had a doctor in Greenbrier. I've sure missed Doctor Williams since he passed away."

To keep herself busy, Ollie pours several buckets of water underneath the tree to dilute the clotting blood, milks the cows, feeds the chickens, and cooks supper—all the time silently praying.

Red sunset spreads across the western sky, and lightning bugs spark across the yard as Roy stops the truck close to the house. John holds one of Patty's arms near the shoulder, and Roy takes the other as they help her up the steps and to the couch.

Roy takes off his hat. "She got a tetanus shot, and several stitches to reconnect her toe."

Ollie looks at her and frowns. "Didn't I tell you it was dangerous to climb trees?"

Patty, pale from losing so much blood, frowns in response. "I wouldn't have fell if you hadn't yelled at me, and I would have landed flat-footed and not cut my toe if that can hadn't been there. Who put it there anyway?"

Ollie draws in her breath. "I did. I was going to plant a flower in it. You weren't supposed to be jumping out of the tree."

"Let it go, Ollie." Roy motions her toward the kitchen. "Have the cows been milked?"

"Yes, and supper's in the oven."

Ollie bends and touches her hand to Patty's cheek. "Would you like some lemonade?"

"Half a glass—I feel a little sick."

One afternoon, Nancy comes in from school with a big smile. "Mother, starting this year, our school will have cheerleaders for the junior basketball teams. Nine girls were chosen, three from each grade, and I'm one of them. I'll have to buy a uniform, but I think I have enough money."

"Don't be worrying about a uniform. You're not gonna be running around at night going to ballgames."

"But, Mother, I was chosen! That's an honor."

"Consider yourself honored, but you're not going on that school bus to ballgames. How do you think you would get to and from the school to catch the bus? Your daddy works long hard days. He can't sit up nights waiting on a bus. Besides, he may have to go to Kansas City again."

Nancy does not like Ollie's decision, but there is nothing she can do to change her mind. The next day she goes to school and tells the teacher she cannot participate. Her grief is another girl's joy.

Chapter 25
Well-done Tenderloin

In the late fall, before Roy goes away again to look for work in Kansas City, John stays home from school to help butcher the hogs. While Roy disposes of the entrails and waste, John, in the smokehouse, grinds scrap pieces of meat into sausage. In the kitchen, Ollie rushes to fry meat and cook lunch.

Having placed the last piece of floured tenderloin into a heavy skillet of bubbling grease, she turns on water at the sink to wash her hands, and then hears John yelling. She grabs a dishtowel, drying as she rushes out the kitchen door to the smokehouse.

"John, what's wrong? Did you cut yourself?"

"No. No," he angrily snaps. "I need some help. My hands are a mess with this meat, the pan is full, and I need another one."

"I was busy cooking. When I finally heard your call, all I caught was 'help'. I thought you were hurt."

With the towel on her shoulder, she places a clean pan under the grinder to catch the sausage, steps out the door, and sees flames at the kitchen window. "The house is on fire!"

She runs to the house. The cast-iron pot of grease has boiled over and caught on fire. With only the dishtowel in her hand to throw over the skillet's thick wire handle, Ollie grabs the pot, runs to the back door and tosses the flaming container into the yard.

Ollie yanks the blazing curtain from the window, pushes it from the rod into a pan of water left in the sink, and then beats at the flaming wallpaper with the remainder of the curtain.

Wiping sausage grease from his hands onto his shirt, John dashes to the outside faucet to catch a bucket of water, but Ollie left the water running when she heard him yelling. Nothing comes out the spigot. After all the water they used throughout the morning, the well is drained.

He runs to an old well that is still set up with a rope and a bucket. He draws a bucketful and rushes into the house, grabbing a towel from a rack as he goes. The kitchen is full of flames.

John drops the bucket of water and flings his sopping towel over the walls. Ollie dips her curtain in the bucket. Working together, they soon extinguish the flames, but the ceiling is smoking.

Stepping onto a chair then to the top of a buffet cabinet, John lifts and removes the crawl-hole cover that goes into the attic. "Mother, hand me a wet towel. The raw sides of these boards are glowing—they're ready to burst into flames."

With the soggy towel, he mops the boards, and the thick two-by-six supports that hold up the ceiling. Satisfied that all of the embers are extinguished, John climbs down to find Ollie with her hands in the bucket of water. "Mother, let me see your hands."

Briefly, she lifts them from the water. Her right hand is blistered past the elbow. The shoulder of her dress is scorched, and the right side of her hair is singed.

John gets a pan from the cabinet, pours water from the

bucket into it, and then goes to the well for a fresh bucket of water.

"That cool water feels better. Thanks, son."

"Mother, remember those old newspapers that were in the attic when we moved here?"

She nods. "Some were dated in the 1800's. I should have kept those."

"I wish you had. I'd like to read them, but I'm glad you didn't have them in the attic. If they had been up there today, they would have caught on fire."

She removes her hands from the bucket, takes a clean dishcloth from a drawer, and lightly pats her palms against it. "I'd better try again. I burned that pan of tenderloin. We need something to eat. It's been a busy morning."

"Keep your hands in the water. We can eat leftovers from last night. Nancy can fry the tenderloin for supper. I'll come in later and heat something for us to eat. Now, I need to go back and tend to that sausage before the dog gets in the smokehouse and has herself a snack."

It is over two weeks before Ollie's hand and arm heals enough to work on repainting, and hanging wallpaper in the kitchen. Through the years, she has frequently reminded the girls not to step away and leave a skillet of grease unattended. Therefore, she is anxious to start on the room and remove the traces of her own negligence, but instead of criticism, when the girls see her hands, they look as if they could cry.

That night, as the family sits at the table in front of fried tenderloin, mashed potatoes, and gravy, Roy looks over at the bare window. "Ollie, before you and the girls paper this room, why don't we see if Jarrell will help us build some real kitchen cabinets out of knotty pine? Then we can get rid of that old curtain hanging in front of the sink."

"Yes." Nancy nods. "That old thing looks awful and it doesn't keep the dust off the pots and pans."

Dipping her blistered hands into a bowl of ice water, Ollie follows his gaze to the curtain covered sink cabinet. "I would like that, if it doesn't cost too much."

"Next week, I'm going away to find work, but you can ask Jarrell what it will cost. Since it's inside work, maybe he can do it this winter when he can't get out doing other carpenter work. I could build you something that would hold the pans, but I'm not a finish carpenter, and I don't have the tools to make pretty cabinets."

Jarrell builds Ollie new kitchen cabinets, and replaces the old single sink with a double one that is white and shining. The new sink and cabinets make the old house look more modern— especially with fresh paint and new wallpaper in the kitchen.

Chapter 26
Tornado

Roy is gone most of the fall and winter. When he comes home, he applies again for the government loan program, hoping he will not have to mortgage the farm to get money to finance a dairy.

Roy drives the truck up close to the back door, and time after time climbs the steps with his arms full of groceries. He does not say a word, just places the bags onto the cabinet and goes back for more. After the last armload, he gets in the truck and drives it to the shed.

Ollie recognizes his disappointed look. Not wanting to ask questions in front of the children, she meets him under the walnut tree as he walks toward the house. "Roy, what happened at town? I can tell you're upset about something."

He shakes his head and his frown deepens. "You have to keep this to yourself. I mean strictly to yourself. My friend would get fired if it gets out that he gave me this information."

She gives him an angry look. "Who do you think I'm gonna tell? I rarely get off this farm."

"You can't tell your mama or your sisters."

She lets out her breath in a huff. "What is this big secret?"

"We're not getting the Production Credit loan. I have an old friend that works there. Somehow, he found out that one man blackballed my name."

"No! Roy, I thought surely we'd get it this time. Did he tell you who did it?"

Roy nods. "Yep, the very man we thought would help us."

Ollie looks up at him. "We haven't received a rejection letter yet. Maybe he's mistaken."

"He wouldn't have said anything if he wasn't sure." Roy shakes his head. "It wouldn't bother me half as much if I'd been denied by a stranger, but that man knows me well enough to know I'd do everything within my power to repay that loan. I considered him a friend."

Ollie sits on a bench under the shade of the walnut tree, and pats the wood beside her. "Sit down, Roy."

Sitting, he leans forward, elbows on his knees. "I don't know what to do now. I can't understand why he would deny my loan. Do you think it's because of my age? I may be fifty years old, but I'm still healthy. Could it be because our only boy will graduate soon, leaving us with four girls to help with the work?"

"If he knows anything about our family, that shouldn't be the cause—our girls are *workers*. They can do any of the work in a dairy except lift heavy feed sacks. I think it's because he has a dairy. He doesn't want more local competition."

"Maybe so, but there's not a thing I can do to defend myself. I'm not supposed to know who rejected the application, and I would surely get a friend fired if I say anything."

"Don't let it get you down. God works in mysterious ways. This wasn't meant to be."

Roy frowns. "Mysterious ways? Do you think He's purposely keeping me away from my family year after year?"

She shakes her head. "No! Nature and the droughts are

responsible for our crop failures."

Without speaking, he sits breaking a small stick into tiny pieces, and letting them fall.

"Roy, you need to disk and seed the pastures to replace what that fire burned. After you get some good grass growing, apply for a bank loan. Ben Clark at the Quitman Bank knows you, and he knows how we've worked through the years. If we can get the building up on our own, I'm sure he'll loan the rest of what you need, and use the cattle and equipment as collateral."

"I can do rough carpenter work, but I'm not a plumber, electrician, framer, welder, or mason. I can't build a dairy barn without paying high wages for skilled workmen."

"Jarrell can do all of that. Get him to show you how."

"Ollie, if it was that easy, everyone would be building their own houses and other structures. Our building has to pass inspection for a Grade 'A' milk barn. It can't be thrown together like a hay shed. Maybe, Jarrell can help me lay out the foundation. Then after John and I get that poured, we can get a truck to bring out the cement for the floor on a Saturday so Jarrell can help us get it smooth. I'll have to hire someone to lay the concrete blocks. It might fall down in the first strong wind if I tried to do it myself."

"All right. It may take us a year or more, but we'll do what we can as we have money to do it."

Roy shakes his head and rubs his neck. "I don't know, Ollie. I just don't know. We may be jumping into something way over our heads."

"No we're not. I know we can do it."

He stands, arches his back to stretch and ease tense muscles.

"I've got to get that tractor and disk going, and plant grass seed. If Jarrell comes out this weekend, I'll ask him to help measure and show me what to do to start on the foundation."

"School will be out next week. John and Nancy can help dig out the trenches for the concrete."

He sighs and shakes his head. "There's a lot to do."

"Oh, Roy, I meant to tell you, the insurance man stopped by while you were gone. He said tell you that we need to think about getting more coverage on the house and barn. We haven't increased it since the original mortgage. He said, at today's prices, the two thousand dollar coverage we have wouldn't build a barn one quarter the size of ours, and it wouldn't even start to build back a house."

He spits tobacco and turns to look at her. "We can't afford to pay for what we have. Insurance is merely a way to swindle poor people like us." Striding fast, he goes to the tractor shed.

Ollie stands watching and listening as the John Deere tractor starts loudly, and—with a steady popping rhythm—backs out of the small red barn and starts toward the pasture. She smiles, touches the hearing aid fastened inside the front of her dress, and remembers when she could not hear a noise that loud.

Monday morning, Roy listens to the weather report on the radio: heavy rain, thunderstorms, and possible tornadoes through the central part of the state by noon. "It sounds like those grass seed are gonna get watered. I hope it doesn't wash them away."

"Roy, I wish we'd kept the kids home from school. Today and tomorrow are not much more than play-days. They've already taken semester tests. Do you think you should go get them so they'll be close to the storm cellar?"

"Ollie, if we kept them home for every storm forecast, they'd never graduate. They'll be inside."

"Inside, but the school doesn't have a tornado shelter, and I don't like the feel of the air and those black clouds rolling in."

"You worry too much. Do I have time to give that sick cow some fresh water before you get the food on the table?"

"If you hurry." She looks out the window. "You may get wet."

Ollie takes a pan of cornbread from the oven, pours strong sweet tea over ice, and scoops fried potatoes from sizzling grease.

Roy comes in the back door. "We need to eat fast. That storm's rolling in, and the sky has a green tint like it has hail in the clouds." He reaches for a bowl of beans, serves himself, and adds a helping to Ollie's plate.

Ollie goes to the living room to look out at the clouds before sitting down to eat. "I wish you had gone to get the kids."

They gulp their food like starving children. Ollie places leftovers in the warm oven while Roy piles dirty dishes in the sink. Ollie grabs a jacket from a hook on the porch and slips it on while she runs to get her purse and a bag containing insurance papers and other vital information she might need if a tornado hits the house.

The wind howls, shaking windows and rattling doors. Roy holds the cellar door open as Ollie pulls hard on the kitchen door, making sure it fastens. Trixie, their half-Britney Spaniel, half-Collie looks up at Roy and whines.

"Go to the barn, Trixie."

The dog shivers, and turns her head to the side with a pleading look.

"Roy, let her in the cellar with us. She's not wet, and we've got plenty of room without the kids. I don't really believe that old saying about dogs drawing lightning."

He snaps his fingers and points at the steps. Trixie darts in front of Ollie and lies down under the potato bench. Rain beats on the cellar door as Roy hooks the latch. He pushes on the door covering the small window. The rain is so dense that they can barely see the orchard. Almost as quick as it starts, the rain stops. Trixie whines, and lays her head between her paws.

They hear the roar in the distance. Roy yanks the small door closed, and pushes down on the hook to secure it.

Ollie puts her hands to her face. "Oh, Lord, protect the children and our home." The roar continues until it sounds like a train going over the top of them. Then it fades into nothing but soft rainfall.

"Oh, Roy, what if our house is gone?"

He walks up the steps, unlatches the door, and pushes it open. The breath goes out of him in a quick wheeze. "The barn's down."

"Oh, Lord, please not the house."

Roy's voice quivers. "I'm afraid to look." Slowly, he advances up one more step, turns his head and looks over the cellar door. "It's there! His words come faster. "The house is standing. The truck and tractor barn is still there."

Stepping up behind him, Ollie barely hears him whisper, "Our big barn is gone, and most of the fruit trees are broke off."

"I've loved that old house since I was a kid, but I've never been so proud to see it. I just want to run and hug it."

"I wish I'd listened to you about getting more insurance."

Trixie stands beside Ollie, whimpering. "Roy, this dog

sensed that storm was coming. She always goes to the barn to get out of the rain, and she knows we don't let her in the cellar, but today she stood begging to go with us."

Ollie runs her hand over Trixie's head. "Girl, I'm glad you weren't in the barn."

Roy takes Ollie's hand so she will not trip and fall over limbs and debris in the yard. They walk around the house, looking at the roof. "Several shingles are gone. I can replace those. The pecan trees have a few broken limbs, nothing serious there."

"Do you think we'll have to cut the silver leaf maple? It's leaning."

"I'll trim it. Maybe it'll straighten on its own."

"Look at the smokehouse, Roy. The wind pushed it off the corner stones."

"That'll be easy to fix, and we can replace that missing tin from the tractor shed." His voice drops again to a whisper. "The big barn is a total loss. We can never rebuild a barn like that." He jerks his hand loose from hers. "I better go check on that sick cow. She's probably dead."

"Roy! The kids! Get in the truck and go check on them."

"The storm didn't go that way." He points. "Do you see the path? It went northeast."

She grabs his hand as they walk through the limbs toward the mangled barn wreckage.

"Ollie, look at that cow. She's calmly laying there chewing her cud."

"How are we gonna get her out of all that mess?"

"I'll drag the boards around and lead her to the pasture."

"You could put her in one of those stalls on the north side of the tractor shed."

"I've got tools over there. She's better now, and will be fine in the pasture. I'm gonna need every inch of dry space to store harness and things we salvage from this wreckage. "

"Do you think we should get in the truck and go see about the other cattle?"

"They'll be coming up in a couple of hours, or more. If they don't, then I'll go looking, but I don't want to drive through the pasture now. We might run over a board with a nail in it. Within the next few days, John and I will go through with the wagon and pick up all the boards we can find."

"Is the wagon all right?"

"It looks like the storm lifted that side of the barn over the wagon. It's scooted a little from where it was, but its fine."

Ollie turns her head, looking from left to right. "I hardly know where to start."

"Let's go to the house and get a sweet snack before we do anything. My legs are awfully weak and shaky."

"I feel like a limp dishrag myself. I made some fried chocolate pies this morning. With that storm coming in, I forgot about them. They'll be good with a cup of coffee."

Roy and Ollie are sifting through the rubble when the kids get home from school. John runs from side to side, looking at the broken boards and rubble. Nancy stands biting her lip, her eyes full and shining.

Patty exclaims, "We'll never again get to jump from the loft into a manger of hay or swim in the oat bin."

Ollie rubs her low back, and calls to the older girls, "Nancy, you and Patty, take the twins to the house. They might get on a nail out here. After you change clothes, you can gather shingles from the yard and put them in a tub. Then go to the orchard and drag all the loose limbs into a pile where we can burn them."

Roy lifts a wide board onto a stack beside the fence before speaking. "John, I want you to drive over and notify the insurance man about the tornado. Tell him I want him to come over and write a claim. When you get back, change into work clothes and come help me sort through this."

The tornado has cut a wide swath through the community. More than a mile away, a neighbor finds tin from Roy and Ollie's big barn. They hear reports of numerous damages to roofs and outbuildings, and learn that the home of Mr. Tom Spears was destroyed during the storm. Mr. Spears and his wife were in Marshall picking strawberries.

Roy, Ollie, and John separate boards and tin. All tin is stacked. Planks damaged too much for reuse are thrown into a pile for burning. Boards that have salvage value are stacked for Nancy and Patty to knock out the nails.

Roy looks at the burn pile and calls out, "Save all of the two-by-fours. We'll need a lot of small pieces when building the new barn. What we don't use, we'll cut into firewood."

Weeks pass while the family labors to tend crops, clean up after the storm, and prepare to build a new barn. Pete McGinty and Doy Cardin, Roy and Ollie's neighbors from Happy Valley, show up with tools and volunteer a day of their time toward rebuilding the barn.

Before winter, it is constructed, but is only about one quarter the size of the old one.

After nailing down the last boards, Roy steps back to look. "I'm about to get too old to toss hay into a high loft like that of our old barn. We can stack square bales in this one and easily drag them over to the feed trough, but I sure miss those big corn and oat storage bins, my tack room, that big manger with troughs on both sides, and the extra stalls for milking, or for holding sick animals."

Ollie looks up at his face, recognizing the pain he feels. "It's sort of like losing the best neighbor you ever had, and having someone you don't even like move in beside you."

He grins. "Yep, but we'll get along."

Chapter 27
Getting Ready

The children leave the table one at a time. Roy and Ollie sit to talk.

"Roy, I need to go to town soon. I have to make school dresses for four girls. When Ann was Nancy's age, she was making her own clothes, but Nancy's never had much interest in sewing. She would sit and read all day long if I'd let her."

"Why not, if she's got her work done?"

"She's reading those old romance magazines that Syble brought up here, and she doesn't always have her work done. Today, I caught her standing behind a door reading instead of sweeping the bedrooms like I told her to do."

"I'd rather talk about having a well drilled, instead of romance magazines and sweeping."

"What about a well?"

"If we still plan on starting a dairy, we'll need to have another one drilled. The one we have won't begin to furnish enough water for a dairy. Another thing required for a Grade 'A' dairy is indoor plumbing with a bathroom and septic tank."

"We need that anyway, but the question is—how to pay for it all?"

"The well will cost the most. This time I want it drilled twice as deep as we think we'll need. The last time, that guy talked us out of going deeper when he hit hard rock, and that well is not nearly deep enough to supply a dairy with water."

"What do you think one will cost?"

"We have enough left from the sale of those cattle. John and I can dig the septic tank and the lines for it. Jarrell will show me how to lay tiles for the drain-lines and build a tank out of concrete blocks. He said it doesn't cost a lot to put in a nice bathroom if you do the work yourself."

"When are we gonna start on it?"

"I'd like to have the well drilled right away, while the yard is dry. Those big trucks and drilling equipment would make awful ruts in the yard if we wait until the rainy season."

"You're right about that."

"I'll go talk to the well diggers tomorrow and set up a time. As for the septic tank and lines, John and I will dig those when I come home from Kansas City. That will be easier after we have rain to soften the ground."

"You've never built a septic tank and run drain lines before. Are you sure you and John can do that by yourselves?"

He grins. "How hard can it be to dig a hole and a ditch?"

"There is more to it than that."

"Jarrell explained how he does it. It sounds simple. I'll ask him to look it over before we cover it with dirt."

Within a week, the well diggers are set up halfway between the house and the future location of the milk barn. The agreement is for a certain amount per foot, whether they are digging in soft ground or hard rock. The work goes fast for the first day. The second, they are in soft rock. At two hundred feet, they tell Roy he will have plenty of water.

"I had one well drilled and built a washroom over it with a thick concrete floor. It was supposed to furnish plenty of water, but it does not. This one will have a well house over it, and I'll need enough water for a Grade 'A' dairy. Drill another two hundred feet, and then we'll talk."

"Man, you've got about one hundred eighty feet of water now."

"I want three hundred eighty feet."

They keep trying to talk him into letting them stop. "Mr. Glenn, if you don't have enough water, we'll come back and drill another for free."

Roy insists they continue. "Mister, cows won't wait on you to drill another well if this one doesn't provide enough water. I have to *know* it won't fail. Keep drilling."

After Roy pays and releases the drillers, he and John start digging a ditch for the water pipes running to the house. The ground is hard, and walnut tree roots are in the path. It takes a long time to complete the job.

John straightens to wipe sweat from his face. "Daddy, our yard is gonna look like a plowed field by the time we get water lines to the house, water lines to the milk barn, and septic lines running away from the house."

"We may wait on the lines to the new barn. If we can afford it, I'd like to hire those men north of the Cadron to do the foundation and barn floor. With their backhoe, they can dig that water line pretty quick."

Running a bucket of water from the faucet beside the new well pump, Ollie pushes back her bonnet. "Roy, I thought we were gonna dig the foundation, have a cement truck deliver the cement, and get Jarrell to help us do the floor."

"We! Where's your shovel? That floor has to be just right so it'll drain. Otherwise, we'll be sloshing in water all the time we're in there. I'll do better working in Kansas City and paying somebody that knows what they're doing."

"The other part of '*we*' has been washing your dirty clothes and cooking your dinner." Ollie grabs the bucket of water and walks toward the house."

Chapter 28
Grade 'A' Dairy

Morene and Jarrell are saving money to build a house. They offer to loan money for the dairy barn at the same interest rate that the bank is paying them. Roy and Ollie want to avoid mortgaging the farm, so they make the agreement.

Ann has worked in Washington D.C., for over two years, and saved her money. She loans most of it to Roy and Ollie at no interest, telling them they can repay it when times are better.

John graduates from high school in May 1958. He wants to go to Little Rock and earn money for college, but Roy needs his help to build the dairy barn. Jarrell helps on his days off, giving instructions and showing Roy and John, what they need to do. What they cannot do, Roy hires skilled workmen to accomplish.

Ann worked for the Department of the Navy when she first went to Washington DC in 1955, but soon transferred to the Department of the Air Force. She was selected to work on a special project for the State Department and was honored with a request to go to the Geneva Conference as a stenographer. She is in Switzerland for almost three months. Ollie and Roy are proud of her accomplishments, but they are so busy trying to succeed with the dairy that they have very little time to brag.

The barn is complete in the fall. Roy purchases a stainless steel milk tank and some equipment from a man who is retiring from the dairy business, and buys a herd of dairy cows from Mr. Marshall Adams, who is also retiring.

He hires a man with a commercial cattle truck to haul the cows. With the large truck and trailer following their pickup, Ollie begs Roy to stop on the way home, pull the man over, and make sure the cows are all right, but he is in a hurry. "Ollie, they're fine. It may be midnight before we get these cows milked. Mr. Adams said we'll probably have trouble with them until they get used to us and the barn, and until they establish a social order of entering the barn."

"I don't care how late it is. I have a bad feeling that something's wrong."

"Ollie, I'm not gonna stop. That trailer's made for hauling cattle."

"But you've got an awful lot of cows crammed in there. If one gets down, she won't be able to get up."

When the cattle are unloaded, Ollie and Roy discover one little Jersey's hoof caught in a hole next to a wheel. The truck's movement has worn the hide off the side of her leg. They pry her loose and release her into the orchard where Ollie will doctor, feed, water, and milk her until her foot and leg heals.

The first week of work in the dairy is one long nightmare. Mr. Adams was right: the cows are afraid of the family, the new barn, the milking machines, and even the feed buckets. With the help of a long pole, Roy forces each cow into the barn. Every cow kicks at the person washing her bag and putting on the milking machine, and then kicks at the machine.

Nancy is afraid of the kicking animals, her jumping only make the cows more nervous.

Roy, tired and annoyed at everything that slows the milking

process, shouts, "Nancy, go to the house and cook supper. Tell your mother to come out here. She's not afraid of cows."

The first night, the vacuum on the milking machines does not work properly. They take the equipment apart and reconnect it numerous times before it will pump milk through the lines. It is after eleven before the process is complete. Now, Roy and Ollie must take the equipment apart again, and wash it and the pipelines with disinfectant. Afterward, they have to wash all the floors, except the feed room.

The ritual starts over the next morning at four. It is more than a week before the cows calm down and voluntarily enter the barn to eat the sweet feed and release their milk. It is equally as long before Roy, Ollie, and the children learn how to put the equipment together without vacuum leaks.

Nancy makes cornbread and cooks supper without any trouble. Her first attempt at breakfast is not so good. Roy taps the bread against his plate, pushes it aside, takes a bite of bacon, and dips gravy over his eggs. "Nancy, be careful at tossing these biscuits out the door. If Trixie tries to catch one, it might knock her teeth out."

Ollie frowns at him. "Roy, she's just a kid. She never needed to make biscuits before. They take practice."

"The rest is all right, but I'm almost too tired to eat." He props an elbow on the table and leans his cheek against a fist. "If I thought we'd have this much trouble for more than a few days, I'd give up and sell out, right now."

"People told you, it'll take a week to get problems worked out."

"I'm tired too." Ollie looks at the clock. "Kids, you're going to miss the bus if you don't hurry."

Calling bye, the kids rush out the door. For several minutes, the house is silent except for the ticking of the clock. "Do you want to rest while I wash the breakfast dishes?"

"No. If I close my eyes, I wouldn't want to get up. I'll go hose down the milking room and the ramp. We can wash the equipment when you come out."

"It won't take me long in here. Nancy didn't leave a big mess."

"I've got to go to the feed mill after we get the barn and pipelines washed. After this load, I think I'll have them deliver feed for a while—at least until we get organized. Their truck can haul more than my pickup can. Do you want to go with me today?"

"Not this time. I have things here that I need to do, but we need another bottle of peroxide and a jar of salve to put on that cow's leg. You can get those at the feed store."

Most days, Roy takes an hour-long nap while Ollie is washing dishes from the noon meal, but there is always something to do when the weather allows. He disks and plants fields of winter wheat and rye for grazing during the cold months; manure must be scooped from the cow lot every day; and Grade 'A' rules require that the dairy barn, inside and out, is washed with disinfectant and repainted often to prevent mold and mildew.

John goes to Little Rock and gets a job to earn money for college. He stays with Syble and JB, her husband. John rides to work with JB until he earns enough to buy himself a car.

After a few weeks, the family works out a routine concerning work in the dairy. Roy and Nancy get up at four and do the morning milking. Nancy is still afraid of several cows—ones she calls kickers. Roy tends to those while she fills the feed troughs. Roy and Ollie clean the barn and equipment after the children leave for school. In the afternoon, Patty and Ollie help milk and clean the barn and equipment while Nancy cooks supper, washes dishes, and looks after the twins.

When Ollie is not feeling well, Nancy has to help in the afternoon—she hates that shift. Not because she minds the work, but because she fears someone besides the family will come to the farm and see her in the faded jeans, old flannel shirt, knee-high rubber boots, and a headscarf that protects her long hair from the swish of a cow's dirty tail.

Patty, a typical tomboy, does not care who sees her in work clothes. She will rush into the lot from the exit door, hop over the fence her long brown ponytail swinging from side to side as she darts around driving the cattle into the barn, and the meanest kickers do not intimidate her.

After several days, the cows work out an order of entering the barn, and calmly line up waiting for someone to pull the rope and open the door. Only a few of the most nervous linger outside.

It does not take long for rats to discover the room full of sweet feed—and not long for the girls to discover the rats. The long-tailed rodents are daring. When someone enters the room, they stand upright, showing long yellow teeth, and hiss a warning.

When Patty first sees them, she backs out the door. "Daddy, there's rats in the feed and they're not afraid."

"Beat your hand on the bottom of that bucket and keep walking toward them. They'll disappear. I'll get some traps and poison tomorrow, but we'll have to be careful. We can't use poison in the feed room. If any of it got into the feed, it would kill a cow."

"Let me get the BB-gun and shoot them."

"No, Sis. You can't shoot inside a block building. One of those BB's could ricochet off the wall and hit you. I'm sure every dairyman has had this problem. I'll find out how others have handled it."

Patty walks through the feed room door, slams the palm of her hand against the bottom of the metal bucket, and the rats disappear. "You were right, Daddy. One loud bang on that bucket and they disappeared like I'd waved a magic wand over them."

Ollie and Roy are extremely careful to measure disinfectant, wash the cow's bag before attaching the milking machines, and wash the milk lines and equipment. They are greatly puzzled when they get a high bacteria count on a tank of milk, and a Grade 'B' classification. Grade 'B' milk brings a much lower price.

Roy and Ollie ask Mr. Adams what could cause the high count.

"It might be mastitis. When is the last time you checked your cows?"

"I run those tests," Ollie answers. "It's been a while, but we haven't had any cows showing signs of soreness or infection."

Mr. Adams takes off his hat and frowns. "They won't always show signs until it gets bad." He shakes his head. "I know how it hurts to get a tank of milk knocked down a grade. Usually it's two tanks, because you've run infected milk into the second before you find the problem. It's cheaper to buy the cards and check your cows often."

That evening they check every cow, and find one showing infection.   They treat the infection, milk her by hand, and dispose of her milk until she is well.

Roy frowns, and props his elbow on one of the stanchions. "Like everything else, there's always something to take our money—boll weevils in the cotton, cut worms in the corn, drought, and now infection in a cow."

"I guess I'll have to check them every week."

Milking is not bad on nice days, but on stormy days, when lightning flashes about, it is frightening to be standing on a damp concrete floor lifting a milking machine from a bucket of disinfectant to put on a wet cow that is lashing out with her rain soaked tail. In freezing rain and snow, that long whip the cow keeps popping is often filled with sharp icicles.

Chapter 29
Time

Roy insists on lights out by nine, but Nancy complains that she does not have enough time to do her homework after she cooks supper in the evening.

"You have a couple of hours after supper. That should be enough. Turn that TV off and you can study."

"Daddy, I hardly ever watch TV, except on the weekend. I have five classes where I have to do homework. Can't I stay up until I finish it?"

"You only get seven hours of sleep if you go to bed at nine. Do it on the school bus or at lunch. You'll get sick if you don't get enough sleep."

Nancy comes rushing in one day after school, and drops her books on the desk, her lips drawn tight around clenched teeth. "I hate my last period teacher."

Ollie looks up from her mending. "You're not supposed to hate."

Nancy's frown grows deeper.

"What did she do to make you so furious?"

"She assigned me to write 'I will not be late for class' five thousand times. We're having semester tests this week, and I have a book report to write."

Ollie grins. "Why were you late for class?"

"It's not funny." Nancy turns and treks toward the bedroom

to change out of her school clothes.

Ollie is putting her boots on when Nancy comes out of the room she shares with Patty. "I'm going to help set up the milk barn. Before I do, tell me why you were late for class?"

"My Home Economics Class, on the south side of the school, is the period before that—that woman's class. I have to go from the south side of the campus to the gym on the north side. Her class is upstairs in the gym. I hurried as much as I could. After passing the main building, I caught up with, and walked the rest of the way with her—right into the room and was about to sit down when she yelled, 'Everybody that's not in their seat has to write a theme.' I tried to explain after class, but with her nose in the air, she blinked and hatefully said, 'You weren't in your seat.'"

"Did you stop to talk to anyone?"

"No. I even ran until I caught up with her. I have to walk that every day, and I barely make it into my seat before she stomps into the room. Mother, I don't have time to write a theme. I was already worrying about how I was going to study for tests and get my book report."

"Turn it in next week."

"If it's late, I'll have to write it ten thousand times."

"My, she is a little rough."

"A little! Everyone I know hates her. She whipped Linda with a thick board, and I've never known of Linda to get in trouble before."

"I guess you'll have to write it, and hurry a little more from now on."

At supper, Nancy asks her dad if she can stay up later to study.

"No, do the best you can, but you'll have to get in bed by nine."

"That's not fair. Most parents would be glad if their kids wanted to do homework."

"You make good enough grades."

"I'd make all 'A's if I had time to study and didn't have to get up at four every morning to milk cows."

Patty has learned to ride Ann and John's old bike. John never rides it anymore, but he helps Patty keep the tires patched. Robbie and Bobbie want a bicycle, but do not have money to buy one.

"Learn to ride John's." Patty holds the bike and motions to Robbie. Within a short time, she is wobbling it around the yard.

"Bobbie, it's your turn." Patty holds the bike steady while Bobbie gets going. She snakes around the most level part of the yard until Patty grabs her.

"See, both of you did it. You can ride this bike, even if it is a little too tall. When I first started riding, I would stand one foot on that step in front of the chimney and push off."

Ollie watches Patty helping them, but suddenly feels afraid. "Girls, get off that bicycle until you're a little bigger. We can't afford any more broken arms."

The girls park the bike, but at every chance they get, they try again—usually when Ollie is busy in the kitchen. Soon they can ride around the yard without wobbling.

Ollie has noticed them several times, but Roy tells her to let them be. After school, she watches Bobbie ride the bike down the lane toward the county road, turn, and ride back toward the yard. She pedals hard, but the hill is too much for her, and she falls. Leaving the bike lay, Bobbie gets up and grabs her arm, trying to straighten it.

From the front door, Ollie can see the strange angle of Bobbie's arm. It is broken. "Patty! Run to the field and get your daddy. Bobbie's broke her arm."

Ollie grabs a towel, wets it in cold water, and meets Bobbie as she comes to the porch, gasping for breath, tears streaming down her face. "I couldn't get it straight."

"I see that. Sit down in this chair and let me wrap a cold towel around your arm. Patty's gone to get Roy to take you to Conway."

Bobbie shivers, pales, and leans her head against Ollie, her breath coming in little puffs as Ollie wraps the cloth around her arm.

"Robbie, go get one of those white flour sacks from the kitchen. I need to make a sling for this arm."

Robbie hands her the cloth. "Now, go get that bicycle out of the road, so Roy won't run over it—although that might be the best thing that could happen to you kids."

Robbie brings the bike to the house and parks it under the walnut tree.

Roy drives to the barn on the tractor, Patty hanging on behind him. Long strides bring him to the house quickly. "Let me wash my face and arms, and put on a clean shirt. Nancy, get yourself ready and go with me. She might need you to help."

Nancy is ready by the time Roy has changed his clothes.

"Ollie, it could be dark before we get home. You and Patty may need to start the milking."

Half of the cows have come through the barn by the time

Roy drives up to the house. He changes into work clothes, parks the truck in the shed, and walks to the barn. "Both bones were broke. The doctor had to put her to sleep to set it. She was terrified and struggled against the ether, gasping for breath. I was afraid they were gonna give her too much. Nancy was, too. She looked as scared as I felt."

"I knew both bones were broken. It was hanging almost straight down before she grabbed it. Did the ether make her sick?"

"Not yet. She's still sleeping. Nancy said she'd put her to bed and keep an eye on her."

"Did Nancy complain that she wouldn't have time to get her homework?"

"No. She didn't say a word about it. I'm sure she'll do fine."

Ollie cannot hear after she takes her hearing aid off at night, but she gets up once or twice every night and goes to the children's bedrooms to make sure they are all right.

Nancy and Patty's bedroom is on the west side of the kitchen. Light from the bedroom windows is only visible from outside the house and from the living room. Nancy pushes a rug against the bottom of the door to stop light from shining underneath; the top and sides fit tight preventing light from shining around them. If Roy gets up to go to the bathroom, he cannot tell Nancy is studying unless he goes into the living room, but Ollie knows.

Ollie has seen Patty's face turned toward the wall, a quilt pulled over her head. Patty would never complain. Nancy gets away with studying late for a few months, but one night before six-week tests, she stays up until one o'clock. The next morning, Roy calls her at three instead of four. She knows better than to go back to bed; she heard the screen door slam as he left for the barn. Nancy gets dressed and goes to help milk.

That afternoon, Ollie sees her taking aspirin. "Do you have a headache?"

"Yes, I had some hard tests today and stayed up to study, then Daddy woke me at three to go milk. I think he did it on purpose."

"You need to try harder to get in bed on time."

When the grade reports come, Nancy looks at hers and tosses it on the desk with a disgusted look. "I shouldn't have tried to take so many subjects with no study hall."

Ollie stares at her. "Your grades are good enough."

"Good enough for you, but not even close for a scholarship." Nancy shakes her head and walks toward the kitchen with a frown. "I would like to go to college, but I'll never have a scholarship, I don't have any money, and I'm sure not gonna stay here and try to go like Ann did with Daddy making me turn the lights out at nine."

"You might do like Morene and decide to get married."

"Married! You won't even let me date."

"You're only fifteen."

"You started me to school a year early, and expect me to compete with older kids, but you won't let me go places and do things like the other girls in my class."

"You've got plenty of time."

"Maybe, but I'm sure not having any fun."

The day is warm with a soft breeze that carries the scent of fresh-cut hay. Roses, zinnias, daisies, and marigolds bloom in various flowerbeds around the yard. Fat from grazing the green hillsides, black and white dairy cows, lift their heads as Roy turns the John Deere tractor near the pasture fence.

Ollie and her mama sit on the front porch. Ollie ties a knot in her thread and clips it before pinning the needle into the cloth.

"You and Roy have a nice herd of cattle, and everything around here looks so clean and well-kept. Ma and Pa would be proud if they could see the farm now."

Letting her eyes wander across the hills Ollie smiles. "It has to be clean for a Grade 'A' dairy. We have to paint the milk barn often, and shovel out the lot every day, but Roy and I both like things to look nice."

"You deserve a nice place. You've worked hard for it. With health problems, drought year after year, fire, a tornado and eight children—I don't know how you did it."

"We've had some rough years." Ollie sighs and looks toward the meadow where Roy is mowing. "The fifties were almost as bad as the thirties for us. Although, during the Great Depression, it was hard to find a job anywhere in the country. At least during the dry weather of this decade, Roy was able to find work in Kansas City. Thank God, things are going better for us now."

Ollie turns to look at her mama, thin and fragile with age. "Mama, I'm so glad you came to visit. I want you to do this more often. The years have gone fast. It's hard to believe we've lived on this farm for thirteen years."

"I love visiting here. It's coming home. You've made a lot of changes, but every time I come down that road, I can almost see Ma and Pa sitting here on this porch in their rockers, smiling and waiting for me to run up the steps." Mama laughs. "Of course, now I can only run in my mind."

From ceiling to floor, Ollie studies the wide porch. "When the weather was nice, they were always waiting here on the porch. Those are the first memories that come to me about Grandma and Grandpa—that and Grandma telling me about guardian angels. I've called on my angels many times through the years."

"Tell me about the children. Did Morene and Jarrell ever get their house finished?"

"Yes, they have a nice brick home, and Jarrell's building houses to sell. Morene helps when he gets down to painting and finishing the inside. Syble and JB have a nice home, but they're looking for a larger one now that they have two children. Syble works in the Credit Department for the big Sears store in Little Rock. Ann writes that she's doing well, and is considering moving to California to work for the Air Force. John plans to start college this fall. He's decided he wants to be a pharmacist. Nancy will be a senior in the coming school year. She wants to go to college, but hasn't decided on a major. She is my argumentative teenager. The older kids went through it, but Nancy always wants to *go* somewhere. Roy and I work hard. We can't run around at night taking these kids to ballgames and school programs."

"Let her go with friends. Eldridge's girl, Linda, was in all kinds of doings at school. Her friends picked her up and brought her home when Eldridge couldn't."

"I don't intend to let these girls run around at night with boys."

"Ollie, you have a nice family, but there comes a time to let young birds fly. I let you go to church, school and community functions."

"Things are different these days."

For several minutes, both women are silent. "Mama, as a child I believed guardian angels watched over me and warned me of dangers. As an adult I've had several things happen that I'm sure were warnings. The trouble is, I worry, and I'm cautious—too cautious, Roy says, but when I keep the children home, I know they're safe."

Mama, face creased with worry, looks intently at her daughter. "Ollie, a bird in a cage is safe, but is it happy?"

Ignoring Mama's question, Ollie stares at the hillside. "I'm proud of my children. I hate they've had to work so hard, but it seemed the only way to survive. Roy and I started out dreaming of a farm like this with lots of healthy children, but my dream won't be complete until all of them are grown and settled into respectable lives."

Eight Souls

Years of raising children, always hoping to win
A godly record, eight souls free from sin.
She made us learn, she made our beds,
She sewed our clothes and baked our breads.

Up before dawn, last to say it's done,
Her hands were busy past set of sun.
Worried, as she touched a fevered brow,
Eight survived; only God knows how.

Tools in hand, at her side a baby,
Working like a man, definitely a lady.
No time to cultivate friendships of her own,
With positive will, she boldly pushed on.

When the gates open, her prayer is mine—
Eight souls in heaven will someday shine.
Please Lord, not only eight souls for Thee!
We're gathering in more for heaven to see.

Dear Lord, as children bowed on our knees,
Look favorably on us and answer our pleas.
Stretch out mercy, forgiveness, love and grace,
And prepare in heaven each grandchild a place.

Nancy Glenn Powell

That Farmer's Eyes

On spring days when silver curtains came drenching
with excited winds boldly twisting and wrenching
to pull budding life from each slumbering limb,
he whittled hickory whistles under a wet hat brim.

As summer sun warmed the earth, crops were laid-by,
welcome shade buzzed with June bug and horsefly;
with a sea grass rope, he hung a swing in the walnut tree,
and there elated children soared, careless and free.

When autumn painted color to take your breath away
and lonesome geese weaved through clouds of gray,
he trekked dark woodlands hunting squirrels for stew,
and thundering wing coveys that huddled then flew.

While snow fluffed meadows like a giant feather bed
and the potbelly stove glowed orange and red,
he mended old harness or a worn-out farm tool,
conservation, in all things, is the farmers rule.

He had firm looks of discipline, hands always strong,
gentle arms to hold babies, a clear voice for song,
quick jokes to chase despair when we wanted to cry,
and faith for pledged rainbows to clear a dark sky.

More than the color of seasonal skies,
memories bring love from that farmer's eyes.

Nancy Glenn Powell

- Title: Dark Secrets
- Author: Nancy Powell
- Publisher: TotalRecall Publications, Inc.
- Format: HARDCOVER, 6.14" x 9.21"
- Number of pages in the finished book: 288
- 13-digit ISBN: 978-1-59095-585-7
- Month and day of publication: Jan. 2, 2013
- Distribution arrangements: Ingram, Baker Taylor, Amazon.com, Barnes and Noble, etc.

Dark Secrets is the first book in a series based on the life of a farm girl born in 1908 when the United States was becoming a world leader, and farm families made up over half of the population. Conditions for the Negro had worsened, women rallied for the right to vote, and social change in music, dance, and fashion filtered into rural areas. This book shows prejudice faced by Negroes, Gypsies, Jews, and women of that era.

The book begins with Ollie trying to get home after receiving a head injury in an attack by two boys—the same boys that she thinks raped her friend and murdered a girl in a nearby community. She remains in a coma for five days, recalling vivid events of her first fifteen years.

Ollie is competitive and contends with schoolmates, and her older brother and sister, but is eager to help with younger siblings. With a gift for premonition and healing, her ambition is to be a nurse, but when her papa has to pay a promissory note signed for a friend, he cannot afford to send her away to school. With no money for schooling, she worries about becoming a spinster. Still, she rejects all the young men—until she meets Roy.

- Title: Angels For All
- Author: Nancy Powell
- Publisher: TotalRecall Publications, Inc.
- Format: HARDCOVER, 6.14" x 9.21"
- Number of pages in the finished book: 288
- 13-digit ISBN: 978-1-59095-588-8
- Month and day of publication: May 28, 2013
- Distribution arrangements: Ingram, Baker Taylor, Amazon.com, Barnes and Noble, etc.

Angels for All is the second book in the Ollie's Angels Series. It continues the story of a young couple in love. Ollie believes in premonitions sent by guardian angels, but has no warning of the hardships to come with drought and the Great Depression.

Roy and Ollie start married life on a sharecrop farm, striving for a better future and a place of their own. Each chapter is an episode that illustrates difficulties imposed by farm life. Almost every year, Roy goes away to other states working to earn money for the mortgage and other necessities.

Ollie stays on the farm to harvest crops and care for the children. She struggles against wild animals, foraging pigs, sickness, storms, hunger, and neighbors that prowl night and day stealing everything they can, including diapers, garden vegetables, harness, and cottonseed.

Ollie offers thanks for blessings she receives, giving credit to guardian angels for helping, but sometimes berates herself for discounting premonitions of impending danger.

About the Author

Nancy Powell has won several writing awards for short stories and poetry. Dark Secrets (under the name Ollie's Angels) won first place in the 2010 Mainstream Novel category at the Oklahoma Writers Federation, Inc. (OWFI) Contest. Also, the second book in the Ollie's Angels Series won an OWFI award in 2010. Dark Secrets was also awarded the 2012 third quarter Grand Prize at the "Books Without Publishers" writing contest sponsored at www.UltimateHeroContest.com

Nancy Powell is married, the mother of two children, and has seven grandchildren. She is a member of the Church of Christ, River Valley Writers of Fort Smith, Oklahoma Writers' Federation, Inc., Greenwood Writers, and Round Table Poets. Nancy is a graduate of the University of Arkansas, Little Rock.

In addition to writing, Nancy loves gardening, sewing, and painting. The paintings and book cover backgrounds are her interpretations in oil paint.

www.ingramcontent.com/pod-product-compliance
Lightning Source LLC
Chambersburg PA
CBHW020336120726
47904CB00002B/427